Dog Crazy

"Wonderful! Anyone who has ever loved and lost a dog will find wisdom and comfort in this sweet, smart story."

—Allie Larkin, author of *Stay*

"Donohue has written a delightful tale with heart-wrenching emotions (both high and low), entertaining high jinks, and a well-deserved happy ending for the many vivid characters you'll grow to love. . . . An entertaining, can't-put-down page-turner you'll want to share."

—RT Book Reviews (top pick)

All the Summer Girls

"A fast-paced novel about the enduring friendship of three young women who spent their summers in Avalon on the Jersey shore before dispersing across the country. . . . A good beach read."

—*Kirkus Reviews*

"Beach Book Extraordinaire! Donohue's three protagonists are irresistibly sympathetic as they try to unbury their true selves from the ruinous secrets of their shared past."

—Elin Hilderbrand, *New York Times* bestselling author

"*All the Summer Girls* celebrates the healing power of friendship for three very different young women with a shared past and different roles in the same guilty secret. . . . [A] compassionate portrait of what it means to be adrift—in love, and in one's own sense of self—with engaging heroines both flawed and utterly real."

—Nichole Bernier, author of *The Unfinished Work of Elizabeth D*

"An honest and engaging look at the complicated and powerful bonds of female friendship. Donohue takes us on a weekend reunion full of secrets, resentment, and regret—in other words, once you start this book, you won't be able to put it down!"

—Jennifer Close, bestselling author of *Girls in White Dresses*

"Donohue captures the beauty and frustration of reconnecting with old friends—they know you so well, and they don't know you at all. Perfect for a staycation for readers who like the beachy drama of Elin Hilderbrand and Susan Wiggs."

—*Booklist*

"Engaging."

—*E! Online*, "The Best Summer Reads 2014"

"Donohue gives the chick-lit buddy trope an appealing twist and a lot of depth, turning a familiar yarn of regret, trust, and loyalty into an elegant ode to late bloomers."

—*Publishers Weekly*

How to Eat a Cupcake

"Beautifully written and quietly wise, Meg Donohue's *How to Eat a Cupcake* is an achingly honest portrayal of the many layers of friendship—a story so vividly told, you can (almost) taste the buttercream."

—Sarah Jio, author of *The Violets of March* and *The Bungalow*

"Deliciously engaging. Donohue writes with charm and grace. What could be better than friendship and cupcakes?"

—Rebecca Rasmussen, author of *The Bird Sisters*

"Donohue has written a sharp little novel featuring the subtle characterizations of two appealingly flawed young women."

—*Kirkus Reviews*

YOU, ME, AND THE SEA

Also by Meg Donohue

Every Wild Heart
Dog Crazy
All the Summer Girls
How to Eat a Cupcake

YOU, ME, AND THE SEA

A Novel

Meg Donohue

WILLIAM MORROW
An Imprint of HarperCollins*Publishers*

P.S.™ is a trademark of HarperCollins Publishers.

HarperCollins books may be purchased for educational, business, or sales promotional use. For information please email the Special Markets Department at SPsales@harpercollins.com.

FIRST EDITION

Designed by Diahann Sturge

Library of Congress Cataloging-in-Publication Data has been applied for.

ISBN 978-0-06-242985-8 (paperback)
ISBN 978-0-06-291356-2 (hardcover library edition)

19 20 21 22 23   LSC   10 9 8 7 6 5 4 3 2 1

For my family

YOU, ME, AND THE SEA

THE PARTY

On the morning of the party, rain hit the bedroom windows in blustery waves. It had a sly quality, that rain, tapering to near silence before striking again. I lay awake, listening. Even during the storm's quiet lulls, I was aware of it breathing, building, returning.

Will stirred beside me. "No," he groaned. "Not rain."

He propped himself on his elbows and looked toward the large bay window. A thick curtain of rain blocked the view of the Pacific Ocean.

When Will noticed that I was awake, he kissed my shoulder. "You haven't been up all night worrying about the party, have you?" he asked. "This storm—"

"No." I wrapped my arm around him and rested my head on his bare chest. I wasn't worried about the party, and it wasn't the rain that had roused me from sleep. I'd dreamed of swallowing a red bird whole and then awakened abruptly, heart racing. I'd had the same dream many times, but it never failed to leave me unnerved. It was so *real*. I'd felt the flutter of the bird in my throat, the weight of its still-beating body in my chest.

When I was a little girl my father told me that red birds held the spirits of departed loved ones. *The past never leaves us,* he'd say. *It only changes shape.* He'd meant to comfort me, but instead the image haunted me. And how could it not? Even now, there were people from my past I would have done anything to see again—and others who the thought of seeing again left me blinking up at a dark ceiling, terrified.

Another letter had arrived that week, its envelope smudged and ragged. I did not need to open it to know that it had come from Horseshoe Cliff. I wondered how he had found my new address so quickly. I hid the letter with the others. Even the handwriting on those letters was menacing, a tangle of fishhooks glinting at the back of a dark drawer.

I know what you did, Merrow Shawe.
All that you have, I can take away.

Will eyed the rain-streaked window. Despite the heavy morning light, despite his pensive expression, his face seemed to contain a glow. Even when he was worried, Will emanated optimism. Of all his fortunes, this seemed to me the most valuable. It certainly made him charming company, beloved by many, his gaze so kind and blue, his temperament so calm and compassionate. He was also intelligent, a walking encyclopedia, a curious student of the world who loved history, art, and literature. What I liked most about Will was how much he enjoyed reading, and how serious his expression turned with a book in his hand.

I often experienced a strange longing when I looked at him, a feeling of coveting something that was already mine.

Now, I hugged him. My skin was dark against his. I swam every day, and my arms were brown and freckled from the sun. I swam even on the days when I knew I shouldn't, when the surf teemed with rage and the undertow threatened to make every stroke my last. The ocean swept through my mind, swelling it with memories, and then cleared it, dumping me on the sand exhausted and sore. Over the years, my body had been marked countless times by wayward waves that knocked me against rocks and jagged shells. You had to know where to look for my scars, hidden as they were among freckles.

Will had the sort of smooth, creamy skin that showed every bruise. His skin was always cooler than mine, too, a perpetual comfort when I tossed and turned through the night, overheating. It was our differences, I thought, that made us such a good match.

"Don't worry," I told him. "The rain will stop."

Will looked at me. His smile filled his eyes first. "'*The . . . rain . . . will . . . stop,'*" he intoned. He could no longer contain his grin. "Cancel the tent! The Oracle has spoken!"

I rolled my eyes but laughed. It was a long-standing riff of his, this idea that I was part soothsayer. Over our years together, I had come to understand that he wasn't entirely joking; Will really did believe that my "rustic childhood" (his words) had given me a unique connection to the workings of the earth, a mystical ability that seemed to toe the line between hippie and witch. (I suspected there was some self-preservation hidden within his teasing; he also liked to claim that I'd ensnared him with a love spell when I was still a minor and he an otherwise law-abiding adult.)

"The Oracle also sees breakfast in bed in her future," I said.

"Oh, does she?"

I nodded, but when he moved to get out of bed, I held him closer. "Not yet."

He settled back onto the pillows. "The caterers arrive at three?"

"Four. The band will be here at five. Valets at five thirty. Guests at six."

He shook his head. "When I suggested that we throw this party, I thought we would plan it together. I never meant for you to do it all yourself."

"I know. I wanted to."

I was eight years younger than Will, and I had no idea where I would be—*who* I would be—if I had never met him. My thoughts moved incessantly between the past and the present, my heart beating in two worlds at once. And so when Will suggested we throw a combined engagement, housewarming, and wedding party before eloping, I had thrown myself into the planning with the hope that I would land, finally, solidly, in the present.

Will smoothed my hair from my forehead—a sweet but fruit-less gesture as my hair would never be so easily tamed. *Seaweed,* my brother used to call it, usually punctuating the insult with a tug hard enough to make me yelp.

"Everything will be great," Will assured me.

Wind rattled the balcony door, bringing with it a feeling of unease about the night ahead. A fervent wish that I had never agreed to the party, that Will and I were married already and enjoying our honeymoon in Morocco, shuddered through me.

I had never told Will that sometimes when I stood on our balcony and looked out at the sea, I felt sure someone watched me. I did not tell him of the red bird in my dreams. I did not tell him how guilt grasped me, yanking me back to a room that I longed to forget. I did not tell him about my feelings for a boy who had been missing for nine years but was with me every moment of my life, so real that I felt his breath on my neck in the night. And I had not told Will about the letter that had arrived that week or any of the letters before it.

How could I tell him one thing and not everything?

THE MARTINI BAR was at one end of the living room and the band at the other, with space for dancing between the two. In the dining room, there was a shimmering display of raw oysters, which admittedly were more to my taste than to Will's. (Earlier I had walked into the kitchen to find two of the caterers shucking those oysters with detached efficiency. The twist of the knife; the air sharp with brine; my senses immediately quivering and alert.) Our home had filled with guests, and after two glasses of champagne, my nagging worries faded and I began to enjoy myself. As a kid, if I had come across a photograph of a fancy party like this, or an illustration in a children's book, it would have fueled hours of delighted fantasy play and feverish writing in my journal. Now, I passed a mirror and saw a woman in a beautiful pearl-colored dress who appeared flushed with excitement and she was, of course, me.

Will was in a corner speaking to his mother, Rosalie, and the sight of them together made my heart swell in a way that frightened me. I knew how far I was willing to go for love, how capable I was of blindly clinging to it.

I stepped outside and breathed in deeply. On the patio, over-looking the ocean and, to the north, the Golden Gate Bridge and the distant hills of Marin, servers weaved through party guests with trays of champagne and perfectly round tartlets baked to a rich shade of gold. The rain had cleared, leaving in its wake wispy clouds that captured and stretched the pink glow of the gloriously setting sun.

The group outside was mostly comprised of Will's former classmates and law firm colleagues. When I first met Will, I would never have guessed that someone so serious could have so many friends. I had thought that perhaps only I noticed his charm, or even that he turned it on only for me. But I was wrong—laughably wrong. Will's life was crowded with friends that he had made easily at every turn.

I scanned the crowd, my gaze landing on Will's sister.

"Emma!" I called.

She turned, her blue eyes shimmering with boozy excite-ment. Emma was nineteen years old, but I suspected that her ability to hold her liquor would not improve with age. There was a purity about her that simply did not mix with alcohol; two sips in, and she would tell you all of her secrets, not one of which was any deeper or darker than a puddle of spilled milk.

On the evening of our engagement party, she had chosen to wear a shapeless brown dress, and yet she looked lovely, her blond curls soft and shining. Even in her drab attire, it was clear that she belonged among the smart crowd that surrounded her—she had, after all, been attending parties like this all her life. Emma's low regard for fashion prompted the only moments of tension I had ever witnessed between her and her mother, Rosalie, who had a wardrobe full of beautiful clothes that I'd never seen worn twice. The first dress I ever owned was a gift from Will and Emma's mother, selected from her own closet. (I was sixteen at the time, and Rosalie's Doberman had recently taken a chunk of flesh from my calf.) I had not worn that dress in years, but I cherished it still and kept it wrapped in tissue paper and safely stored with my most treasured possessions.

"This weather!" Emma exclaimed, landing a light kiss on my cheek. "It's beautiful. Where did you put the rain?"

"Will persuaded it to come back another day."

"Lawyers!" Emma laughed. "But just look at that sunset."

Between the sunset and the alcohol, everyone seemed to have fallen under the illusion that the evening was warmer than it actually was. Men's cheeks were pink below their sunglasses; women's bare shoulders glowed. The ocean was an expanse of light. Voices engulfed the air, nearly but not quite drowning out the waves that crashed against the shore.

I caught the eye of a waiter passing with a tray of champagne flutes. He stopped so quickly that the glasses wobbled, bubbles multiplying. Emma and I each took a glass.

"We haven't seen enough of you lately," I said. "How are the seals?"

Her eyes grew round. "Oh, Merrow, they're *wonderful*. So playful and funny and smart. You have to come visit soon. The little one I told you about—the one born with the mangled flipper? She's as strong as any other seal now." After a sip of her champagne, she added, "Actually, she could end up being the strongest of them all."

I felt a pang of indignation before quickly forgiving my future sister-in-law. It might have been difficult for her to imagine how a creature born at a disadvantage could manage to thrive, but Emma's heart was in the right place. Besides, her love for the sea rivaled mine, and I found that this connected us every bit as much as the fact that I was on the cusp of marrying her brother. Emma was a sophomore at Berkeley with an internship at the Marine Mammal Center in Sausalito. I still remembered how I'd felt when I'd heard ten-year-old Emma announce with utter confidence that she planned to be a marine mammal veterinarian. When I was ten, the idea that I might one day become a marine mammal veterinarian would have seemed as likely as someday becoming the supreme leader of a distant galaxy.

"And how are *you*?" she asked. "How's work?"

I hesitated. That week I'd worked with a nine-year-old boy named Assim whose scrawny limbs and milk chocolate eyes had made my heart contract. He'd asked, quietly, if I could help with an essay he was writing about bullying, and we'd waded steadily deeper into a conversation about the ways that life might shape a person, the possibility that inside every bad person was someone good. *Every action is a link in a much longer chain of events,* I'd said. I knew that Assim had recently been placed with a foster family, but I didn't ask him about that. Not yet. Over the years that I'd been working at the after-school program, I'd learned that if I asked too many questions early on, the children would not return.

It was difficult to talk about certain aspects of my job with Emma, or even with Will. The conversations I had with the children felt private.

"I'm trying to get everything in place before our trip," I told Emma. "I don't want the kids to lose momentum while I'm away."

"Morocco." She sighed. "It's so romantic. When do you leave?"

"Three weeks."

"And then you'll finally be a Langford."

"Well, I don't know if I'll change my name, but I'll officially be your sister-in-law, and that's a much greater cause for celebration." I meant this, truly. The Langfords were a tight-knit tribe that I had longed to call my own almost from the moment, years earlier, when I'd met them.

Emma grinned. "I'm going to need to see that ring again."

I held out my hand. Will had given me a ring with a large blue sapphire. Its color reminded him of the sea that our hotel room in Italy had overlooked five years earlier. We were falling in love before that first trip together, but our vacation had solidified our feelings. It was as though breaking from our regular lives had allowed us to see each other, and the possibility of our future, in a new light. Since that trip, we'd traveled together as often as our jobs allowed.

"It's *so* beautiful." Emma touched the stone lightly with her long finger. "And unique. Like you." She tilted her head and looked at me. "And you deserve it," she added firmly, as though I might argue with her. Even sober, Emma was prone to make sweeping, sentimental statements. I knew she meant that I deserved not only the ring, but *all* the many gifts that Will had given me over our years together, and she probably meant even Will himself, really, because my parents had died when I was young, and my brother—

Enough. The past was a fast-moving current that perpetually threatened to sweep me from my feet.

Emma was effortlessly generous with her affection, just like Will. I loved this about them, but sometimes I could not help but wonder if kindness meant as much when it came from someone who had never experienced anything else. My doubt made me feel ashamed, as though something small and petty and hateful had shaken loose from where I'd hidden it and fallen to the floor for all to see.

When I tried not to think of the letters, I failed. The words haunted me, as I knew they were meant to.

I know what you did, Merrow Shawe.
All that you have, I can take away.

INSIDE, AFTER TOASTS were given, after Rosalie and Wayne Langford and their posh, silver-haired friends hugged and kissed Will and me and wished us well, the band switched from the toothless jazz it had been playing throughout the evening to music we could really dance to. I moved through the house, turning down the lights, leaving a blur of candles in my wake. The rooms grew warm. When someone passed me a drink, the glass was so beaded with sweat that it nearly slipped from my hand. A caterer refreshed the rapidly melting ice in the raw bar, each piece a glittering, diminishing diamond in the candlelight. Most of the men had shed their suit jackets; a few women had already taken off their heels. I flung open the windows, as I often did late at night. I liked how quickly the salt air seeped in, making the dark floors gleam like tide pools below the moon.

I was only dancing by myself for a moment or two when Will found me and wrapped his arms around my waist. "You're a sight for sore eyes," he murmured in my ear.

A loud crash interrupted us.

In the dining room, the tiers of the giant raw bar had toppled over. Oyster shells and ice cubes spun across the floor. Caterers rushed from the kitchen with trash bags and brooms and kitchen towels and I knelt to help, the wet floor cold beneath my bare knees. I moved a towel over the floor and when I lifted it I was jolted by memory.

A lifeless weight in my arms; blood, not water, soaking through my clothes; in my chest, rage rising from grief like a flame from kindling.

I dropped the sodden towel to the floor and stood, swaying and desperate for air. Nearby, a caterer filled a trash bag with soiled ice and oysters.

"I'll take that," I said, ignoring his protest as I grabbed the bag and hurried toward the door to the garage.

I SET THE garbage in the bin and replaced the lid. Then I opened the garage door and stepped onto the sidewalk.

Above San Francisco, the stars were always small. I wasn't sure I would ever get used to this. I breathed in the air, feeling the city moving around me. I thought of the kids I worked with at Learning Together and wondered if the noises of the city floated through their dreams. It was hard for me to imagine a childhood here, below stars that did not insist you look up with wonder.

I had hoped that a party would solidify my hold in this place, but all it had taken to summon the past was the weight of a wet rag.

When I looked down from the sky, he was walking toward me. At first, I felt annoyed. I'd had too much to drink; my mind was playing tricks; of course it was not him. I had seen him so many times over the previous nine years . . . everywhere Will and I traveled, I saw him . . . only to be wrong.

But now . . .

If this was him, a powerful new silhouette had swallowed his wiry body. He moved in a new way, too, gliding from the shadows with confidence. His beautiful dark hair was shorn close to his scalp.

And then he was before me, and I saw the silver scar near his temple, as pale as a sliver of winter sky. Up close, the boy he had been at sixteen was no longer hidden in his face.

"Merrow," Amir said, and the sound of my name in his voice made me feel as though he were rousing me from a long sleep, whispering "fire."

PART ONE

CHAPTER ONE

The thing that I'd said to Assim at Learning Together about every action being a link in a longer chain of events was something I had learned from my father. For my father, there was always a larger story; every action was a reaction. Assim and I had been discussing violence, but my father had always been speaking of love. My father believed that our lives were bound together—and to the past, and to the earth—through a web of connections both seen and unseen. *Whenever you are lost*, he'd tell me, *search for that web. In the right light, it shimmers.*

ALTHOUGH HE WAS typically soft-spoken, Dad's voice changed when he spoke of the past. He would start slowly and gain momentum, his stories unfolding with both drama and poetry. I wondered, when I was old enough to do so, whether his memories returned him to a time when he was a different sort of person. A bold dreamer. An optimist. A romantic. Through his stories, I came to know my father, and also—more exciting still—my mother. When he told me that my mother used to draw swirls on my skin with her finger, I remembered it. I remembered, too, the ecstatic frizz of her blond hair escaping its braid, and how her eyes held a promise of adventure that drew people close.

"Your mother never wanted to put you down," he told me. "It had taken nearly a decade to have Bear, and we'd waited even longer for you. Our little girl. A sister for Bear. When you finally arrived, your mom almost couldn't believe it. When Bear was born, he was covered in fuzz, like a little cub. When you were born, your skin was slick as silk. You were perfect and strong and glowing, like something born of the sea. Our very own Merrow. All your mom wanted was to lie in bed and hold you." At this point in the telling, he would smile. "And feed you. So you quickly became a fat baby. Fat and happy, like you knew how much you were loved right from the start."

I remembered the tight cradle of my mother's arms as we lay together in bed for weeks, for months.

This was the power of my father's stories; they made me feel that I had been with him all along, a part of Horseshoe Cliff since the beginning. His stories made it seem as though the past were something I could step into, like a room in the house that was always there, its door unlocked by a combination of words.

My father purchased our land for a steal at an auction in 1969. His expression would become gleeful, even cunning, when he told this particular story, the story of how he'd surprised my mother with a gift of seventeen acres, a quarter mile of which hugged the coast.

I would eventually learn that some of the people of Osha felt the dupe had gone in the other direction. They thought that no one in his right mind would spend eight thousand dollars on a crumbling bluff with no water meter or well. Osha, with its tiny downtown made up of a natural foods co-op, a café with early-morning hours that catered to fishermen and surfers, and a schoolhouse, considered itself an oasis of peace in a troubled time, and they intended to keep it that way. The inhabitants regularly dismantled the street markers that newcomers needed if they were to have any hope of navigating the winding, coast-bound roads that would deposit them in sweet and stubborn Osha. And to discourage development in an area where the water supply came from a single creek, the town voted to limit the number of water meters available. No land that didn't already have a water meter in 1961 had much chance of getting one in the future, and the Horseshoe Cliff parcel eleven miles north of town, uninhabited for as long as anyone could remember, had none.

A spirited, adventurous child, I sided easily with my father on the subject. As though to make up for the water that it lacked, Horseshoe Cliff offered an overabundance of alternative treasures—beaches full of shells that whispered the steady song of the sea, dark and echoing caves carved into cliffs that glowed golden at sunset, the towering eucalyptus grove that was perpetually draped with fog like a fairy queen cloaked in mystery. And of course, spanning to the horizon and roaring with excessive enthusiasm as it reclaimed the land foot by foot over the years of my childhood: the Pacific Ocean.

What the people of Osha did not know was that my father had walked Horseshoe Cliff under the cover of darkness the night before the bank's auction. Contrary to what neighbors might have thought, he'd done his research. He knew that the land had no water rights and never would. Yet, as my father picked his way through scrub grass with his flashlight bobbing before him, he felt possibility humming up toward him from the land. He trekked through fields of golden yarrow and wild daisies and poppies and bluff lettuce until he met the curving line of jagged cliffs that fell to the ocean. There, he turned off his flashlight and breathed in the salt air. Forty feet below, at the bottom of a drop so sheer it made his heart race, the sea swelled in the moonlight. The steady waves that hit the rock-strewn beach below made him think of an animal breathing.

He was walking back toward his car and had nearly reached the road when his foot hit something hard underneath the brush. An iron pump. The pump handle joint was rusted over, but he got it to move, and after pumping for some time, water fell from the spigot to the land. He knelt down and found it tasted sweet on his tongue. I always felt a twinge of envy at this point in the story; the water from the well had never tasted like much of anything to me.

The bank that had found itself in possession of Horseshoe Cliff had no idea that this well existed. When my father moved the beam of his flashlight in a circle around him, it landed on the remnants of the foundation of a small house. He felt willing to bet that the well would provide water for the cottage he

planned to build, the horses he expected to buy, and the children he and my mother hoped to have.

The septic tank he would have to dig himself, but he was
young and strong enough and, having spent the previous three
years living among a group that called themselves the Freedom
Collective, he had plenty of friends to call on for help. My
mother had been with the Freedom Collective even longer.

My father met my mother on his first day in San Francisco.
Until then, he'd lived his entire life on his parents' sugar beet
farm in the western panhandle of Nebraska. He'd been born
prematurely and as a result suffered from weak lungs and
chronic pneumonia throughout his childhood. Bedridden for
weeks at a time, he'd had an unusual childhood for a farm kid.
Like so often in life, he told me, what at first seemed likely to
close doors actually opened them. In order to provide my father
with an activity while in bed, his grandmother taught him to
whittle when he was just six years old. It was not long before
my father handled the knife even better than she did, creating
fanciful creatures that delighted his family.

When he wasn't whittling, my father's mother read him stories of the sea. My grandmother had convinced herself that the
ocean air might cure my father, but without an ocean in sight,
she decided that books were the next best option. My father's
lungs were not strong, but his mind was; my grandmother believed it held the power to heal him. She told my father to
imagine himself in the world of the stories, to imagine standing
barefoot in the sand as the ocean crept toward his feet.

Close your eyes, she'd tell him, even once he was old enough to read the stories himself. *Breathe.*

They favored myths and folklore and came to believe that the surprising overlaps between diverse native peoples' stories were proof of a universal and ancient truth: the power of the sea. As he slept, my father, who had never stepped foot off the arid Nebraska plains, dreamed of the ocean, of cool salt air that would fill his chest as steadily as a bicycle pump does a tire wheel, making movement that was once hard, easy.

And so he came to believe that while the land was in his bones, the sea was in his heart—and with it a yearning for the mystical and the mysterious. He knew that the farm would always be his home, but that it would eventually belong to his older brother, Nate, who had worked hard enough for both boys during those long spells when my father was confined to his bed. His family did not want him to leave, but my father craved adventure. The coast pulled him westward.

In 1966, San Francisco was in the news. The city was home to the musicians my father listened to on the radio, the writers and poets whose books he read, the protesters of a war that had already taken the lives of two of his childhood friends. He'd been left out of so much of life while lying in his bed as a kid; now that he was stronger he didn't want to miss anything more. San Francisco seemed the center of the Now. And it stretched right to the ocean.

In Nebraska, the summer sky hugged the land in a tight, airless embrace, but in San Francisco my father was surprised to find that the sky appeared demure and distant behind a veil of fog. The bus station was crowded, and the streets roiled with cars. He'd planned to find another bus to take him to the ocean, but now he felt too excited by the number of people surrounding him to leave their swell. He hitched his backpack on his shoulders and began to walk, following first one person and then another on a jagged westward stroll.

The news had prepared him for swarms of meandering young folk, dreamy kids around his own age in dungarees and T-shirts, but from where he found himself on Market Street everyone seemed older. Men with crisp haircuts wore suits. Women wore belted dresses and high-heeled shoes. All possessed a purposeful pace that made my father feel slow and conspicuous. When he stopped to catch his breath, he watched a security guard chase a pigeon from a hushed lobby with a stone floor that gleamed. The air was thick with car exhaust, and he felt his chest tightening. It seemed possible that he'd made a terrible mistake and San Francisco was nowhere near the ocean. He blinked up at the office buildings, walked into an intersection, and was sent reeling back to the curb by the blare of a yellow taxicab.

"Damn cabs," said a man beside him on the curb. He had eyes like my father's grandfather, a soft brown that shone with kindness. His hair was the same color gray beneath his hat, too, but his skin was pale and smooth, where his grandfather's was cragged by lines. Still, the resemblance between the two men was enough to make my father feel as though his grandfather were sending him a sign of encouragement.

"That one had you in his sights," the man said. "Are you in one piece?"

My father nodded, thanking him. He wondered how near he'd just come to the end of his adventure.

The man looked him up and down, his eyes lingering on his backpack. "I'm going to take a wild guess and say you're looking for Haight Street."

Haight Street. My father recognized the name. "Could you point me toward it?"

The man laughed, not unkindly. The light turned green, but still he stood on the curb beside my father. "I'll do you one better." He took a small notebook and silver pen from the inside pocket of his suit jacket and scribbled a quick map. "Good luck," he said, tearing the sheet from the notebook. He seemed on the verge of saying something more, but instead nodded and crossed the street.

"To this day, I wonder what he was going to tell me," my father would say at this point in the story. "I suppose I always will." He had a way of finding a bit of mystery even in the smallest moments of life. Or if not mystery, exactly, perhaps what he sensed was possibility—glimmering threads that spun out in every direction, forever unbroken, connections that existed whether seen or not.

By the time he made it to Haight Street, his backpack was beginning to dig into his shoulders, but here at last were the kids from the newspapers, the young people with their long hair and colorful clothes. Music poured from the shops that lined the street. The buildings were lower than on Market Street; the sky didn't seem so far away; my father felt the knot in his chest begin to loosen. The people on the sidewalk moved more slowly, and there was something different in the air—it vibrated with excitement.

A few blocks before the spot on his map that showed Haight Street meeting Golden Gate Park, a crowd had gathered on a corner. In its center, a beautiful woman stood beside a large cast-iron pot. Her dress was long and white and snaked with red embroidery. A blue scarf hung around her shoulders. The crowd whistled and laughed as she spun a tin mug around the long neck of a metal ladle above her head. My father watched the mug spin, impressed, and was momentarily blinded when sunlight hit the metal with a bright flash.

This was my favorite moment of this story, the moment my father met my mother.

When my father opened his eyes, she was looking right at him. "Hey you," she said. The hum of metal on metal slowed and then stopped as she lowered the ladle to point it at him.

Hey you, I would say in my head along with my father, my mother.

He stepped to the front of the crowd. The leather sandals on the woman's feet were flecked with dried mud. Her toenails were painted citrus orange. She emptied a ladleful of what appeared to be stew into a tin mug. When she handed the mug to him, she cupped her fingers around his.

"This," she said, "is the best Free Stew you will ever eat." Her smile was warm. The mug she'd given him was not. My father, hungry and in no mind to disappoint this woman anyway, drained the mug of its contents and was surprised to find that the stew was delicious even cold. He tasted potatoes and bell

peppers and buttery greens, and there was not a single sweet beet in the mix. It was only once he'd handed the mug back to her that it occurred to him to wonder if there were drugs in the stew.

"Well?" she asked.

"You're right. I will never in my life have better Free Stew than that."

She smiled, as he'd hoped she would. Her eyes, my father saw now, gathering the courage to look, were a surprising green-brown color that seemed to glow against her suntanned skin. They moved from his face to the bag on his shoulder.

"Where are you coming from?"

"Nebraska. Just got here."

A line had formed behind him, but she seemed in no hurry to move on. "Nebraska." She chewed her lip. "Then you need to see the ocean."

This was the moment, my father told me, that he fell in love with my mother.

"Louie!" she called, not taking her eyes off my father.

A man emerged from a knot of people who were handing out slices of dark bread from baskets. "Marigooold," he said, drawling the name into song. His lips were hidden behind his beard.

Marigold. A fitting name, my father thought. There was something bright and bold and a bit wild about her, like a flower that held the colors of the sun.

"I'm cutting out to see the ocean," she said. "Can you dish the stew?"

The man named Louie ran his hand down the length of Marigold's tangled blond hair and my father felt his heart drop. But then Louie dipped the ladle deep in the pot and smiled an easy smile at him. "Sure thing," he said. He filled a mug with stew and handed it to the next person in line.

When Marigold held out her hand to my father, he took it. A current of energy flowed from her. He sent a message of thanks to the man with his grandfather's eyes for drawing the map that had led him to her.

As they rode a streetcar toward the ocean, she told my father that nine months earlier she had left a girl named Mary Simon back in New York City. Now she went by Marigold.

So my mother had been just like my father, chasing adventure, brave enough to change her whole life.

Her people called themselves the Freedom Collective. "Emphasis on the free," she said. She had not yet let go of my father's hand, and she squeezed it now and again in percussive backdrop to her words. When he told her his name, she repeated it and squeezed his hand three times: *Ja-cob Shawe.*

At this point in the story, my father would reach for my hand and squeeze it three times. *Mer-row Shawe.*

"We have a big piece of magic earth up north of the city," my mother told him. "The plants burst out of this dirt all big and green and beautiful. We work in shifts up there on the farm. Then we take turns coming down here to the city to give away what we've grown." She squeezed his hand. "I should have given you some of our Free Bread. It's even better than the Free Stew."

"The best Free Bread in the world, I bet."

Marigold laughed. An elderly woman sitting in front of them turned to stare, and Marigold offered her a radiant smile.

"Free is our special ingredient. It's not a secret, but you'll have trouble finding it anywhere else." She looked through the streetcar windows at the rows of low, pale homes that lined the long avenue. "There aren't really any sights to point out to you on this route. This is just where ordinary people live ordinary lives. It's so calm, isn't it? It's beautiful just to be on this car driving through all these ordinary lives."

After a thoughtful beat, her smile grew sly. "But the ocean will blow your socks off. And if the ocean blows your socks off, our land up north is going to leave you wearing nothing at all." She laughed. "Which is the way most of the Collective likes it."

She said this as though there were no question in her mind that my father would see the land, that he was one of them now. The idea didn't bother him a bit.

"Freedom Farm has a bunkhouse if that's your thing, but most of the time we just sleep under the stars. When the clouds clear, the stars look so close they could just about blind you. And it's quiet up there, but not quiet at all, you know? Because the land is breathing and moving all the time. You're alone and never alone. There's so much space, but every time you stretch your hand you touch something alive."

My father had felt this way many times about the farm in Nebraska, but he had never heard someone who spoke quite like Marigold. He had poetic thoughts like this, too, and listening to Marigold made him think that he ought to have the courage to start saying some of them out loud.

"You like the shifts on the land more than the shifts in the city," he said.

She thought about this. "I guess I do." The bright way she looked at him made him glad he'd said it.

When they stepped off the streetcar, Marigold's long hair whipped around her head. She lifted the blue scarf from her shoulders and tied it around the billowing brown and blond strands.

The ocean pulled at my father. If the sky here was smaller than he expected, the ocean was bigger. The waves rose and crashed with a roar; the water seemed both darker and more sparkling than it had in any movie or photograph. It was loud and powerful and riotous in a way that made his heart race. But the air did just what he'd always thought it would, filling up his chest like it belonged there, like it was returning home.

They took off their shoes. My father dug his toes into the sand and found it warm on top and cool below. He rolled up his dungarees. Marigold knotted her dress above her knees. They waded in. The water was bracingly cold, surprising him, but Marigold didn't hesitate. He couldn't believe he was finally here.

"That's where our land is," Marigold yelled through the wind. He shielded his eyes and followed the line of her finger north. In the distance, beneath a trace of fog, a stretch of golden cliffs stood tall despite the battering of the waves.

"On the cliff?" At that point, it was impossible for him to imagine a farm by the sea.

"On the cliff," she said. Her hand found his and squeezed, and as he told me this, he always squeezed mine again, too, and I was right there with them, looking north toward the land by the sea.

FOR THREE YEARS, they lived and worked together at Freedom Farm. The farm had a disorderly beauty that spoke to my father. The soil required the kind of steadfast attention that reminded him, happily, of his home, but there were so many surprises, too: the bunkhouse with its cots that glowed in the dark, the colorful banners that fluttered from the trees, the spiky wild-flowers that looked like they'd been dropped from outer space, the purple tractor with its crackling radio, the distant roar of the ocean, the thick and romantic fog, the bluff-top meadows of wind-stamped shrubs, the fancy hens with their pale blue eggs.

Marigold was unlike anyone he'd ever met. She believed wholeheartedly in the Free Movement, and thought that the path to world harmony would be found through binding person to person in a string of kindnesses and generosity, giving and receiving and passing on, a sharing of warmth (*like stories,* my father thought, remembering those ancient myths of the sea, passed on for generations, that had brought him such relief as a child). Marigold loved the ocean, and her skin seemed always speckled with salt, her blond hair just a little bit wet. She could hold her breath underwater longer than my father had known was humanly possible; just when he grew frantic, she would surface, calm and satiated as an animal after a meal. When he watched her swim, he thought of the merrows in the Irish folk-tales he used to read with his mother—mermaids whose true home would always be the sea.

When he missed his family, the big sky of Nebraska, his quiet childhood bedroom with its filmy white curtains that billowed at the slightest whisper of breeze, Marigold's kindness buoyed him. In truth, he was not sure how he felt about the Freedom Collective—Louie and the others were welcoming in a boisterous, zealous way, but living among so many people felt unnatural to him. As much as he loved living on the coast, he missed the quiet thrum of family life as he'd known it. Freedom, he was learning, did not mean the same thing to everyone. In the early hours of morning before the rest of the group was awake, he helped a neighboring farmer with carpentry work. Someday, he thought, it would be time to move on from Freedom Farm, and when that day came, he wanted to have some cash saved. But he knew that he would stay with the group as long as Marigold was happy. He loved her.

After a few visits to San Francisco, my father traded his city shifts for farm shifts, content to stay up north. More often than not, Marigold stayed with him. She was not always animated and talkative. Sometimes the light behind her eyes flickered and dimmed. Her spirit grew heavy, each hard-won smile seeming to surface from a dwindling supply of joy. The color drained from her face. When my father saw the early signs of these mood shifts, he learned to take her by the hand and walk with her along the beach. His silent company seemed to help. The sea air dampened her skin, making it shine.

Sometimes he took her for long drives in one of the slowly

rusting cars that were always parked along the side of the tractor barn. He'd pack her favorite sandwiches, hummus and cucumber on Free Bread. She liked listening to the Byrds as the
car's wheels stuttered over the crumbling roads. They drove
past small, shaggy farms and stopped for lunch on hidden
beach coves. In Osha, my father traded Freedom Farm eggs for
fresh blueberry muffins from the café. In front of the co-op, he
found a soft, knitted shawl in the bin of clothes labeled FREE.
He draped it around Marigold's beautiful neck and kissed her.
They walked the dirt road that ended at the beach, passing cot-
tages with surfboards on their porches and clotheslines bowed
by beach towels and the violet-colored schoolhouse with the
sign, stuck in the dirt out front, that read LITTLE EARTH. He
could not imagine this part of the country ever not seeming
remarkable to him. Nebraska no longer claimed him in the
way this land by the sea did. He felt as enchanted as one of the
characters in the myths he so loved.

"Look," my mother said one day as they drove. My father
turned to her, relieved. It was the first time she'd spoken in
hours. She pointed through the window and he pulled the car
onto a patch of weedy dirt on the side of the road. Even before
the car had completely stopped, she'd opened the door.

My father stepped out and circled the car to join her at a
split-rail fence. A field rose gently away from them. On it, a
handful of cows grazed on the sort of scrubby brown grass that
would have made Nebraska stock turn up their noses. At the
end of the field there was a red barn painted with a huge white
peace sign.

There was yearning in the deep breath that Marigold took then. "This looks like a happy home," she said.

My father felt his heartbeat quicken. He had been waiting for her to give him some sign that she was ready to leave the Freedom Collective and start a different sort of life with him. After three years of carpentry jobs and living for free at Freedom Farm, he had saved eight thousand dollars.

He managed to take his eyes off her face long enough to look at the farm before looking back at her. "Is this the sort of place *you'd* like to call home?" he asked.

Her brow wrinkled. For a moment my father felt disappointment looming. But then she put her arm around his waist and drew him closer to her. "Wouldn't it be perfect," she said, "if we lived in a place like this with a view of the sea?"

THE NIGHT BEFORE the bank's auction, after he'd walked Horseshoe Cliff, my father lay awake thinking of stories his grandfather had told him. The bank believed Horseshoe Cliff was like a fruit that was flecked with rot, that only the most desperate would seek juice below its puckered skin. After walking the land, my father didn't feel desperate, but he knew that the water from the well would not be enough to farm the land at Horseshoe Cliff. In the morning, hours before the auction, he called his grandfather.

Dry farming, his grandfather told him, involved tilling and pressing the soil during the rainy season so it formed a crust that held in the moisture accumulated during the wettest months. It was risky business to be at the mercy of nature, most successful when farming low-water crops that could survive on the moisture provided by the coast's summer fog when the land below was driest.

"Potatoes," his grandfather recommended. "Tomatoes. Onions. Garlic. Sunchokes. Most greens. Pumpkins. Watermelons, believe it or not. Oh, and apples, sure. They won't be big or pretty, but see if they're not twice as flavorful as any irrigated orchard pickings. The water deficiency stresses the fruit, concentrating the sugars and nutrients. Small but mighty fruit is what you'll grow. 'Good for pies,' your grandmother is saying in my other ear."

By the time my father hung up the phone, he was already pacing out the orchard in his mind, mentally tilling the sandy soil until it became a sponge that pulled water from secret depths and the fog above. He envisioned the neat rows of an ambitious garden, the first green sprouts striving toward the sun. Barrels that could store the winter rain. A farm stand by the road where anything more than they needed could be given away for free to those less fortunate.

My father was young and full of hope for the future. With the clouds of my mother's latest dark mood parting, he would not allow himself to see anything but happiness ahead.

CHAPTER TWO

One of my earliest memories was of my brother promising me chocolate cake. It was my fifth birthday. Bear told me the cake was in the eucalyptus grove, and I believed him. So many wonderful treasures could be found in the grove; why not, among them, chocolate cake? I loved the grove as I loved all of Horseshoe Cliff, my home by the sea.

My father sat in his chair on the back porch, whittling one of his tiny houses, looking out from time to time toward the line where the land fell away. From the back porch, the ocean was an enormous silver sail pulled taut. The eucalyptus grove was on the other side of the house, closer to the road. My father couldn't have seen what happened.

As Bear and I walked away from the house, the distant rumble of the waves seemed to rise up through the soles of my feet.

The grove was a different world from the sun-bleached coast. Above, fog clung to shaggy trees; below, my feet rustled a blanket of decaying, dagger-shaped leaves. At five years old, I already knew that my father worried over the grove during lightning storms, that the oils in the trees and the dry footing of leaves could easily spread wildfire. But butterflies, orange-hued and polka-dotted, flitted through the grove, and I loved to chase them, imagining they were stars that would float into the sky at nightfall.

As Bear led me along a winding path through the ancient-looking trees, I searched for fairies in the shadows. I felt my stomach growl. The warm and minty air of the grove, its sleepy stillness, always made me hungry.

My father gave the pumpkins that we grew to our friend Rei from town, and sometimes Rei returned to Horseshoe Cliff with a pumpkin pie that had a whipped cream smiley face on top. *Maybe,* I thought, *she'd taught Bear how to make that pie, and he planned to give it to me for my birthday.* So what if it wasn't really a cake? I would be happy with a pie. But I hoped there would be candles. I wondered if Bear would keep me company while I ate it. This idea excited me. My brother never wanted to play with me. I would gladly share the pie with him, I decided.

"Look, Merrow, there's the cake." Bear was ten years older than me and lately his voice had become strange, falling and rising and falling like a bat hunting something I could not see. He pointed at a canvas bag tucked into a nook among a tree's roots. I called these nooks "tree pockets" and spent hours of my days hiding little treasures within them. More often than not when I returned, sure I'd remembered the right spot, I would find the treasures gone. I would press my hand against the cold dirt and wonder how I could have forgotten something so important.

I raced to the bag. Overhead, the trees shivered in a breeze that didn't reach me. I looked in the bag and thought, *Chocolate!* But what I pulled from the bag was a fistful of black mud. A pale worm as thick as my thumb dropped onto the bare skin of my thigh. I yelped and fell backward. The ball of mud hit the ground beside me, writhing with worms.

Bear was laughing. "Did you really think I'd put a cake in a bag? God, you're dumb. It was only a joke."

My legs were streaked with mud. I looked up at my brother and began to cry. "I want Daddy."

Bear's face changed when he became angry. "'I want Daddy,'" he whimpered, imitating me.

Something inside of me went still when my brother looked at me like that. A thumping sound began in my ears. I stood to walk back toward the house, but Bear grabbed my wrist and pulled. I fell and then he was above me, one knee on each of my arms, pinning me down. It was hard to breathe.

I already knew to be careful around Bear. He was more than twice my size, and you had to be alert around people and animals that were bigger than you because they could hurt you without meaning to. Like when my pony, Guthrie, whipped my eyes with his tail when he'd only been trying to get a fly off his back. Bear was like Guthrie, I thought. He had patches of whiskers around his lips that made his face always look dirty, and his hair hung around his neck like a mane. I admired how strong and brave my brother was, how he always had blood beading from some scrape on his arm or the purple stain of a bruise on his shin. I'd never seen him cry. He couldn't help that he was so big, or that I so often ran into his hard elbow and wound up on the ground, or that his long feet clipped my ankles and made me fall. His eyes were always empty when he looked down at me, like he couldn't even see me because I was so small. Bear was a horse and I was a fly, as difficult to see as any fleck of dust.

But now, something was changing. Bear looked right at me and he had knives in his eyes. "Stop crying," he said.

"I can't." I twisted below him. My arms and my belly hurt. There was a sour taste in my throat, but I fought it, sensing how angry it would make Bear if I became sick.

"I'm not letting you up until you're quiet." He put his hand over my mouth. It smelled of the grove, this place that I loved, and the smell made me cry harder. I thought about biting him, but then I looked up into his narrowed eyes and couldn't.

"Stop crying," said Bear. "Stop."

"You're hurting me!" I managed to say beneath his hand.

My brother's face was flat and hard. "I don't care. You're not allowed to cry. You know why."

How did I know, suddenly, that the "why" was our mother? No one had told me when our mother had died, or why. It was a question that I carried around with me, always and never asking at the same time. It was what I was asking my father when I sat next to him on the porch and listened to his knife scrape against wood. It was what I was asking Bear when I followed him around the orchard, hoping he'd play with me. It was what I was asking Rei when I thanked her for that pumpkin pie.

Why is Mama dead? When will she be back?

"I want Mama," I said, releasing the words quickly.

Bear's knees pressed down on me. I could hardly see him through my tears, but I thought I heard him say, "It's your fault she's dead." His knees dug into my arms.

I closed my eyes and thought of following butterflies as bright as stars. Something happened to time after that. When I opened my eyes, Bear was gone, and the light in the grove was fading. My arms ached. Bear had never hurt me like this before.

Later in my life, I would think of this moment often. It seemed to me that it was the first time I felt true fear. True fear was different from worrying over howling wind outside my bedroom at night. It was different from the feeling of looking at an empty plate after another meal that wasn't quite large enough to satisfy my hunger. It was different from the hard ball of loneliness that rolled around in my heart from time to time. This fear did not feel like the sort of thing that came and went; it felt like something that was meant to last, like a rope with a double knot.

Still, I loved Bear. It was a strange and awful and confusing feeling to love someone I feared.

I found my father sitting on his chair on the porch just where I'd left him, but now he was asleep. The tiny house he'd been carving had fallen off his lap. So had his knife. I picked up the house and turned it on my palm. It was a miniature farmhouse with a peace sign carved into its tiny door and a cat curled on the top step. There were holes bored into the chimney so I knew that the house was meant to hold salt, and he'd soon whittle a matching barn to hold pepper. Sometimes my father tied a red ribbon through a notch as small as a sliver and turned the house into a Christmas ornament. Other times he nailed tiny brass hinges below the roofline, and the house became a jewelry box. Our friend Rei sold the houses at the fairs she traveled to every month. The orchard had not borne much fruit that fall, and my father spent more and more time working on the houses.

I wondered where this one would end up. Not a single toothpick-wide spindle on the house's tiny porch railing had broken in the fall from my father's lap. I longed to keep the house for myself, to hide it deep in a tree pocket where I could play with it during the long hours of the day that I spent alone. But if I put it in a tree pocket, I would probably only end up losing it. I set it down beside my father's chair.

The knife handle had smooth indentations the size of my father's fingers. The blade curved like a fang from the handle. I turned the knife in my hand, studying it, wondering over the fluttery feeling that was released in my belly as I held it.

When my father stirred, I set down the knife and crawled into his lap. His head rolled up from his chest. He blinked at me a few times and then shifted back in his chair. He didn't ask where I'd been. I was just five, but I had free roam of the property, including the curve of cliff that hung over the ocean. Whenever Rei visited, she told me not to go near the cliffs, and I would laugh at how scared she sounded. Rei was a grown-up and grown-ups weren't supposed to be scared of anything.

"Bear sat on me," I told my father, tears welling with the

words. My arms were sore and streaked with dirt. "He wouldn't let me up. He hurt me."

"Poor girl," Dad said, pulling leaves from the tangle of my hair.

I sunk against his chest. His arms were warm around me.

"Is it my fault that Mama is dead?"

"Of course not. Did Bear say that?"

I nodded. I couldn't look at him.

My father held me with one arm as he leaned to the side and lifted the cans on the porch one at a time and shook them, releasing small clouds of wood dust each time he set one down. When he found a can that suited him, he sat back in the chair again and drank.

"Bear misses your mama a lot, but it's no excuse to say those things to you."

"He hates me." The truth of my own statement caught me by surprise. I squirmed in my father's arms. It was true. Bear hated me. That was why he had those knives in his eyes when he looked at me in the grove. It was why he never played with me.

"He loves you. I know it. If you don't feel it, you'll just have to believe me." My father hugged me. "You're full of light, Merrow. When you're full of light, it's easy for you to love and be loved. Even Horseshoe Cliff loves you. Did you know that? It turns your little footsteps into heart-shaped stamps in the dirt. I see the hearts you leave everywhere I go.

"Do you know what happens when Bear walks on the land? Dust rises up and makes him cough. He's not easy to love like you are, and there's a reason for it. He was born chock-full of complicated emotions that make him do things neither of us would ever think of doing. The things he has done have welded together to form an anchor that he has to drag around everywhere. He's heavy with the things he has done, the things he has seen. But you are light, little Merrow. You are as light as a bird. Nothing holds you down. Whenever you choose, you can fly."

I loved when my father spoke this way, with poetry instead of plain words. But at that moment I did not understand him. My encounter with Bear had left me exhausted. The sun hung just above the ocean, and the sight of it made me tremble. My days were full of adventure, but at night my imagination got the best of me, and I hated being alone. The wind whistled against the side of the house outside my bedroom, and the blanket on my bed scratched me, and I didn't like to walk outside to the toilet shed alone, so I lay awake and worried I would wet the bed. The mice came alive at the prick of the first star, their feet always whispering, their eyes always searching. I would grow hungry lying awake, and the only good thing about that was that my stomach groans kept the mice from climbing onto my bed. Bear wouldn't let me sleep in his room, and my father cried out in his sleep in a voice that scared me even more than being alone. On warm nights, my father used to let me sleep in the pasture with my pony, but ever since half the chickens had been killed, he wouldn't allow it.

"It's my birthday," I reminded him now.

"I know it."

I searched his face, but he was looking out at the scruff of meadow that spread from the porch to the sea, and he didn't meet my gaze. He had soft brown eyes and a dark beard and dark hair to his shoulders and skin that was sort of pink—the color that a strawberry turned after it stopped being green but wasn't quite ripe yet. He said that Bear and I took after our mother with our green-brown eyes and golden skin that never burned and pale brown hair that striped yellow in the sun. *My little acorns,* my father called us, which made me laugh because Bear was anything but little.

"Let's go for a walk," he said.

We walked together every day. We checked on the chickens frequently because we'd lost half of the old brood to coyotes over the summer, and even though the new chickens were settled in now with the old, the blood that stained the coop ramp had not faded. We fed and watered the horses, Old Mister and Guthrie. We often walked the garden rows, rewarding ourselves with tiny sweet tomatoes that burst between our back teeth. Or we looked for wood for Dad's miniature houses. Or stuffed steel wool into holes to keep mice out of the cottage walls and sang about answers that blew away in the wind.

I always felt my father's love for the land as we walked it. If he saw my footsteps everywhere, I saw his handprints everywhere. He had built our cottage and planted every tree in our orchard. Later, when he was gone, he was never really gone, because he was everywhere.

Now, we ducked between the rails of the paddock fence he had built years before I was born. A strange sound came from the lean-to at the end of the pasture. I dropped my father's hand and ran toward it, worried for the horses. There were hunting animals all around—animals I'd seen, like the mean, bold coyotes that had eaten the chickens, and ones I hadn't seen, like mountain lions. Diana, my father's old dog, used to guard the land at night, but she'd died a week before the coyotes attacked the chickens. Bear told me that the coyotes must have been watching us all along, waiting for Diana to die. Now I sensed the coyotes' invisible eyes following me around the land just as I sensed the moon peeking from the sky all day, impatiently waiting for its turn to shine.

My mother had died, Diana had died, and the chickens had died. Still, it had only lately occurred to me to wonder what might happen next.

"The horses are fine," I heard my father call behind me as I ran.

And he was right; the horses were fine. In a corner of the lean-to, separated from the horses by a bank of hay bales, I was astonished to find a puppy.

I clambered up and over the hay bales into the makeshift pen and lifted the puppy, a wriggling, yipping whirl of black and brown, into my arms and laughed.

"This little guy," Dad said, looking down at me, "is all yours."

When the puppy licked my chin, his sharp teeth raked my skin, but I didn't mind one bit. I couldn't believe he was mine. He squirmed in my arms, pressing his body against the bruises left there by my brother. I thought of Bear kneeling over me, pinning me down, the knives in his eyes. My mouth went dry. The puppy was mine. I looked up at my father.

"What about Bear?"

He ruffled my hair. "It's not Bear's birthday, is it?"

I shook my head and tried to smile. My stomach felt knotted. I hugged the puppy tight to my chest. Bear didn't want a dog, did he? Had he cried like I had when Diana had died? No. I had never seen Bear cry over anything. I guessed he was too old for crying, like my father. Dad's eyes were only wet when he stared too long at the horizon at night. Bear said I did all the crying at Horseshoe Cliff while he did all the work. I decided then and there that I would take on more chores, and I wouldn't spend so much time wandering around lost in imaginary games, and I wouldn't cry. The puppy was already mine. He licked my chin, cooling the scrapes he'd left there. He smelled of hay, of home, and I could feel his little heart skittering around as though trying to reach mine. *I will love this dog forever,* I thought. What could Bear do about that?

My father leaned over the hay bales and rested his big warm hand on my shoulder. "Happy birthday, Merrow," he said. "Enjoy your new pal."

CHAPTER THREE

I was born in 1988 but since I never spent much time anywhere but Horseshoe Cliff, where for many years there was no television, my childhood never felt connected to the times in which I was living. It was only when I entered kindergarten at Little Earth School in Osha that I became somewhat aware of pop culture and the larger world. From the beginning, I loved school. I was not the sort of child who was afraid of new experiences. My father told me that I was like my mother in this way, always up for an adventure. There were other young students who clung to their mothers and sobbed on the steps of the school in the morning; I hopped out of my father's truck and ran right past them. My schoolmates did not know what to make of me at first, but after some effort on my part, they came around.

Little Earth occupied an old Victorian house. The upper school was upstairs, and the lower school was downstairs, with only twenty or so children enrolled in each. I had no idea, of course, that it was a little hippie school in a little hippie town.

Little Earth might as well have been the whole earth—that's how big and exciting it seemed to me. The raucous clatter of dozens of children talking and laughing at once was as wonderful a sound as I had ever heard. Until then, my only playmates had been covered with fur or feathers.

It did not take long for me to understand that I was not like the other students at Little Earth. My classmates wore different outfits every day of the week. They had clean hair that smelled of flowers. They left school with blackened fingernails and streaks of dirt on their knees from playing in the schoolyard and returned the next morning wiped clean, all signs of the previous day's activity erased. They had more food than they could eat in their lunchboxes, packed neatly by their mothers.

They were kind to me, often offering me half a sandwich or a cookie when they saw how little I'd brought.

"Here you go," a talkative girl named Daphne said to me on our second day, handing me a plastic bag full of celery sticks covered in peanut butter. "My mom told me to be *extra* nice to you because you don't have a mom and you're poor." Daphne spoke in a matter-of-fact tone. A few of the other children at our table glanced at me and smiled in a way that revealed that they, too, had been told to be nice to me.

I'd known the mom part, of course, but the poor part surprised me. Was I poor? No one had mentioned it before. It made sense, though, upon reflection. I was often hungry, and the shelves in our kitchen were closer to bare than full. I wore clothes that my brother had worn years earlier, or things that we found in the free box in front of the Osha co-op. We did not have a television. We occasionally endured a week or more without the lights working. The only new things I had ever owned were presents from our friend Rei, and though my father sometimes protested her gifts, in the end he always accepted them.

With the word *poor* echoing through my mind, I felt a sudden impulse to impress my new friends. When Teacher Julie had gone slowly through the letters of the alphabet the day before, I had not spoken up to let her know that I could already read, but now, I did. I had learned to read when I was four. We did not have many toys at Horseshoe Cliff, but stuffed bookshelves lined my father's bedroom. He and Rei frequently traded books, discussing their most recent reads at length on the back porch while watching the sun set. When Rei noticed that I had taught myself to read, she started bringing me stacks of books that she had borrowed from a library some distance away, though she was less inclined to do so as of late because I had lost the last few books she had given me. The books were beside my bed when I went to sleep, and when I woke up, they were gone. Rei was softspoken but serious; she had never before scolded me the way she did when I lost those books.

After only a few days at Little Earth, it became clear to me that I read far above the average level for my age. I offered to tutor my new friends, but they declined my help.

My stories, on the other hand, delighted my classmates. I told them about the mermaid sisters who swam alongside the whales just off the coast of Horseshoe Cliff and the civilization of fairies that had been living in the eucalyptus grove for a thousand years. These were complicated tales with devious villains and plucky heroines. Not every character made it to the end alive. In the yard, my classmates would gather around me to listen to the latest installment of life under the sea, or in the trees. My audience swung from gasps to laughter. Sometimes, they clapped.

When Teacher Julie would come outside to collect us from our recess, she would wait until I'd reached a suitable resting point in my story. One day, after sending the other kids inside, she handed me a clothbound journal.

"You're nearly bursting with these stories, Merrow," she told me. "Why don't you try writing them down?"

I ran my hand over the journal sadly. I adored Teacher Julie, but how could I explain to her that the only way for me to keep my stories was to save them inside of me? If I wrote them down, I would only lose them. I was so forgetful I could hardly remember half the things I'd forgotten. Just a week earlier, one of the older girls at school had presented me with a doll that she'd sewn from old cloth and bits of ribbon. Within a day of bringing it home, the doll disappeared. I was sure I had left it at the kitchen table when I'd gone out to feed the chickens, but when I returned to the cottage, the table was empty.

"I'll lose it," I told my teacher. "I lose everything."

Teacher Julie studied me, thoughtful for a moment. "Why don't you keep it here at school?" she said at last. "You can write during quiet time and store the journal in your cubby when you're not using it. I'll help you remember to put it in the same spot every day, okay? Nothing is lost for very long at Little Earth."

Her words filled me with hope. I gave her a tight hug before hurrying to place my new journal in my cubby.

As MUCH AS I loved school, Bear hated it. In the morning, after Dad drove away from Little Earth in his truck, Bear would lumber off toward town. On those days, he smelled like beer in the afternoon when our father picked us up. Dad would tell him that if he skipped school again, he would have to drop out permanently and stay home to work in the orchard. But he kept giving Bear another chance and another chance until the Friday came when Bear learned he was all out of chances.

I sat between Bear and my father in the cab of the truck. Since I refused to sleep during naptime at school, not wanting to miss anything, I was always tired on the way back to Horseshoe Cliff and usually nodded off. That afternoon, I awoke to hear my father telling Bear that from then on, he'd remain at home to help in the orchard. As Dad spoke, Bear's elbow pressed sharply into my side. I looked up to see my brother glowering at me. I felt a chill around him that would not thaw; I'd seen the knives in his eyes every day since that first time in the grove. His elbow pressed into my side so hard that I gasped. He had never hurt me in front of our father, and I think I was surprised as much as I was hurt.

"Bear!" Dad said.

"She's taking up all the space."

I squeezed my eyes shut and pretended to sleep.

"Ugh, she smells terrible," Bear said. "She has fleas."

"Your sister doesn't have fleas."

On cue, the red bumps along my arms began to itch. Once I started scratching, I could not stop. I had fleabites. It was true. Fleas loved Pal as much as I did, but I'd endure the bites of all the fleas in the world if it meant I could keep my dog with me at night.

"Oh, Mer," I heard my father say. "Are you letting Pal in your bed again?"

I pretended to snore. I couldn't stop scratching though. The scratching, at least, gave me something to do other than cry, which I knew would have made Bear only angrier. The kids at school never pointed at my fleabites or yanked my hair or told me manure smelled better than I did. Only Bear. My father told me that Bear loved me, but what I felt from him seemed the opposite of love. It seemed to me that before my fifth birthday, when Bear had sat on me in the grove, I had walked around in a kind of fog. I had not been able to see all the ways he mistreated me. But now I felt a kind of clarity. I knew Bear hated me and wished me only harm. I knew I should stay as far away from him as I could.

As the truck tires rumbled from the paved road onto Horseshoe Cliff's dirt drive, I hugged my backpack and kept my eyes tightly shut. I imagined that I was still sitting on the rug in Little Earth, surrounded by other kids, listening to Teacher Julie tell us how the Earth turned. I wished the Earth would speed up just this once, delivering me back to school faster. I shuddered at the thought of a weekend at home with Bear, especially now that he had been sentenced to full days of the farmwork he hated.

OVER THE NEXT couple of years, I became more adept at staying out of Bear's way. Still, the anger that I sensed simmering within him would boil over unpredictably, and there were times when I could not avoid his rage. These assaults felt random, but some calculation must have gone into them; Bear never shoved me to the ground or twisted my arms behind my back within sight of our father. And he never went so far as to hurt me so badly that my father could not dismiss my complaints as within the realm of normal sibling squabbling. I loved my father more than I loved anyone, but it always seemed that he was only half listening, only half watching. He did his farmwork and he put plates of food on the table and at night he sat on the porch, exhausted, coughing, whittling those tiny houses and staring off at the horizon and drinking beer until his words softened. He was a vague presence much of the time, benevolent but preoccupied. And what preoccupied him? The farm, of course, which needed near constant attention, but I also came to believe that my father's thoughts never strayed far from his memories of my mother.

When I thought of my missing treasures, I thought of a list as long and old as an ancient scroll, and at the top of that scroll was my mother. Of all that had gone missing, she was, of course, the most important. Of all the mysteries that hounded me, the mystery of *how* she had been lost was the most unrelenting.

When I finally worked up the nerve to ask my father outright what had happened to my mother, the look on his face was so pained that I ran away from him and never asked again.

It was Rei who at last gave me some hint of my mother's demise. Rei had a quiet energy much like that of my father, but where my father's attention was inconsistent, when Rei was near, I felt my every move observed. She wore an armful of colorful bangles that I admired and an enormous straw sun hat and a rotating assortment of overalls that always looked so crisp and clean that for a time I was convinced she stopped in Osha to buy them on her way to Horseshoe Cliff. She never raised her voice, but when her face went very still, and her eyes roved from my bare, dirty feet to my uncombed hair, her displeasure was palpable. She worried over me in a way my father did not, and never once came to our house without pressing some treat she'd baked into my open and eager hands. She worried over my father, too, bringing him strange-smelling teas and pots of honey for the cough that increasingly bothered him. Rei, I sensed, would have believed me if I'd told her how Bear treated me. And yet I never told her. I couldn't say why, exactly, except that I had developed a notion that to do so would hurt my father, and I could not stand to be the one who made him sad.

Besides, though I would not have traded her delicious presents for nearly anything in the world, it annoyed me that Rei treated me like a child far younger than I felt myself to be. It was Rei who convinced my father that I should not be allowed to ride Guthrie beyond the limits of the pasture without an adult to keep watch, and that I should not be allowed to swim in the sea alone. (Thankfully, he lost track of these rules as easily as he was convinced to make them.)

And the cliffs. Rei was perpetually warning me to stay away from the cliffs.

She said it again on a day that she brought me a new blue swimsuit. When I tried on the suit, her keen black eyes clouded with a faraway look.

"Your mother loved that shade of blue," she said. "She wore a blue scarf that was so light it seemed to float on her shoulders. Your father would laugh and ask her how it felt to have her head in the clouds." Rei blinked. She looked down and brushed invisible lint from her overalls. "She was very beautiful."

She had promised to watch me swim. I ran across the bluff toward the steep path that cut down to the beach, ignoring her calls for me to be careful. When I neared the cliff, Rei's nagging grew urgent. I spun around to confront her.

"I'm not stupid, you know. I never go right up to the edge."

Half of this was a lie. I did not believe myself to be stupid, but I did go right up to the edge of the cliff. I liked the thrill of it, the way it made my fear grow so big that it shook my heart and wrenched my stomach and pounded on my ears. I bellowed out at the sea and the sea bellowed back at me, and when I stepped away from the cliff's edge the fear would drain immediately out of me and I would feel better—exhilarated and exhausted, like I'd won something for which I'd fought hard.

Rei pressed her lips together and gave me a look that told me she knew I was lying.

I shrugged and turned to keep walking. "Seriously," I said over my shoulder. "What's the big deal?"

"The big deal," she answered, "is that the land at the edge of the cliff is not secure. Pieces of it fall into the sea every day. *People* fall into the sea."

This made me stop. "Who?"

Rei made a shooing motion with her hands and didn't respond.

She meant my mother. I knew it like I'd always known it, like I suddenly remembered something that had been told to me long before.

My mother had died falling from the cliff.

This was the reason my father grew sad at night as he gazed out at the horizon—it was not the horizon he was watching, but the cliff.

And this was the reason my brother hated the beach so much that he had never learned to swim.

Knowing how my mother had died should have made me sad, but I felt a weight slipping off my shoulders: the weight of the unknown. For the first time, I'd found something I'd lost, and it was the most important thing of all. I understood then that I was drawn to the cliffs, and to the sea, just as my mother had been. I had always felt my father's presence with me as I explored Horseshoe Cliff, but now I felt my mother's spirit, too, surrounding me, emanating from the earth and the sky and the sea.

My brother's attacks grew fiercer around the same time that I learned how my mother had died. It was as though he sensed my new peace and it aggravated him. But understanding why my brother had never learned to swim helped me see that my brother not only avoided the ocean; he avoided the entire beach. From then on, I knew that when Bear threatened me, I could run down the path from the bluff to the sand below and he would not follow me. When I stepped onto the path down to the sea, I grew so light that I felt as though I'd sprouted wings. I was free.

I ran from Bear to the beach many times over the following years, and each time I did I looked up at the cliff and imagined my mother standing there on the edge, watching over me, keeping me safe.

CHAPTER FOUR

On a Saturday morning when I was eight years old, my father announced that he needed to go to the airport. No matter how I begged, he would not bring me with him. Nor would he tell me why he had to go.

"Take care of your sister," my father told Bear.

We stood on the front porch. It was still early in the morning and the sun was low enough in the sky that we had to squint at each other. It would be a rare hot day. The fog that blanketed the land at night had already burned away, and at my side, Pal swung his gaze from one of us to the next, panting.

In response to my father's request, Bear only grunted. His hands were shoved deep in the pockets of his jeans. He did not have a shirt on, and his wide chest was covered in swirls of brown hair that turned amber in the rising light. He was eighteen now, but it seemed to me he was the same non-child, non-adult he had forever been. He would not play with me, and he would not take care of me. He must have felt me studying him because he turned toward me, and I dropped my gaze to my feet.

"I'm serious, Bear," Dad said. "See that Merrow gets something to eat. I might not be back until late tonight."

I looked up and stared at my father. I could not remember him ever leaving us for so long a stretch of time. My father was steadfast in his routine, and he seemed as much a part of Horseshoe Cliff as the cottage, or the cliffs, or the sea. Would the whole place disappear when he drove away? It did not seem impossible.

Tears threatened to spring to my eyes, but I held them back. I could see that Dad would not bring me with him, and if I began crying now it would only serve to stoke my brother's disgust of me. It was the last thing I wanted to do before we were alone together.

"'Something to eat'?" Bear echoed. He coughed up a wad of mucus and spat it off the porch. "What do you suggest?"

"I'll make myself an egg," I said quickly. "And an apple."

"There's a loaf of bread in there, and peanut butter, too," said my father. My spirits lifted. I loved peanut butter, and Dad knew it. "Don't let Bear eat it all," he told me. Then he looked at my brother and muttered something under his breath. My father usually had patience for Bear's sullen moods, but lately he seemed more frustrated with my brother than usual. I thought that perhaps he was just tired. It had been another poor season for the farm. He whittled late into the night and used the money that Rei gave him when she sold his tiny houses to buy provisions from the Osha co-op.

The chickens were my responsibility, and it seemed to me that their eggs were more important than ever. I took good care of them, singing to them each evening at dusk. I did not go so far as to give them names. There were nights when we ate chicken, and I did not want to connect a name to my dinner.

As I watched my father's truck grow small along the drive away from our home, the rumbling of the wheels along the dirt path echoed within me. I decided I would spend the day pulling weeds from the garden. This would serve the double purpose of pleasing my father and keeping me far from Bear, who was unlikely to do anything resembling work without my father's urging.

After weeding for most of the morning, I joined Pal in a patch of shade under the row of cypress trees that I called the Old Ladies. My skin was hot from the sun, and the cool dirt below the trees was a welcome relief. I snacked on a few of the small tomatoes I'd found while weeding. Though I craved a peanut butter sandwich, I had not seen Bear leave the house and I did not want to cross his path. I wished I'd thought to bring a book with me. I curled up beside Pal and looked at the tree's crooked spine. My father had told me that he and my mother chose this spot for the garden because the line of cypresses protected it from the gales that blew onto the land from the ocean. I called the trees the Old Ladies because they looked like a huddle of tough old grandmothers, their green bouffants flattened into funny shapes by the wind.

Hidden within the shadow of the Old Ladies, I soon fell asleep.

I was not sure how much time had passed when I awakened. My stomach felt hollow with hunger; it drove me toward the house. I breathed out in relief when I saw that Bear was not in the kitchen, and quickly set to making myself a sandwich. Bear had already made a dent in the peanut butter, but there was plenty left to spread a thick layer on two slices of the brown bread that my father always purchased. I was not particularly fond of that bread, with its strange, seedy lumps and thick crust, but my father had once told me that it had been my mother's favorite, and knowing this allowed me to take some pleasure in it. I sat down at the table and took a large bite. As I swallowed, I heard a racket coming from Bear's bedroom. A moment later, he threw open his door and stumbled toward me. Even if I hadn't seen the cans of my father's beer that littered the floor behind him, I would have recognized the smell. On my father, the odor of beer was a light presence that arrived only after sunset, but Bear smelled like he hadn't so much drunk the beer as bathed in it.

I felt the urge to run, but my legs would not work. I sat very still, holding the sandwich in midair, wishing myself invisible.

Bear's bleary gaze narrowed. He lurched toward me and swiped the sandwich from my hands.

"Who said it was lunchtime? I'm in charge." He kicked at the chair beside me and sat down heavily in it. Then he began to eat my sandwich.

"Hey!" I cried. "That's mine."

"No shit," he said, and kept eating. In three bites, the sandwich was gone. He stretched his long arm to the counter and picked up the peanut butter jar. Why hadn't I hidden it some-where? I was full of regret as I watched my brother jam his dirty fingers into the jar and scoop out an enormous lump. He wrinkled his nose as he ate it and spoke with his mouth full.

"I don't know why you like this stuff." His mouth was a dank cave of wet peanut butter. He began to clear his throat so loudly that at first, I thought he was choking, and I felt my body seize with worry for him. I put my hand on top of his, but he swatted me away.

Then he spat a huge brown wad of phlegm into the peanut butter jar.

A noise emerged from me, a sort of strangled howl that made Pal jump to standing from where he'd been watching us from the floor.

"Don't cry," Bear warned.

"I'm not," I said, but of course I was. I could not believe that of the entire brand-new jar of delicious peanut butter, I would have only one small bite.

"Stop crying!" Bear bellowed. Specks of spit and peanut but-ter hit my face. "Stop! Stop!" His eyes burned with rage. His hands encircled my arm, and he began twisting it.

I wailed in pain.

And then he was dragging me across the room. He opened the door to the linen closet, threw me in, and slammed the door. I tried the door handle and it turned in my hand, but the door would not open. I pushed my shoulder against the door and shoved as hard as I could. It did not budge.

"Bear!" I screamed. "Let me out!"

There was no light in the closet. The sound of my frantic breathing filled the small space.

I screamed Bear's name over and over again. From the kitchen, Pal scratched at the door and whimpered. There was a ribbon of light at the bottom of the door. I lay down and pressed my face against the floorboards. I could see the legs of the kitchen chair that Bear had wedged under the doorknob. Pal pushed his nose into the crack and sniffed. I could just manage to touch his nose with my finger.

"It's okay, Pal," I said. "I'm okay. Don't worry." It was as much bravery as I could manage before crying again.

Time passed. I didn't know how much. My eyes grew dry. My stomach growled. My bladder began to pinch. I hopped from foot to foot and yelled for Bear, but he did not come. When I couldn't hold my pee any longer, I pulled a towel from the shelf and crouched over it. When I was done, I rolled up the wet towel and shoved it into the corner. I was so hungry that I felt sick to my stomach. I sat on the ground and put my head on my knees. I hated the darkness, the heat of the tight space, the gaping silence beyond the door. I felt myself begin to shake, and the shaking grew until I was stomping my feet against the floor.

I imagined revenge. My father would come home and be horrified to find me in the closet. He would hug me tightly and apologize for leaving me alone. He would cook me an enormous dinner and he wouldn't give any of it to Bear—in fact, he'd tell Bear he would never eat again unless he started being nice to me. He would make Bear say he was sorry. I would not forgive Bear though. I would make Bear go days without food before I forgave him and allowed him to eat.

When this fantasy faded, I was left alone again in the small closet. I closed my eyes and imagined the expanse of the ocean. I imagined the salt air filling my chest the way my father had told me it had once filled his, healing him if only for a time. I felt my mother watching me from the cliff. I saw her become a red bird that called to me in a clear song from outside the cottage.

My head jerked from my knees at the sound, and I realized I had fallen asleep. The ribbon of light around the edge of the doorframe was gone. The inky darkness of the closet caused a new wave of panic to wash over me. What if my father didn't return that night? Would Bear leave me to sleep in the closet? I reached to try the doorknob and gasped when the door swung open. Pal trotted over to me, shimmying and nipping nervously at my hands. Bear's bedroom door was open, and the room was empty.

I hurried across the kitchen and snatched two of the hard-boiled eggs from the bowl my father frequently restocked on the top shelf of the fridge. My hands were shaking. I peeled and ate the eggs so quickly that my teeth crunched against tiny pieces of shell that I couldn't be bothered to remove. The clock above the sink revealed that it was nearly nine o'clock at night. Except for a single bite of the peanut butter sandwich that Bear had stolen from me, I had not eaten since early that morning. After I finished the eggs, I sat at the table and ate one piece of bread and then another, washing them down with a large glass of water. I wished again that I had hidden the peanut butter.

I was still sitting at the kitchen table in a sort of daze when headlights swung through the kitchen window. I ran out to the front porch with Pal at my heels to see my father stepping out of his truck. I leaped clear over the porch steps and threw my arms around his waist. He lifted me easily off the ground and hugged me. When I opened my eyes, I saw Bear appear around the corner of the house. He glared at me and shook his head. The sight of him made me involuntarily bite down on the inside of my cheek. I whimpered from the pain and burrowed my face against my father's neck.

"What is it, Merrow?" he asked, running his hand down the length of my hair. "Don't cry. I'm home now."

"I bit my cheek," I said, muffled. I didn't want to raise my head and see Bear watching me again.

Dad stroked my hair. "Poor Merrow." He set me down gently, peeling my arms from his neck. "Don't you want to know why I went to the airport?" He waved his hand in the direction of the open truck door. "Come meet Amir."

The truck seat was too high to see what was on it, so I climbed into the cab. At first, I saw only a big blue coat, puffy and strangely shaped, and so I thought perhaps the coat was called an Amir. But then the coat moved, and the head of a boy appeared. The boy looked like one of the wood sprites in the book of fairy tales that I had borrowed several times from Little Earth before losing it. His hair was black and silky around his long face and narrow chin; his blocky ears reminded me of my father's wood bookends. His eyes were as dark as the smudges made by rubbing burnt kindling on stone. My skin was brown from the sun, but his was browner.

He studied me just as I studied him. His eyes were big and serious and searching. I liked him immediately. This wasn't something that I decided, just a feeling of happiness that rose within me as I looked at him.

"Hello," I said.

"Who's that?" came Bear's voice, making me start. He stood beside my father with his arms crossed against his chest.

"Bear, say hello to Amir. He's going to live with us," said my father.

I stared at my father, surprised and excited. But when I turned back to Amir, his big eyes brimmed with quivering tears.

"Oh no," I whispered, leaning toward him. I'd never felt a coat like his, as thick as a new pillow below my fingers. "Don't do that. Don't cry. Bear won't like it." I used a corner of the enormous coat to wipe the boy's eyes.

"Amir," my father said, "this is Merrow."

He stared at me and said something that sounded like *Shookdeeyah.*

I stared right back at him. "Is that a fairy language?" I asked. "Will you teach me?"

"No, that's Hindi, isn't it, Amir?" my father asked, sticking his head into the cab. "Merrow, Amir's mother's name was Allison. She was *your* mother's best friend when they were both children in New York. But Amir was born in India. He speaks Hindi, and English, too."

Amir was still looking at me. "I lived in an orphanage in India," he said in a quiet but surprisingly clear voice. "When my mother adopted me, she took me to live in New York City. And now my mother has died."

My mouth fell open. I wondered how his mother had died, and if it had been his fault. I'd never met another child with a dead mother. And he'd been an orphan! And now he was an orphan again, I realized. I'd never met an orphan, either, but Rei had recently given me *Anne of Green Gables* and I'd loved it, finishing the entire book in a weekend. I thought that Anne and I would have been best friends if we'd had the chance to meet. It seemed very likely to me that Amir and I would become best friends.

"You're joking," I heard Bear say to my father. "We barely have enough to feed ourselves."

"We have plenty," answered Dad.

"Plenty! We have plenty of rotten apples and chickenshit. Is that what this kid eats? Because I don't."

"Bear." My father's voice was low but held a warning.

Bear grabbed my arm and pulled me from the cab of the truck. "It's my turn to see our new brother."

His words were so startling that I didn't yell at the pain of being yanked from the truck. I rubbed my arm and looked up at my father. "Is Amir our new *brother*?"

"Well, no, not exactly. But he's going to live with us. I'm his guardian now. That means I'm going to take care of him the same way that I take care of you."

Inside the cab, Bear muttered darkly. I'd read in books of

siblings who were friends and protectors, but I'd been given a dud, a brother who hated me and would happily feed me to a mountain lion. If my brother and I had ever shared a loving moment, I'd forgotten it.

Now, it seemed, my father had corrected the mistake.

"Can he sleep in my room?" I stood on my toes and tried to catch sight of Amir around Bear's back. What was Bear doing to him in there? "Do you want to sleep in my room, Amir?"

"Well he sure as hell isn't sleeping with me," said Bear, finally pulling back out of the truck. He spat once at the ground and then plodded heavily up the porch steps.

Amir appeared unshaken by Bear's inspection.

"Come on out," my father told him. "Most of us don't bite."

Amir crawled across the seat of the cab and lowered himself to the ground. I was surprised to see that once straightened, he was taller than me. He clutched his blue coat in his arms the same way that the kids who didn't know how to swim held rafts at the beach in Osha, and it made me feel as sorry for him as I did for them.

"*I* don't bite," I told him. "Sometimes the chickens peck, but not much. There are coyotes, but they mostly bite the chickens. The horses don't bite unless they think your fingers are carrots. Dad doesn't bite, but Rei says his burps are so loud they hurt her ears."

"Guilty as charged," said my father.

Amir's eyes hinted at a smile. I took a step closer to him. "Rei is our friend from town who bakes pies and sells Dad's carvings at festivals. How old are you? I'm eight."

"I'm almost nine."

I nodded. "That's why you're taller than I am." I turned to my father. "Will Amir go to Little Earth?"

"Yes. Now go inside, both of you. It's cold out here. I'll get your things, Amir."

I wondered what kinds of things Amir had. He trailed after me into the house.

"Did you bring books?" I asked. When he shook his head, I hoped my face didn't reveal my disappointment. "That's okay. You can borrow as many books as you want from Little Earth. That's your new school. It's in town. You'll be the only other eight-year-old besides me. I'm reading *Pippi Longstocking* right now, but if you don't like that there are a lot of other books you can choose. But *Pippi* is really funny. You'll like it."

Amir's eyes were traveling all over the kitchen. I was happy to see that Bear was in his bedroom with the door shut. I followed Amir's gaze around the room. I tried to see it the way he might. I'd never had someone my own age over before.

"Is it bigger or smaller than your house?" I asked.

"I didn't have a house. I had an apartment. This is darker."

I laughed. "Well, we only have the one light on. We like to save electricity. It's good for the earth." Pal was sniffing Amir's sneakers. "That's my dog, Pal."

Amir stroked Pal's head. They looked each other in the eyes, and Pal wagged his tail in a thoughtful way. When Amir straightened, he said, "You're lucky to have a dog."

I swallowed. I thought of his dead mother. "We can share

him," I said quietly. It pained me to offer this, but when Amir smiled the pain disappeared.

My father came in carrying a green duffel bag in one hand and a paper bag in the other. "We stopped for hamburgers on the way home. Here's one for you," he said, handing me the bag.

Normally, I might have asked if he'd brought one for my brother, but in that moment, I didn't care if Bear ever ate again. Even though my stomach was full from the eggs and the bread I'd eaten, I stood right there in the middle of the kitchen and devoured the hamburger.

Dad watched me, shaking his head. "Slow down," he said. The look he gave me almost made me tell him what Bear had done that day, but the sight of my brother's closed door across the kitchen stopped me.

"Follow me, Amir," Dad said, walking toward my room. "You'll sleep on the floor in Merrow's room for now. Rei's dropping off an extra bed tomorrow. We'll get you settled in before you know it. I can tell Merrow is happy you're here."

"I am," I confirmed, swallowing the last of the hamburger as I hurried after them. "Are you tired, Amir? I'm not." I liked saying his name. *Amir is here*, I thought, enjoying the rhyme.

"He's had a very hard few weeks and a long day of travel. Try to let him get some sleep, okay?" My father set the green duffel on my floor and left the room. "You'll show him the ropes, won't you, Merrow?" he called from the kitchen. I heard the fridge door open and knew he was searching for his beer. I wondered if Bear had left him any.

Amir looked around my room, but there wasn't much to see. Most of the toys and treasures I tried to accumulate were lost.

"We brush our teeth in the kitchen sink," I told Amir. "And there's a toilet shed around the side of the house."

Before Amir could answer, my father appeared with a pair of quilts I'd never seen and a new pillow, too. As soon as they were spread on the floor, Amir lay on top of them and covered himself with the big blue coat.

"You'll be all right," my father murmured to the boy. He didn't seem surprised that Amir hadn't brushed his teeth or changed into pajamas. When he turned off the light, moonlight flooded the room. "Get some sleep, and in the morning, we'll show you around the property. You'll like it here, Amir. Horseshoe Cliff is a wonderful place for children."

I was feeling tired myself and it didn't seem like my father was paying attention to me, so I followed Amir's lead and climbed into my bed without brushing my teeth or changing into my pajamas. Pal looked at me with his ears all perked up and expectant, but I shook my head to let him know not to jump onto the bed until Dad had left.

"Good night," said my father, kissing my forehead. The door clicked shut and Pal immediately leaped onto my bed and curled himself around my feet. I turned onto my side and watched Amir. His eyes moved below his eyelids in a way that made me think he was not yet asleep. I longed to reach out and touch the blue coat, to knead it like dough below my fingers. New York must have been very cold to need a coat so big.

"That's a big coat," I could not help but whisper.

"It was my mother's," Amir whispered back without opening his eyes.

"Oh. Was your mother very big?"

Amir was quiet for so long that I thought he had fallen asleep. I rolled onto my back and stared up at the ceiling. What a strange day I'd had. First my father had left on a mysterious errand. Then Bear had locked me in the closet for hours. And now an orphan had come to live with us, bringing not much more than his mother's enormous coat. Had my own mother been big or small? I wondered. There was a stack of her clothes on the top shelf of my father's closet. I would lay them on the floor in the morning, I decided, to see how big my mother had been.

"She wasn't very big," I heard Amir say then, so quietly that I wondered if the words had come from my own lips, if I'd drifted off to sleep and murmured the answer to my own question. But when I rolled back onto my side and looked down, I saw that the boy's eyes were dark jellyfish in shimmering twin seas. I felt a connection to him that I could not explain. On an impulse, I reached out my hand to him, and he held it.

CHAPTER FIVE

Amir took to Horseshoe Cliff like a fly to washed-up seaweed. It was hard for me to believe that before we met, he'd never ridden a horse, or held a just-laid egg, or eaten something pulled straight out of the dirt. He'd never even *planted* something in the dirt.

When we walked around the property on his first day, he kept stopping to crouch down and examine things. We saw all kinds of rocks and sticks and plants and bugs that day, including a small, strange, gold-winged bug that I'd never seen before. Amir didn't say a lot, but his eyes shone with curiosity. Everything was new to him, everything a discovery.

When we stopped at the pasture, Amir looked up at the mural on the side of the horses' lean-to.

"My mom painted that," I told him.

My father had told me the story. He'd worried about my mother standing on a ladder because she was pregnant with Bear at the time, but she'd said a little daring made a baby strong. And then Bear had turned out to be as big and strong a baby as had ever existed, and by the time he turned one our mother could barely carry him.

"My mom was a painter, too," Amir said. His accent made his words sound even and pure. It reminded me of rain falling into a half-full barrel.

"I wonder if our moms became friends because they both liked to paint," I said. "Or if one of them taught the other how to do it."

Amir stared off for a moment, thinking. "Maybe they met each other in a class."

I threw a stick in the air but didn't manage to catch it. Pal scooped it up and shook it a few times before stretching out in the dirt to gnaw on it. I looked up at the mural.

"My dad wanted my mom to paint the solar system," I said. "He said if you linked all the peace signs in Osha, they could circle the planet. He thought we should be different, but my mom said that someday someone was going to paint the peace sign that did the trick. The peace sign that worked. What if that person was her? My dad couldn't argue with that."

Amir stood very still as he listened to me. I could tell that he liked this story as much as I did.

The horses had been walking lazily toward us from the far end of the pasture.

"How about I teach you how to ride?" I said. It would help us become best friends like our mothers had been if Amir liked horses as much as I did. I climbed the rails of the fence and paused at the top, waiting for him to join me. The horses snorted warm bursts of air onto my legs, saying hello. "You can ride Old Mister, the bigger one. He's my dad's horse. Guthrie's mine."

As soon as Amir climbed up beside me on the fence, I grabbed a fistful of Guthrie's gray mane and swung my leg over the pony's back. I pressed my leg into his side to move him toward Old Mister, corralling the horse closer to where Amir sat on the fence. "Go on," I said. "Grab his mane. He won't stand still forever."

Amir grabbed Old Mister's mane and swung his leg over the horse. Seated, he grinned at me.

I laughed. I was a little surprised by how easily he'd done it. "There! Now all you need to do is hold on. Old Mister's in love with Guthrie. He'll follow him anywhere." I pressed my sneakered heels into Guthrie's sides and made little kissing noises with my mouth. For as long as I could remember, Guthrie had been my pony, but my father had once told me that Guthrie used to be Bear's. Only Bear never liked to ride him. He didn't like any animals, as far as I could tell, not even Pal, who was the most likable animal in the world.

I planned to ride down to the beach, but when I turned Guthrie toward the paddock gate Rei and my father were standing there, watching us.

"Rei!" I hollered, waving. Her face was pinched under her big hat. She was a terrible worrywart. For a moment, I forgot that Amir was behind me on Old Mister. I squeezed my heels into Guthrie and trotted across the paddock, dodging the gopher mounds below as best I could. Pal ran along as though on springs beside us, tail going in circles, barking even with that stick still in his mouth.

A quick tug on Guthrie's mane was all it took to bring the pony to a halt right in front of Rei and my father. I was proud of my clean, rein-less stop, but Rei wasn't even looking at me. I turned to see Old Mister hurrying toward us. Amir looked loose on the horse, his elbows jangling at each bounce, his body slipping from side to side, but his expression was set with determination and he managed to keep his seat. His shaggy black hair rose and fell around his big ears. When Old Mister stopped behind Guthrie and gave the pony's rump an annoyed nip, Amir laughed. His laughter was a full, rich sound, and his eyes were so bright with joy that it seemed to me you could have seen them in the dark.

"You're taking to this place like a fly to seaweed," my father said. I must have learned the saying from him.

"Where is your helmet? And the bridle?" Rei asked. The way she spoke was the thing I liked third best about her, after her pumpkin pies and the books that she gave me. Rei was from Japan. Each word she said was as crisp as a bite of fresh cucumber.

"We're fine," I assured her. "I'm teaching Amir how to ride." I tried to make my voice sound low and calm like my father's. Rei never scolded my father.

"You just sprinted across the field without the boy!"

"'Sprinted'!" I laughed, already forgetting to keep my voice low. "Rei, you're so funny! Horses don't sprint."

Rei huffed. She turned her attention to Amir. "It's you I came to see, young man. Are you all right up there? Would you like to come down?"

"No," said Amir.

Rei frowned. "No, *thank you.*"

Amir nodded, but didn't repeat her words. Later, I would have to tell him what my father said about Rei, which was that she'd never had time to have her own children because she was too busy raising everyone else's. My father had said this with a smile because he loved Rei just as I did. At dinner one night back when Bear still ate with us, Bear had said that Rei was in love with Dad and the idea of this had made Dad laugh so hard that I was surprised his chair survived the meal.

"Rei lives in Osha, the nearest town," my father told Amir as he gave Old Mister's forehead a massage. "She brought over a bed she wasn't using. I set it up in Merrow's room for you."

"We love Rei," I added. The thought of Rei helping to make Amir's stay in my room permanent made me contrite. After only one night together, I could not imagine ever again being able to fall asleep without Amir nearby. "Sometimes she visits Little Earth and reads stories to us. She was a teacher in Japan."

"Many years ago," Rei said. When she was pleased, her black eyes gleamed like wet rocks in the sun. I'd forgotten that seeing this was nearly as fun as seeing her rub her hands together with worry. *She's going to start a fire doing that someday,* I had murmured to my father once, making him duck his head and smile.

"Thank you for the bed," said Amir quietly.

Rei nodded. "You're welcome. Do you like lemon bread? I just put a loaf in the house. Make sure you kids have a piece before Bear gets a whiff of it."

I hoped Bear hadn't seen Rei's car pull up. "Follow me, Amir," I shouted. "We can ride to the house." I tapped my heels against Guthrie's belly, waking the pony from his doze.

"To the house?" Rei cried. "The boy's never ridden before! Jacob, talk some sense into her."

"It's not far, Rei. They'll be fine. Just walk, Merrow. Don't make Amir eat your dust."

I gave a frustrated groan but walked Guthrie toward the paddock gate. Old Mister and Amir followed behind us.

We had not made it far when Rei said in a clear voice, "Saying 'no' to that child every once in a while would do her some good, Jacob."

If my father replied, I didn't hear it.

I WISHED I could press Guthrie into a gallop, but lemon bread or no lemon bread, I was Amir's guardian now. Without my encouragement, Guthrie was in no hurry; *his* home and hay lay behind him. Old Mister plodded along with his chin practically resting on Guthrie's haunches. Guthrie swished his tail in a show of annoyance, but I knew that in truth nothing made the pony happier than feeling the weight of his friend's adoration.

"Is Rei your mother?" Amir asked. "The one who painted the barn?"

I looked back at him, surprised. "No. My mother died when I was little."

"Oh." His expression shifted, and I guessed he was thinking of his own mother.

"I can tell Old Mister likes you," I said. "Maybe my dad will give him to you. He hardly ever rides with me. My dad still likes riding, but his ass doesn't anymore."

I was learning that when Amir laughed, a burst of delight as sweet as any of Rei's pies spread through me.

We left the horses grazing on a patch of weeds along the dirt driveway. True to Rei's word, a loaf of bread drizzled with icing awaited us on the kitchen counter. Within moments we were eating hunks of it from our hands.

"Mmm," I said. "Thank goodness for Rei."

There were heavy footfalls outside and then Bear's voice, muttering, "If those horses run away because no one bothered to tie them up, I'm not going to be the one . . ."

I grabbed Amir's arm, but it was too late—Bear was already inside. His muttering ended abruptly, and his eyes narrowed as they fell on my hand encircling Amir's arm. He walked toward us. I pressed my eyes shut and waited for the blow, but it was Amir who crumpled beside me with a grunt, falling first against the kitchen table and then to the floor.

"Bear! No!" I cried, but he didn't bother to respond. He scooped up what remained of the loaf of bread and ambled out of the cottage.

Amir stood, cradling his elbow.

"Are you okay?" I asked.

He managed to shrug and wince at the same time. "Is he always like that?"

"Only when my dad isn't around. He hates me."

Amir didn't seem surprised by my statement. I peeked at his elbow and sucked in my breath when I saw the cut.

"Hang on. I'll get you a Band-Aid."

My father kept a first aid kit in his bureau. When I shut the drawer, I heard muffled voices. Rei and my father must have stood just outside the house. I pressed my ear to the wall and listened.

"Was she sick for a long time?" Rei asked.

"That's what her father said when he got hold of me. I haven't spoken to Allison in ages. Not since Marigold died."

"And Allison's father wouldn't take the boy? Who would not take his own grandson?"

"He didn't approve of Allison adopting Amir. But Allison was never close with her parents. Back when we knew her, she hadn't spoken to them in years. Her father said she didn't get in touch with him until she got sick and moved home from India. He's been helping them out for a while, but once Allison died . . ." His voice lowered. I pressed my ear against the wall. "He wanted to try to send Amir back to the orphanage in India, but someone found Allison's will. She had set me as Amir's guardian if anything happened to her. I guess Marigold had told her, years ago, that Horseshoe Cliff was a good place for a child to grow up."

"But to have you—a single man—take on this responsibility. How could she ask this of you?"

"I must have been her only option."

"That poor boy. He seems strong at least. Did you see the

way he stuck on your horse? He is a determined child. I suppose that is what happens when your childhood is all death and dislocation. Eight years old and to have lived through so much already." She was quiet for a moment. "And *you* . . . well, now you have another child to take care of on your own."

"He'll be fine. We'll all be fine. We have land for him to run on and a perfectly nice bed for him to sleep on, thanks to you. He'll go to school with Merrow. What more could a boy need?"

Rei said something I couldn't make out.

"I know you will, Rei. You always do. You're good to us."

"True goodness," she responded, "is shown by those who have nothing to give but what comes from their heart."

Amir appeared in the open door of the bedroom. I lifted my finger to my lips and without any other encouragement he joined me in pressing his ear to the wall. I smelled the lemon bread on his breath, the dusty horse scent on his skin. His big eyes blinked inches from mine. They were not as dark as I'd thought them to be; there was honey within the brown, softening them.

My father and Rei must have moved closer to the house, because suddenly Rei's voice was as clear as if she were in the room with us.

"But what about *your* health, Jacob? When did you last visit the doctor?"

I heard my father laugh.

"I'm serious," Rei said. "I don't want to embarrass you, but you were wheezing when you lifted that bed and—"

"Rei, I'm not a young man. I'm meant to huff and puff—"

"And if something happens to you? What will become of these kids then?"

Amir and I stared at each other. Despite the fact that he looked nothing like me, there was something about Amir's face that made me feel as though I were peering into the dark water of a tide pool and seeing a different version of myself in the reflection. I knew how he felt in that moment listening as Rei speculated about our future; I felt the same way.

Rei said, "Just promise me that you'll take care of yourself as well as you take care of these children. That's all I ask."

"Promises." I knew my father was smiling; I could hear it, and it reassured me. "You know what I can promise, Rei? I can promise to cut myself an extra big slice of that lemon bread you made. How's that?"

The sounds of the adults moving away from the window made us straighten.

"Poor Dad," I said. "He doesn't know that Bear took off with the rest of the lemon bread."

I licked my thumb and used it to wipe away the blood on Amir's elbow. I carefully pressed a bandage over his cut, the way I imagined Allison might have done for him, the way that my own mother might have done for Bear's scrapes and skinned knees in the years before I was born.

AFTER A WEEK of evenings on the porch watching my father work on his tiny houses, Amir asked if he would teach him how to whittle.

I had learned from Amir's first day at Little Earth that he

was not a strong reader. He did not listen to Teacher Julie's lessons with rapt attention as I did, but instead gazed toward the window. At home, though, Amir had taken great interest in my father's work, following him around the garden and the orchard. He kept his face very still, but his eyes took in everything. He asked questions that I had never thought to ask. Teacher Julie always told us that there were no right questions, but I could see from the way that my father looked at Amir that Amir was asking the right questions. My father showed us every tool in the shed and explained how to use them. In the orchard, there was dusty soil below our boots and plump apples above our heads. Dad told us how our trees—trees that drank the coastal fog—grew deep roots in order to find moisture where they could, seeking out hidden reserves far below the dry surface soil.

Adversity makes them stronger, my father said. *Heartier.*

Now, my father opened the leather whittling kit his grandmother had given him and handed Amir a knife. I looked up from my book. Amir's spine straightened. The blade caught the lantern's light as he turned it in his hand. His expression was unreadable. Then he nodded at my father, ready.

I listened as my father talked about how to safely handle the knife, but I soon returned to the book I was reading. I'd finished *Pippi Longstocking* and had moved on to a book of Greek myths that I'd found at Little Earth. I loved the goddesses' dresses, the way they flowed to the ground in silky folds and glittered with shells and pearls. In my entire life, I'd only worn clothes that had been worn first by other people. Without a television, I rarely caught glimpses of what people outside of our little corner of the world wore. It was only Rei, with her pretty bracelets and wide-brimmed hats, and the characters in the books that I read, who showed me that fancier clothes than mine existed.

I read to my father and Amir as they worked their knives. I noticed that my father smiled when he looked over at Amir's progress; it made me happy to see him smiling during those hours around sunset when he usually fell quiet.

Amir surprised us with how quickly he became adept at carving. He looked at a piece of wood and saw something else within it. Wood turned into shells and flowers and animals in his hands. Except for a fairy that he'd made for me, he gave all his carvings to Rei to sell along with my father's. The fairy he made for me had such wild hair and tiny toes and ornately detailed wings that I could not bear to tell him how swiftly I lost her.

The only one of us who was not taken with Amir was, of course, Bear. It seemed to me that the sight of the three of us happily sitting together on the porch each night drove him to an even darker place than he had been previously. My father asked him to join us, but he looked over at my father and Amir with those twin knives in their hands and refused.

Some nights, Bear shut the door to his room and turned on the radio that he had taken from the kitchen. Others, he would walk down the driveway and I'd watch the night close around him and wonder if he would come back. He fought with my father almost every day. It was clear to me that he hated Horseshoe Cliff, hated working the land and answering to my father. I didn't understand why he stayed.

It wasn't long after Amir arrived that I realized I'd stopped flinching when my brother approached. I was no longer his target. Amir took the brunt of my brother's violence from the moment he came to live with us. Every time Bear shoved Amir, I cried out, expecting to hear Amir's bones cracking as they hit the ground. But Amir seemed made of rubber. He'd once made the mistake of scrambling to his feet while Bear was still nearby, only to find Bear's thick hands on his shoulders again, tossing him back down. After that encounter, Amir learned to wait where he'd landed until Bear was gone. When I yelled at my brother, he just swatted me away like I was nothing. I would kneel to the ground and wait with Amir until Bear was out of sight, my whole body throbbing in anger as though I'd been knocked down, too.

When my father was nearby, Bear ignored Amir. I waited for Amir to tell my father what was happening, but he never did. He seemed so content when Bear was not around, and took such obvious pleasure in life at Horseshoe Cliff, that it was almost possible to believe that he forgot Bear's abuses as quickly as he was subjected to them. But there were nights when he groaned as he fell into bed, and I knew he was not sore from his chores. Without my father stepping in, I worried Bear's aggression would only worsen.

"I'm going to tell my dad," I said one night, blinking through the darkness toward Amir's bed in the far corner of our bedroom. "Bear is hurting you."

Amir sat up. "No. It doesn't matter what Bear does to me. You can't say anything to Jacob."

The desperation in his voice surprised me. From across the room, the bedsprings complained as he lay down again. I heard him turning from side to side, restlessly.

"It's quiet here," he said. "At the orphanage, I slept in a room with fourteen other children. Some of them would yell and cry in the night. It was hard to sleep. In the morning, I was always tired. I was small, and the bigger kids took my food. There was a courtyard to run and play ball in, and that was the best part of the day. A lot of the children were nice. Some were not. The man who watched us was not a good man. We called him Uncle. From one minute to the next, I didn't know what might happen to me. Uncle didn't like to hear us—singing, whispering, chewing our food. He didn't like our smells. He laughed to Cook about how dirty and stupid we were, about how nobody wanted us or would ever want us because just look at us. We were disgusting. When we looked at him wrong, he took our food away. Or he hit us on the shoulder or the back of the head or behind the knee.

"One day, I convinced Cook to let me deliver Uncle's lunch to his office. I was quick and quiet and I stood completely still outside Uncle's door while he ate. When he called for his plate to be taken, I did so silently. After that, I delivered Uncle's lunch every day. He never hit me again. His bowl always had a few bits of rice left in it when he was finished, but I never ate them.

"Maybe Uncle told my mother to choose me, or maybe she

had no choice at all. One minute I lived in the orphanage, and the next I lived in a house with my mother and three other American women who were in India to help children like me. They said they had waited a long time to be able to take me in, and I still can't understand that because all that time they were waiting, I was waiting, too. If we were all waiting, why couldn't we have waited together, away from that man at the orphanage? I was six then, I think, but I don't know. Maybe I was older and I lived even longer in the orphanage than I remember. I hope not. All I know is my mother and her friends cooked food that I had never had before. I grew bigger in that year but a part of me always thought it could not last because it did not feel real to live with them in that quiet house.

"I was right. When I was seven, my mother became sick. We moved to New York City. Her father didn't want me to call him Grandfather. He didn't like me in his home. He wrinkled his face when he saw me. I tried to stay out of his way so he could pretend that I wasn't there. It was cold in New York, and then it was hot, and then it was cold again. And then my mother died, and I came here to live with you."

I listened, astonished. It was the most Amir had said about his past. I understood that Bear's treatment of me over the years was small compared to what Amir had been through. Even at eight years old I understood that I was listening to something profound. Bravery and strength had resided quietly within Amir the whole time that we'd been running around Horseshoe Cliff, exploring and laughing and playing.

And then I understood what he was trying to tell me.

"You love it here," I said.

"Yes."

"My father wouldn't make you leave. He's not like your grandfather."

"Bear is his son. If he learns Bear doesn't like me—"

"Bear doesn't like anyone! And anyway, that doesn't matter. My father wouldn't send you away. I wouldn't let him!" This was true. In that moment—and, really, from the moment I met him—I felt fiercely protective of Amir. It was why I felt the urge to step in front of him when Bear approached—I'd rather Bear hurt me than him. I was used to it, anyway. But I guessed what Amir was trying to tell me was that he was used to it, too.

But he was not done with his story. "In the orphanage," he said, "there was a corner of the courtyard where bird droppings streaked the wall. Every day, I used a rock to scrape the poop from the wall onto a little slip of paper, and then I folded the paper and kept it in my pocket. Cook saw me do this. It was why he let me bring Uncle his lunch. Uncle always complained about Cook's food. Every dog is a tiger in his own street, Cook used to say. I did not know if he meant Uncle was the dog believing he was a tiger, or if I was. When I dropped that bird poop into Uncle's lunch each day, I felt like the tiger."

I laughed until my cheeks ached. My body was still tingling with delight at Amir's story when Bear's face flashed in my mind. I thought of the irritated expression my brother wore when he skulked by the three of us sitting cozily on the porch.

"Did you ask my dad to teach you to whittle just to annoy Bear?"

Amir laughed. "I also wanted to learn to whittle. It wasn't *just* to annoy Bear."

I smiled. Amir might not read as well as I did, but he was clever in other ways.

"You won't tell your father about Bear?" he asked.

"No. I promise."

Amir was silent, the bedsprings still below him. "I've never had a friend like you, Merrow."

I could not see him in the darkness of the room, but I knew he was smiling. I smiled back. "I've never had a friend like you, either, Amir."

THE NEXT MORNING, before the sun rose, before my father could tell us not to, we put on bathing suits and grabbed towels and hurried outside. Fog hung in the cold air. Pal barked at our heels, nearly tripping us at every turn. We raced down the switchback path to the beach and straight into the ice-cold water.

Amir was ahead of me, but I'd already discovered that I was a faster swimmer and knew I would easily catch up. The water was black and freezing, and we kept moving so our limbs wouldn't grow heavy with cold. All the while, Pal barked anxiously from the shore. The sea was calm, roiling gently around us. We dove along the surface of the water. Amir's stroke was getting stronger, but I easily swam past him, grinning.

We dragged ourselves out of the water and collapsed breathless onto the sand, teeth chattering. The moon and the sun were both in the sky. The speckled sea stretched out before us like a frost-covered meadow. Glossy ribbons of purple seaweed hung from the rocks, a gift that would be taken back as the tide rose. I pulled off a piece and ate it. Amir watched, wide-eyed, then did the same.

"Salty," he said. He yanked off another piece and handed half of it to me. We chewed and looked out at the water.

"It's beautiful here." Amir pulled his towel tighter around his narrow shoulders.

I nodded. I felt very proud of Horseshoe Cliff and was happy to share it with him. We dug in the sand for a while, building a web of rivers around a fortress with windows of broken white shells. I knew it would be time to leave for school soon, but with the sounds of the waves filling the air, and the sand slowly warming below me, and Amir for company, I did not feel like moving. Amir sat back on his heels and looked up. I watched his eyes follow the curve of the cliff that hugged the cove.

"That's where my mother died," I told him.

His mouth opened. "She fell?"

"Or maybe the cliff crumbled beneath her feet." It did not pain me to talk about her. My father had told me that the dead never really left us, and I had taken his words to heart. "I feel her watching me when I'm on the beach. Bear hates to come down here. I think it makes him sad. But it makes me happy. Anyway, Bear will never follow us here."

As the sun lifted in the sky, it hit Amir's ears and made them glow. I looked at him and smiled.

When our hunger set in, we trudged back up the path. We decided we would fry eggs for our breakfast. But when we approached the chicken coop, Bear was standing outside the pen. He held one of the chickens.

The blank look on his face made me feel as though I'd swallowed a fistful of stinging nettle. On Bear, whose expression seemed so often shadowed by sullenness, that blank stare took on a semblance of pleasure. The muscles of his arms bulged. The chicken was silent and still in my brother's grip, frightened into a kind of trance.

Suddenly, the hen released a panicked squawk and began to writhe. Bear must have been squeezing her, but his blank expression did not change.

I took a step forward, intending to intervene, but Amir's hand on my arm stopped me.

"Hey!" he yelled to Bear.

Bear blinked and looked in our direction. His lips twitched oddly. When he threw the chicken away from him and she landed safely on the dirt, I felt a moment of relief. But then I saw that my brother was walking toward us, and he had those knives in his eyes. Without a word, we dropped our towels and ran. I was faster than Amir on land, too, and I led the way, racing toward the eucalyptus grove. I knew each turn in the path, each knot of exposed root below. Pal ran along at my side. I could hear Amir running behind me, and behind him, the heavy steps of Bear.

And then Amir was gone.

I turned and saw that he lay on his back with Bear heaving above him. I raced back to them.

Bear had one foot pressed into Amir's chest. Amir squirmed like a cucumber beetle flipped onto its back.

"Let him go!"

My brother ignored me. I rammed my body into his, but he didn't move. Pal's hair stood on end and he barked frantically, looking between us in confusion.

I pulled Bear's arm. "Let him go!" I yelled again.

"Why should I?" Bear shoved me so hard that I stumbled backward.

"Because if you don't," came Amir's voice from below, as cold as the ocean we'd just swum in, "I'll tell your father how you hit me."

I looked down at him, surprised.

Bear's lips curled toward a smile. "And?"

"And I'm not the one who complains about my chores. I don't eat much. I don't steal his beer."

Amir's words, coolly delivered, hung in the air. I wondered how he managed to radiate so much anger while appearing so calm.

"Don't fool yourself," said Bear. He ground his heel into Amir's chest. "This isn't your home. Who are you? Some strange Indian kid with no parents." He bent down, pushing his face near Amir's. His lips curled. "*I'm* his son."

Amir seemed to have clamped his teeth together to stop himself from crying out at the pain of Bear's weight on his chest. He narrowed his eyes and said nothing.

"You're really hurting him!" I yelled.

Amir didn't speak.

I sank my teeth into Bear's arm and made him howl. He struck my neck and I sunk to the ground beside Amir, coughing and trying not to cry. My brother looked down at me. His face was twisted and dark.

"If he's ever worth really hurting, believe me, he'll know it." Bear gave a funny-sounding laugh, lifted his foot from Amir's chest, and walked off toward the house.

Amir sat up and rubbed his hand over his chest, watching Bear's back. In his place, I would have been sobbing. I wondered if, like Bear, Amir didn't cry, but then I remembered the tears I'd seen brim in his eyes on the night he'd arrived at Horseshoe Cliff.

"Are you okay?" I asked.

He nodded, rising to his feet. He took my hand and helped me up. "Are you? You bit him!"

I shrugged. "Don't listen to him, Amir. This *is* your home now."

"I know it is. He knows it, too. That's why he hates me so much." Amir stroked Pal's head. "What did he taste like?"

I thought for a moment. "Like a piece of raw pumpkin covered in horseshit."

Our laughter rose up from us in such a rush that the leaves of the whole grove quivered.

"Did you mean what you said?" I asked. "Did you change your mind about telling my father how awful Bear is?"

Amir shook his head. "I was just trying to scare him."

I smiled. I liked the idea of one of us scaring Bear for a change.

"Let's get our eggs," he said. "I'm starving."

A look of hatred passed over his face when he glanced after my brother, who was still making his way toward the house and kicking at every stone in his path. I wasn't surprised by Amir's hatred, or frightened of it. Instead I felt drawn to it, envying the clarity of his emotion, its pureness. His hatred was as bright as a guiding star on a cloudless night. My own feelings for my brother were a murky sky that only left me moving in circles. I hated him. I felt sorry for him. I hated him. I loved him.

There was a frayed rope between us that would not break.

CHAPTER SIX

For the next two years, Amir and I attended Little Earth and helped my father with the many chores assigned to us at Horseshoe Cliff. We spent our free time roaming the land by foot and horseback. We were late for school every morning because we lost the hours after dawn to building forts in the grove, or swimming out toward passing whales, or racing the horses along the bluff. We were inseparable. But while I read more books in a week than all of our classmates combined, at ten years old, Amir continued to struggle to make sense of the words on the page. I helped as best I could, but sometimes I wondered how much it mattered that Amir did not love school as I did—his talents were in the wood sculptures he created, his passion lay with our land.

We managed to avoid crossing paths with Bear for long stretches of time by exploring the areas of Horseshoe Cliff where we knew he was unlikely to wander. It seemed to us that our home protected us, and why wouldn't it? We were sure it felt our love for it and returned the feeling.

There was the one Sunday when we wandered through the orchard, collecting apples that a windstorm the night before had knocked from the trees. Slight wisps of fog came and went. Stopping in a patch of sun, we unwrapped a pair of Rei's gingersnap cookies. I heard Bear's voice before I saw him. Amir and I froze, and as we did, the patch of sun in which we stood flooded with fog. We grabbed our bags of apples and darted silently away. The fog was so thick that we could not see even as far as the trees that stood within five feet of us. Amir reached for my hand. In all my life, I had never seen the weather change so suddenly. Why had the fog rushed through the orchard, if not to protect us? I slowed, pulling on Amir's hand so that he slowed, too. We stopped. Though we could not see him, we heard Bear's heavy footfalls nearby. He stumbled and released a gruff stream of curses that made my heartbeat thunder in my ears. He was so close that I was sure if I reached out, I would touch his shoulder. Silently, Amir and I stood together within that extraordinary, breathing mantle of fog. After a few moments, silence fell. Bear was gone.

And then there was the time when an ocean current held Amir and would not let him go. Something stopped me from swimming back toward him. I scanned the beach and my eyes landed on a snakelike coil of bullwhip kelp. I grabbed it and stepped into the water only to my ankles, throwing one end to him. I sat down hard, digging my heels into the sand. Hand over hand, Amir pulled himself along the length of that rope of kelp toward me. I willed the kelp not to break. It should not have held his weight. But it did. At last, Amir sat beside me on

the wet sand, his dark eyes round with the strangeness of the
sea's hold, the kelp's strength. We leaned against each other. As
our bodies connected, we lost ourselves to long, ragged gusts
of laughter.

There was the night that we sat on the back porch as Rei read
to us. She and my father often exchanged books, but on this
night, he asked her to stay and read out loud. They sat in the
two chairs and Amir and I sat on the steps. My father and Amir
worked their knives; I could not yet tell what either was making.
Rei had brought a book of stories about mythical islands because she knew how my father loved folklore of the sea. I rested
my head against a stair rail and closed my eyes while I listened
to her calm, crisp voice pick a careful path through the legends.
She read to us of King Arthur's elusive Isle of Avalon, where
apple trees grew heavy with fruit and the shape-shifter Morgan
changed from human to bird as she pleased. She read to us of
Buyan, the magical center of the universe in Russian mythol-
ogy, home to the sun and the winds, an oak tree that connected
heaven to earth, and a white stone that granted healing and eternal happiness. It was when she was reading to us of Hy-Brasil, a
bountiful island hidden within a shroud of mist off the western
cliffs of Ireland, that I opened my eyes and looked out toward
the horizon. Fog moved along the coast, suddenly parting.

"Look!"

The others followed my gaze. On the horizon, an island rose
from the sea.

"It's a cloud," said Rei.

"It's very still for a cloud," said my father. I looked at him, unsure if he was teasing me. Though he kept his gaze on the horizon, I saw the smile hidden within his beard.

"It's an island," I said. I looked to Amir, expecting him to agree.

But after a thoughtful moment Amir said, "What if *Horseshoe Cliff* is the island hidden within the fog? And what we see out there is the rest of the world catching its first glimpse of us?"

I could tell by my father's expression that he was as delighted by this idea as I was.

"If we're the hidden island, let's find the magical stone that grants healing!" I said. "We'll use it to get rid of Dad's cough."

My father laughed. "Who needs to heal? On this island, we're immortal!"

I scanned the sky for a red bird, hoping one would appear, but none did. I lowered my eyes to the horizon.

"It's a cloud," Rei said. She was looking out toward the sea, too, and sounded very sad. "It will be gone by morning."

As it turned out, it *was* gone in the morning. But who could say if what we had seen was cloud or island? Or if Amir had been right and we were the ones who were, in fact, on an island? Wasn't that the beauty of magic? Before you could be certain it existed, it slipped away, leaving you full of wonder.

THAT SPRING WE all became sick. The illness started with me and spread to Amir, then my father, and finally Bear. For a week we coughed and shivered and sweated and drank the spicy seaweed and noodle soups that Rei brought us. My father's coughing fits had punctuated my childhood, but these seemed worse than ever before. I remembered the stories of his youth; how he'd spent so much time in bed because of illness. I waited for the sea air to cure him the way he'd told me it once had. I wished for a magical stone of healing.

My father's skin grew pale, and the arms of his shirt grew big. Still, every morning he shuffled out of the cottage with Bear trudging along behind him. Amir and I wanted to help, but my father wouldn't allow it during the week. Our responsibilities were school, the chickens, and the horses. The garden withered; it was as though the land, too, had fallen sick. When Bear drove to Osha to exchange our fruits and vegetables for meat and dried goods at the co-op, the box he came home with was less full each time. Amir and I were quiet around the dinner table at night, our sparse conversation marked by my father's coughs and the sounds of Bear slurping his soup out on the porch. He had not eaten a meal with us in years. He gave no excuse to our father, but he'd grumbled to me that he could not stomach watching Amir eat food that did not belong to him, food that should have been ours.

Even when the rattling sound in my father's chest grew worse, the idea that he might not recover from his illness never occurred to me. Through all the death that had moved through Horseshoe Cliff, my father had been untouched. Mothers died, animals died . . . But fathers? I believed that fathers remained.

One morning we arrived back at the cottage after feeding the horses to find that the truck was gone. My father was not in his usual chair on the porch waiting to take us to school. The sight of that empty chair made my stomach clench.

I remembered now that my father's cough had seemed particularly relentless the night before. Why hadn't I checked on him before I ran out to feed the animals? Inside the cottage, the noises of the land and the ocean fell away, revealing an unsettling quiet. All the windows were shut, the air thick with the smell of dust.

We hurried to my father's room. He lay in his bed and opened his eyes at the sound of our approach. I chewed my lip. His skin was sticky looking. Sweat beaded on his brow, but his bed was piled high with all the blankets in the house, including the ones from my bed and also Amir's. Bear must have walked around and collected them. This possibility surprised me.

"What's wrong?" I asked my father. I put my hand on his shoulder. "Is your fever back?"

One corner of his mouth attempted to move toward a smile. "Nothing that Doctor Clark can't fix. Bear went to get him."

It was difficult to imagine that little gray-haired Doctor Clark from town with his table full of coloring books and wooden puzzles could fix a man as big and strong as my father. I thought the doctor only saw children whose fevers wouldn't go away or children who felt like rocks were lodged in their throats or children who had cuts so deep they needed sewing. My hand, still resting on my father's shoulder, began to tremble.

Amir stepped up to the other side of my father's bed. "Would you like some water?" he asked. When my father nodded, he ran to the kitchen.

I held my father's hand and decided I would not let go until he was well again. I lifted his hand to my lips and kissed it.

"Sugar-and-Spice," he said. It was his nickname for me. His eyes were locked on mine, but his voice was nearly swallowed by the wind that suddenly rubbed the sides of the house. His breath was loud and ragged.

Amir returned with the water. He stood on the other side of the bed, but when my father didn't reach for the cup, Amir held it to his lips. Some of the water spilled down my father's cheeks. It didn't seem to me that he had managed to drink any. I dried his cheeks with the sleeve of my shirt, leaving behind a shadow of dirt. When I tried to rub the dirt away, my father closed his eyes, but seemed restless, his eyelids moving and flickering.

He licked his lips and spoke. "I haven't done this for years," he said in that strange, croaky, new voice. "When I was a kid, I used to lie in bed for weeks. My breathing was always bad then. I was born early, my mother said. Weak lungs."

A shiver moved down my spine. I didn't like hearing him use the word *weak* to describe any part of himself. I thought of how he worked outside from sunrise to sunset. I thought of our walks together, the beat of our footsteps on the land, the songs we sang.

I began to sing the songs that my father loved, the ones he always sang while striding around Horseshoe Cliff. Amir sang, too. He knew the words now, and our voices sounded nice tangled together, sweet and high.

Eventually we heard the truck rumbling up the dirt drive, the squeal of the brakes as it stopped in front of the house, but we didn't stop singing until Bear and Doctor Clark entered the room. Without a word, Bear pushed Amir from his place beside the bed.

My father opened his eyes and stared up at the doctor. His breathing made a wet, whistling noise.

"Hello, Jacob," Doctor Clark said. He always seemed weary and today he looked no different, his shoulders slumped as though his exhaustion were a heavy coat.

My father moved his lips, but I couldn't make out his words.

Doctor Clark pressed his listening tool to my father's chest. After a few moments, he put his hand on the side of my father's neck, and then his wrist. "I don't like the sound of those lungs of yours."

"He's had that cough for years," said Bear.

I looked sharply toward my brother. Was he nervous? I took a step closer to my father. I had not let go of his hand. My heart was beating so fast that it felt as though it were preparing for flight.

"And the fever? When did that spike?"

Bear shrugged. "We were all sick. It was just a cold. Something *he* brought home from school," he said, tossing his chin toward Amir.

This wasn't true, though he said it as though he believed it. "I was the one who was sick first," I said. I'd been the first to get the cold and the first to recover. Amir moved to my side of the bed.

Doctor Clark's eyes softened when he looked at me. "Well,

everyone gets sick at school—especially in the spring when the weather goes one way and then another. Why don't you two head outside for a bit and let me chat with your dad and brother?"

It didn't seem to me that my father was up for much of a chat. I held tight to his hand and shook my head.

"We don't want to go outside," said Amir.

Doctor Clark looked to Bear, but Bear just shrugged. The doctor sighed. "Fine, then." He took his listening tool from his neck and put it back into his bag before addressing my father.

"Jacob, my guess is you have pneumonia. I won't know the severity of the infection until I see an X-ray of your lungs. That means a visit to the hospital."

The hospital! I waited for my father to protest, but he only nodded.

"We'll come with you," I said quickly.

"No, you won't," said Bear. He'd been slouched against the wall, but now he straightened.

Doctor Clark looked at Bear. "I don't know how long your father will be there," he warned. "It could be days . . . or longer."

"They'll be fine here," Bear said.

The doctor's brow furrowed. "How old are you now, Merrow?" he asked. It occurred to me that he'd hardly glanced in Amir's direction.

"Ten."

"Well, that's older than you look, but it's still young to be left home alone."

"I'll call Rei Ishikawa when we get to the hospital," Bear

said. "She'll keep an eye on them. Anyway, someone needs to stay here to mind the animals."

"No," I said. "I want to be with Dad."

"No one cares what you want, Merrow. I don't need to be watching the two of you *and* looking after Dad at the hospital. You're staying here."

The doctor shot Bear a look and walked around the bed to where I stood. He put his hand on my shoulder. "There, there," he said. "Don't cry."

"I'm not crying."

"Don't cry, little one," my father said, blinking up at me.

"I'm not crying," I insisted again, but now I *was* crying. Hot tears rolled down my cheeks. Bear's jaw grew tense, and he turned away from me. I was shocked at how easily Bear and the doctor lifted my father from his bed, my father who had always seemed so large to me. I lost my grip on my father's hand as they lifted him, but in the moment we lost touch, Amir took my other hand in his. He held my hand as my father was carried out of the house and placed in the backseat of the doctor's car, and he held my hand as the doctor drove my father away, and he held my hand as Bear got into his truck without another word to us, leaving behind only dust and the faint sounds of the chickens squabbling and, farther away, the surf breaking over and over against the rocks.

REI DID NOT come for two days. We never knew if Bear had forgotten to call her or if his neglect was intentional. Either way, by then we really were old enough to fend for ourselves.

We ate tomatoes and greens from the garden and we scrambled eggs with beans from the cans in the cupboard. We did our best to look after the animals and the garden. At night, I could not hold my tears any longer, and Amir sat beside me on my bed and patted my back. Pal whined and shivered and looked back and forth between us for an answer we could not give.

The second day was longer than the first, and still no one came. Amir and I did not venture far from each other. The view of the ocean from the back porch might have given us comfort, but for the first time I preferred the front porch with its view of the driveway. I wanted to see my father the moment he returned.

When a car finally came toward us down the long drive, my father wasn't in it.

If we hadn't known the shiny white car belonged to Rei, we might not have recognized her. She looked so much older than she had when we'd seen her earlier in the week. Her perfect posture was broken in a way that looked irreversible, her shoulders sagging so heavily they seemed to pull her spine. She did not have on her usual sun hat, and the sight of the thick gray streaks in her black hair made my eyes sting.

Amir and I stood from our chairs. We were so close to each other that our elbows touched. We did not speak.

Rei walked up the front steps and grasped us both in her embrace. I twisted my body so that I could look up at her. Her black eyes glistened in the shade of the porch, and then tears were running down her cheeks.

"I'm so sorry, my darlings," she said. "Bear just called me. Your father is gone. He died an hour ago. I did not even know . . ." Her lips kept moving, but a buzzing noise in my ears drowned her words. Amir's hands found mine. Cradled in Rei's arms, we clung to each other.

CHAPTER SEVEN

$\mathbf{M}$y father's death released something within Bear. He planted himself on the front porch facing the road and drank all day long. It seemed to us that he never moved far from that spot, but one evening after we watered the horses, Amir went to fetch the whittling knives and returned to the back porch empty-handed.

"He took them," he said. "Your father's knives. I put them on the floor right next to my bed last night. They were there this morning. Now they're gone. *He* took them."

The moment Amir said this, a wave of understanding passed through me. For so many years I had blamed myself for misplacing the things that I loved, for forgetting which tree pocket in the grove held my stored treasures, for misplacing Rei's library books, for losing the pretty little doll my classmate had given me and the fairy Amir had made for me. But I understood at last that all along it had been Bear who had been taking my things.

"The children need to go to school," Rei told Bear. She stirred a pot of soup at the kitchen's small white stove. "You are their guardian now, and you need to start thinking of their needs above your own. You are twenty years old. A young adult, but an adult nonetheless."

Bear gave no indication that he was listening. Rei passed bowls of soup around the table. Bear set upon his immediately, slurping so loudly that it unsettled a cloud of rage within me. Rei had told him that the soup was only for those who sat at the table, but I wished she'd let him eat on the porch by himself. Before I knew what I was doing, I picked up my spoon and threw it at my brother.

"Hey!" Bear drew back his hand to strike me but suddenly Rei stood between us. Amir was so still that he nearly vibrated; his hand gripped his spoon as though he were readying to throw it, too.

Bear glowered at us but dropped his hand down to the table, where it encircled a can of beer. It was the kind our father had drunk. In a few short weeks, Bear had adopted most of my father's things. He even wore my father's brown flannel shirt and his work boots. I tried not to look at Bear because each glance threatened to erase some memory of my father. It was why the sounds of my brother's slurping had annoyed me so; it was as though Bear were demanding that I look at him and admit that he was all I had left of the family I'd been born into.

Bear took another loud slurp of his soup. Then he said, "They're not going to school anymore."

Rei shook her head. "They *must* go to school. It's the law. You are their guardian. It's you who will be held accountable."

This seemed to surprise Bear. "I dropped out and no one came after my father about it."

"You were fifteen. Merrow and Amir are ten."

Bear shrugged. "I'm not taking them."

Already, Little Earth felt like a memory. We had not been there since my father had died three weeks earlier. I still had a few books from the school's little library hidden in my pillowcase. I longed to exchange them for new ones and to see the faces of my classmates.

Teacher Julie had come to my father's memorial service the week before when we poured his ashes into the sea at the bottom of the cliffs. The ocean had been strangely calm that day. Rain fell slowly, and each raindrop had landed in the water like a stone, a thousand stones, a million stones. Amir and I stood side by side up to our shins in the cold, dark ocean and watched the falling rain. Bear was a little ahead of us. I was surprised when he had walked right into the water; I'd never seen him in the ocean before. His eyes had been as cold and dark as the sea that day. He had not waited long before opening the urn and pouring out the stuff that was our father. Then he turned and walked right by us, out of the ocean and up the cliff path. Amir and I stood there until Rei touched our shoulders and urged us back to shore. Her long skirt had been gathered up in one hand, her exposed knees as pale as bone.

Later that day, before she left Horseshoe Cliff, Teacher Julie handed me a cloth sack that held my journals. She had given me one each year I'd been at Little Earth and I'd filled them with my stories, comforted by her promise to help me keep them safe. I took the bag from her, knowing Bear would steal them and hardly caring. How could I care if I lost my stories when I had just lost my father?

"I'll teach them," Rei told Bear in the kitchen now. She was still holding the soup ladle. "I'll come as often as I can. I was a teacher once. I can arrange the papers to show that I'm in charge of the children's schooling."

Bear set down his can of beer. The look on his face made me sit up in my chair. *"The children?"* he said. "There will only be one of them soon."

"What are you talking about?" Rei asked.

"I'm sending Amir away." He looked at me as he said this. "He never belonged here in the first place. He's not our brother. He's not our problem anymore."

"No!" I slammed my hands on the table. Bear's beer can quivered, and he snatched it up, annoyed. Amir stared at my brother, and I saw his jaw twitch with fury. "Rei, you can't let him do that!"

"Bear, may I speak with you outside?" Rei asked.

"No."

"This land belongs to all three of you. That's how your father left it in his will."

It was the first I had heard of this. Amir and I exchanged a glance.

"Not until they're eighteen," said Bear.

"Yes, but until then your father left you in charge of *both* of them. You are Amir's guardian. It's what Jacob wanted. That is also in his will. I saw it myself."

"Did he put how I'm supposed to feed all of us in that will, too?"

The garden and orchard were in as sad a state as they had ever been. Even in our grief, Amir and I were trying our best to take care of the land, but we were ten years old and our stamina only went so far. Bear knew what to do, he just didn't want to do it. Without my father around to insist on Bear's help, he did nothing.

"Perhaps he meant for you to get a job," Rei said. "Construction, maybe. House painting."

Bear snorted.

"Then you must work as hard as your father did. You are his son, Bear. You have it in you to do just as he did and keep this family together. You were never hungry when he was alive."

"We were never hungry? Is that what he told you? And you believed him? Is that why you were always buying our piss-poor little vegetables and hauling away those stupid carvings, Rei? Is that why you were always bringing us the food you made? Because my father did such a good job providing for us?"

Rei didn't respond. Bear took a long drink of his beer. Then he leaned across the table toward me until he was close enough that his beer breath wet the tip of my nose. I forced myself to look right at him and not blink. "Were you never hungry when Dad was alive?" he asked. "Surprise everyone and tell the truth."

I narrowed my eyes at him. "I was never hungry," I said. The lie came so easily, so enjoyably, that I felt a thrill in my stomach. When I glanced at Amir, I saw that he was struggling not to smile.

Bear sat back and drank his beer. "It doesn't matter. Rei, you know it would be easier for us without Amir."

Rei fell quiet. I stared at her, wondering if she would allow for this betrayal. But then she put her hands on her hips. Her cheeks were flushed with anger. I had known her my entire life, and I had never seen her look so furious.

"Do you know how much money Amir's carvings fetched before you took away his knife? No, I am sure you don't. I'll tell you this: Without Amir, you will not pay your tax bill. And that's not all. If Amir is no longer your problem, then you will no longer be mine. I will not buy your vegetables. I will not help you sell anything made or grown here. You will be on your own."

I wanted to leap from the table and throw my arms around Rei. But I sat still, looking from Rei to my brother and back again. Amir did the same.

Bear took a long drink from his can of beer, glowering at Rei over its rim. He did not say anything.

"Amir stays at Horseshoe Cliff," Rei continued. "You will give him back his knife so he can make the carvings that I will sell for you. And I will arrange to teach the children. You will watch over them in the manner your father expected. The manner that your mother would have wanted, too."

At this, Bear stood so abruptly that his chair fell back and hit the floor. His face was red, and he did not look at any of us. He grabbed a six-pack of beer from the fridge and strode out of the house, slamming the door behind him. As I watched him go, I had to clasp my fingers together to keep them from shaking. I was happy that Rei had spoken up for Amir—but I knew that Bear would punish us for witnessing his humiliation.

It did not take long.

That night, I was reading aloud in our bedroom when the door was thrown open. Bear loomed in the doorframe, swaying.

"Get out," he slurred. "You. *Amir.*" His hand slipped from the doorframe, and he stumbled forward a couple of steps before straightening. I stared at him, frozen in my bed. Across the room, Amir was frozen in his. "I said GET OUT!"

"What do you mean?" I cried. "Where is he supposed to go?"

"The shed."

"The *shed*?"

"It's freezing out there," said Amir. He spoke in the cool voice he always used with Bear, the one that drove Bear crazy. I was never able to stay as calm as Amir, but I was working on it. If I couldn't scare Bear the way he scared me, I could at least try to get under his skin the way that Amir managed to. Amir spoke in a way that seemed disconnected from his skinny body; it was the voice of a bigger man, made calm by the knowledge that he had the upper hand. Of course, his upper hand was only a bluff; Bear had all the power. We were children, and Bear was now the adult in charge.

"You want to stay at Horseshoe Cliff? You'll sleep in the toolshed," Bear said. Spittle sat in the corners of his mouth, threatening release into the room. "You should never have been allowed in the house in the first place. From now on you can live like the other filthy pets that my father gave Merrow." He stepped toward us. With one violent yank, Amir was on the ground. Bear towered over him. *"Move."*

Amir stood and slowly gathered his pillow and blanket into his arms.

I scrambled to my feet, but Amir held up his hand, stopping me. He walked out of the room. When the front door opened, a blast of damp air swept through the cottage. The door shut.

Bear looked down at me. I had learned that he loved to see me miserable, so I tried to hold my face expressionless. I couldn't manage it. My skin felt hot with the rage that seeped up from my chest. I would never be like Amir, who so easily closed his anger into his fists, saving it. *For when?* I wondered when I watched Amir speak to my brother with such control. What moment was he saving up all of his anger for?

"How could you do that to him?" I yelled at Bear. "You heard what Rei said! She's not going to help you if you don't let him stay."

Bear leaned down. I smelled his sour, unclean skin below the yeasty scent of beer. "Amir *is* staying," he sneered. "In the toolshed." On his way out of the room, Bear shoved his knee into Pal's side, making my dog hit the floor with a pitiful yelp.

I rushed to Pal and held him in my arms. He licked my face, reassuring me for a moment, but when he lifted himself off the ground, he would not set down one of his paws. "Poor boy," I cried, burying my face in his warm fur.

I thought of Amir out in the dark shed and when I did something mysterious happened: My room became the dark shed, too, and I lay on the dirt floor among the saws and shovels and picker baskets. I was Amir, without a parent, without a friend, without even a dog. A black loneliness gripped me. I dug my nails into my palm and my room became my room again.

I could not stand to wait—Rei frequently said I was the most impatient child she had ever known—but now I did. I sat beside Pal and stroked his head and waited.

When the tinny thump of Bear's beer can returning to the table finally fell away, I peered into the kitchen. My brother's head rested on the crook of his arms. His shoulders rose and fell with his deep, shuddering breaths. I grabbed my pillow and blanket and hurried outside with Pal limping along at my side. The front door closed with a hushed click behind us. The fog was so dense that I couldn't see the shed until I was nearly upon it.

When I opened the door, I heard Amir suck in his breath, but I couldn't see him in the soupy blackness of the windowless room.

"It's me," I whispered.

He released a relieved choke of laughter.

"Where are you?"

"Here."

As my eyes adjusted to the darkness, I saw that he'd set his blanket in the middle of the shed. Gleaming tools hung on the walls. I spread my blanket beside Amir's and lay down. The ground was cold and damp.

"We'll tell Rei," I said, pulling my blanket around me. My teeth would not stop chattering. "Rei will make Bear let you sleep inside again."

Amir was silent.

"Amir?"

"We can't tell Rei."

"Why not?"

"If she finds out how badly Bear treats us, she'll take us both away from here. I could see she was thinking about it earlier today. She was trying to decide what to do. If she doesn't trust Bear, she'll take us away."

"Then we'll live with Rei! And we can go to Little Earth again."

"Rei doesn't get to decide if she keeps us. That's not how it works. We'll be sent away. Who knows where we'll end up. Or if we'll be allowed to stay together."

"Of course we'd be allowed to stay together," I said. But I realized it was a subject Amir knew more about than I. He had been sent away from everyone and everything he knew before, when his mother died.

"We'll stay together if we stay here." Amir's voice was determined. "Even with Bear . . . even with sleeping in this shed . . ." He folded his arms behind his head and looked up at the ceiling. "I think sometimes of my friends at the orphanage and how they would love it here. The ocean. The beach. The garden and the orchard and the grove. So many places to run and explore and . . . be free. And Rei is a good person. Not everyone is like her. She watches over us. I'll sleep in the shed if it means that we can stay here, together."

I didn't have to see his face to know his expression in that moment. The fierce way that Amir spoke of Horseshoe Cliff, and his certainty that we would never be parted, thrilled me. He seemed older than me then, more confident of his ability to shape his own destiny. His bravery always seemed to me a choiceless matter; it was just who he was.

"Fine," I said. "We won't tell Rei. But if you have to sleep out here, I will, too."

When I told Amir how Bear had kicked Pal, Amir worried over our dog in a voice so gentle that Pal burrowed himself under Amir's arm and licked his chin repeatedly. We talked about the other children and teachers from Little Earth and what they might be doing, how strange it was that we would no longer attend the school. The fog outside must have grown thin because moonlight suddenly fell through the shed's many cracks, brightening the room and making the teeth on the saws that lined the wall glimmer.

"Oooooooo," I moaned, ghostlike.

"Spoooky," Amir joined in, making his long fingers scramble through the air like spiders on a web.

Our laughter excited Pal. He stood and yawned and then tugged at our blankets, growling and playful even as he limped. We shushed him, laughing, but we knew the noise didn't really matter. Bear was passed out in the cottage and wouldn't stir until morning. There was no one else for miles in any direction. We were alone.

MY BROTHER NEVER said anything about me sleeping in the shed each night with Amir, but a few weeks later a silver truck rumbled down the driveway pulling a horse trailer behind it.

When the truck stopped in front of the cottage, a man with a beard as silver as his truck stepped out.

"Hello," I said, hopping down the porch steps to stand before him. Amir trailed after me more slowly, holding one of the wood animals he'd been whittling in one hand and the knife that Bear had returned to him in the other.

"Hello, young lady," the man said. He cocked his head and looked Amir up and down, his gaze resting for a moment on the knife in his hand. "Oh, that's right," he said. "You're that Indian boy Jacob took in a few years back. I see he managed to teach you to whittle."

There was something in his voice that set my teeth on edge. I took a step forward. "Are you looking for Bear?"

The man gave me an amused smile and was about to respond when he caught sight of something over my shoulder. I turned, shielding my eyes from the sun with my hand, and saw Bear walking toward us with Old Mister and Guthrie on either side of him. Their lead lines encircled his hands in the way that my father had always warned us to avoid. If your hands were tangled up in a lead line, a horse could drag you with him if he spooked and galloped away. Bear had never had any interest in the horses, and it showed in the careless way he led them.

"Hey, Lawton," he called gruffly. He didn't look in my direction. "Here they are."

My heartbeat sped up.

"What's going on?" asked Amir.

Bear ignored us. The stranger walked around the horses,

running his hand along their haunches, lifting each of their legs and looking at their teeth.

"Let's see them move. Walk them toward the truck for me," he said.

"Why?" I asked, but the man didn't answer. I ran up beside Bear and tried to grab Guthrie's lead line from him, but Bear pushed me away. I stumbled backward and fell hard against the ground.

"Easy, Bear," the man said sharply. He walked over to me and reached out his hand. I pushed it away.

"What do you want with my horses?"

"*Your* horses?" I did not like the way he smiled. "I thought they belonged to your brother."

"Of course they do, Lawton." Bear's voice was cold. "She's a little girl. She doesn't even own the clothes on her back."

"That's not true," Amir said. He stood beside me, turning that knife over in his hand, his body betraying the emotion he managed to keep from his voice. "Jacob gave Old Mister to me. Guthrie is Merrow's. You know that, Bear."

Lawton's lips were set in a grim line as he listened to Amir, but when he turned toward me, his expression relaxed. "I'm sorry, sweetheart. I'm taking these horses with me. I have grandchildren who are going to take great care of them."

Bear took the stack of bills that Lawton gave him and tucked them into the pocket of his jeans. As I watched Bear load the horses into Lawton's trailer, I felt as though a piece of my own body were being ripped from me and there was nothing I could do about it. I grew hot with a familiar mix of frustration and rage. If I loved something, Bear would take it from me.

"NO!" I screamed. I ran at my brother, fire in my throat, but it was the terrible old man, Lawton, who grabbed me and held me in his arms as I kicked and thrashed.

"Put her down!" I heard Amir say.

"Walk away, boy," Lawton said in a voice as low as a growl. "Walk away if you know what's good for you."

But Amir didn't walk away. Lawton's grip around my waist tightened. "Now, child," he said to me. "Don't be too hard on your big brother. He has a lot on his shoulders. You and that . . . that Indian boy to look after at his young age. These horses are going to a good home. You don't have to worry about them. And in exchange I think you're going to be seeing a bit more food on your plate in the months ahead." When I finally stopped kicking, he set me down. His leathery hand encircled my biceps, squeezing it. "Skinny thing like you needs more food, and now you'll have it. Maybe some new clothes, too. A pretty dress instead of those boys' clothes. Wouldn't that be nice?"

I sniffed. "Sure, that would be nice. But keeping my horses would be nicer. I hope you're happy with yourself, Lawton, taking a pony from a child."

For a second, Lawton just stared at me. Then he broke into a big laugh that made my cheeks burn. He laughed so hard tears came to his eyes.

"Sugar-and-Spice, isn't that what your daddy called you?" he asked. "I just remembered. Boy, he sure hit the nail on the head, didn't he?" He walked to the cab of his silver truck, still shaking his head with laughter.

Amir stood beside me, his face red. We hadn't even had a chance to give the horses a proper goodbye. I couldn't remember my life without Guthrie in it; he'd been my pony since before I could walk.

"We'll get them back," I said.

Amir put his hand on my shoulder, but he didn't answer. In his silence, I realized that it was silly to think that I would ever see Guthrie again. I hated my brother. Lawton didn't know what he was talking about when he said that I should be kinder to Bear; my brother was cruel and bitter. My father had managed to keep us all fed and clothed and happy without ever selling something any one of us loved.

Lawton slowed the truck as he drove past us. He leaned his elbow on the open window and called to me. For a moment, my heart soared. Maybe he'd changed his mind! Maybe he'd let us keep the horses and the money, too, now that he'd seen how we needed it.

But when I ran to the truck he handed me a dollar. The bill was warm and smooth in my hand.

"Get yourself a candy bar." He grinned at me as though he expected me to be delighted. "Add some more sugar to that sugar-and-spice heart of yours."

The truck hadn't even made it to the road before Bear strode over and yanked the dollar from my hand.

"Hey!" I said. But I didn't run after him to try to get it back, and neither did Amir. When Bear wanted something, he took it. There was nothing we could do to stop him.

IRONICALLY, THE SHED turned out to be one of the few places we felt free of Bear. In its dusty corners we stored collections of shells and smooth stones and sea glass, interesting pieces of driftwood, books, and my collection of journals from Teacher Julie. We didn't know why Bear didn't come in and steal these things from us, but he didn't. The freedom made us bold. We wove nests from twigs and strung them from the shed's ceiling with fishing line so they looked as though they were suspended in air. We filled the nests with five tiny birds that Amir carved and I painted red with the old lean-to paint that I found on a shelf. Five birds to represent my mother and father, Amir's mother, and Amir's birth parents, whoever they were. We dotted the shelves with snail shells that we found in the garden. At night, the light from the candles we lit bounced off the shells, making them glow. We spoke loudly in the shed, filling it with our laughter. Sleeping there did not feel like a punishment; it felt like a refuge.

During the day we spent our time studying with Rei, working in the garden and orchard, exploring the caves that pocked the cliff where it met the beach, and wandering through the eucalyptus grove. We avoided the cottage when Rei wasn't there for fear of running into Bear.

When we did cross his path, Bear would mutter insults about us being no better than the feral cats that prowled the alley behind the Osha co-op. He never said anything about the fact that I no longer slept in the cottage. I assumed he was happy to have the house to himself, just as I was happy to know that Bear wasn't under the same roof as me while I slept. Amir and I even briefly considered moving our beds into the shed, but decided not to when we realized that Rei would notice. She'd been looking through the cottage during her last visit and had stopped in the doorframe of our old bedroom. The beds were neatly made with the same sheets that had been on them for months.

"Are the two of you still sharing one room?" she asked. "Even now that there are three bedrooms available?"

We glanced at each other before nodding.

"One of you should sleep in Jacob's room. Or Bear should, and then one of you can take his room."

"But we like to be together," I said. "It helps us sleep."

Rei pursed her lips. "I am aware that you like to be together. I don't know where Merrow's shadow ends and Amir's begins."

Amir and I both smiled at this image.

Rei's expression softened. "But it's time you had your own rooms. It will take some adjustment, but you'll get used to it. In fact, I'm sure you'll soon be very happy to have your own space. A little privacy is good for everyone."

"But—" I began.

"Rei's right," Amir said. "Do you want to move into your dad's room or should I?"

When Rei walked toward the kitchen table, leaving us to discuss it, Amir whispered, "It doesn't matter what room we pretend to sleep in, does it?"

I nodded, but Rei glanced back at us as we whispered together, and the look on her face worried me.

A FEW DAYS after that conversation with Rei, we were returning from a swim in the ocean when we noticed that the shed
door was open. We had been careful to keep the door closed
ever since the day that an opossum had found his way inside.
Now, the sight of the open door sent a tremor of apprehension
through me. We ran toward the shed but stopped short when
Rei appeared in the door.

"Merrow! Amir!"

Her arms were crossed over her chest. We walked to her, our
shoes scraping the dusty ground. She gestured at the blankets and
pillows that were rolled into a pile in the middle of the shed. The
nests of red birds spun in the sunlight that fell from the open door.

"What am I seeing?" she asked. "Because I feel as though I
am seeing your bedroom."

I looked down and kicked at the ground.

"We slept out here last night," Amir said. "The house was
too hot, so we thought we'd try the shed. It was my idea."

Rei studied him. "Oh, Amir. Those big, soulful eyes. You are
a quick thinker but a bad liar." She put her hand under his chin
and lifted his head so that he had to look at her. They were the
same height, I realized. When had that happened?

"Why are you sleeping out here?"

Amir held Rei's gaze, but I could see by the set of his jaw
that he would not answer. When she looked at me, I pressed
my lips together, imitating Amir.

"What will I do with you?" She shook her head. "It weighs on me, the two of you out here, so isolated. And now I find you are sleeping in the shed! You are children. Your father would be furious with Bear . . . and with me, for allowing this to happen right under my nose. No. No, I cannot allow it to continue."

She turned and began to stride toward the cottage. "Bear!" she called. "Bear, where are you?"

Rei was angrier than I'd ever seen her—angrier even than she'd been the day months earlier when Bear had threatened to send Amir away. When I looked at Amir, I was startled to see how pale he'd become. He was frightened. He looked more scared of what Rei was about to do than he had ever been of Bear. I grabbed his hand and squeezed it and he gave me a grateful, sad look. He did not have to tell me what he was thinking; I could read it on his face. He thought he would be forced to leave Horseshoe Cliff, the home he loved. He thought we were about to be separated. I dropped his hand and ran after Rei.

"Please don't talk to Bear," I cried, throwing my arms around her. I buried my face in her neck. "Please! We'll sleep in the cottage from now on. We'll sleep in separate rooms. We'll be good."

At this, Rei laughed. "Don't you start lying to me, too," she said. I breathed out, relieved. I could see in Rei's eyes that my plea was working. She stroked my hair, her fingers sticking in its many knots. Her expression turned serious again.

"I need to know the truth, Merrow. Has Bear hurt you?"

"No," I answered quickly. "He ignores us." It was half true, at least. Bear ignored us right up until the moment that he hurt us. But he was drunk most of the time, and this made him slow. Of course, the drinking also stoked his rage, and one time he'd shoved Amir so hard that Amir's back ended up covered with bruises that looked like gathering storm clouds. *You're nothing,* he'd said to Amir that night. *You're nobody.*

"Ignores you," Rei echoed, doubtful. "And you're getting enough to eat? You don't look like it." She looked over at Amir. "Neither of you do."

I hesitated. We had not seen an increase in food after Bear sold our horses, but Bear did now have a television on his nightstand. He watched it for hours each day. On the rare occasion that Bear worked in the orchard, we snuck into his room and turned it on. I had never watched television before. *Days of Our Lives* mesmerized me. All of those beautiful, devious women with their shiny hair and sharp tongues; the men with smooth faces and bright white shirts. Once, President Clinton was on the television, looking right at me as he spoke. And the commercials! I'd never known there was so much to buy.

Amir was less impressed by the TV. Or maybe he just didn't like being in Bear's room, which smelled of sweaty sheets and beer and stagnant air. *Turn it off,* he would say. *Let's go for a swim.* I imagined that he'd seen enough of the world—India, New York—that the stories the television offered did not impress him. Unlike Amir, I was terribly excited by the glimpses into other lives that television offered. President Clinton and the women of *Days of Our Lives* began to appear in my dreams nearly as often as my father and mother did.

"Well," I told Rei after some thought, "we're still grieving Dad, you know. That sort of sadness doesn't leave much room for an appetite."

"You seem to feel just fine when you're gobbling up the meals I bring on school days."

"But that's because you're such a good cook, Rei! I could have a horrible stomach bug and be throwing up and shitting at the same time and I'd still want to eat whatever you brought!"

Amir snorted with laughter. Rei wrinkled her nose. "You should not use that kind of language, Merrow."

It was difficult to keep my face solemn when I had a clear view of Amir's delight, but I managed as best I could. "I got excited thinking about your cooking."

Rei sighed. "I won't say anything to Bear if you promise that you will tell me if he ever treats you poorly. And I need you both to sleep in the house, in separate rooms, from now on."

Amir and I nodded.

"You have our word," Amir said. I looked at him. Lies came easily to both of us, it seemed.

Rei studied him. "Do not let this one be a bad influence on you, Amir. I know you share everything, but there is no need to share her mischief. You have a wise heart. I have always seen it."

I was surprised to see Amir's cheeks turn pink.

"You are two people, not one," Rei continued. "Beware if you begin to hear thoughts in your head that do not speak in your voice."

"Like a ghost?" Amir asked.

"No. Not like a ghost." Rei threw her hands in the air as

though she were giving up. "Let's go sit on the porch for your lessons. I brought some books on Native American pottery that I think you'll both like."

My mood instantly lifted. Rei, we had learned recently, had not been an elementary school teacher in Japan as I had always believed, but a professor of art at a university. I found the fifth-grade worksheets from the homeschooling curriculum she had acquired fairly dull, but Rei's lessons sprang to life when she supplemented them with her knowledge of the history of art.

As we walked up the porch steps, she touched each of our shoulders. "I am glad you have each other," she said, her voice more gentle than before. "My parents, in Japan, lived through great hardship that they would not have survived had they not had each other. They looked nothing alike, but you could not look at one without seeing the other. They shared something that showed on their faces. There was a special energy between them, joining them. Even when my father died, from a heart attack at far too young an age, I saw him for years in my mother. I felt his presence when I was with her."

I stared at Rei, thrilled. "So your father *was* a ghost!"

"No. A ghost is troublesome. This was a haunting, maybe, but a happy one. A welcome one. A love that runs that deep cannot simply disappear. It lives on. It has power."

On the porch, we each settled into our usual chairs.

"What am I trying to tell you?" Rei thought for a moment. "Only that I believe this friendship the two of you share will give you comfort for your entire lives. Even—maybe *especially*—

when your futures take different paths and you find that you are no longer together."

Amir and I looked at each other. I knew what he was thinking because I was thinking it, too: Rei meant well, but she was wrong. We had been left by too many loved ones; we would never inflict that pain on each other. Already, I heard Amir's voice in my mind when he wasn't speaking, just as I knew he heard mine. In the shed at night when it was very cold, we huddled close under the gaze of the red birds we had made together, and I would drift to sleep unsure whose breath I heard so steady and sure, his or mine.

We would never be apart.

CHAPTER EIGHT

Pal's spirits returned moments after Bear kicked him that night in the bedroom I had shared with Amir, but he was never as physically strong again. By the time I was fourteen and Pal nine, he had the stiff gait of an older dog. He was hesitant to follow Amir and me down to the beach, a place he had once loved as much as I did. The rocky path along the cliff bothered his old injury, as did the shell-strewn sand. Amir and I had learned to ask Pal to wait at the chicken coop while we visited the cove. There he would busy himself with protecting the hens—a grave insult that infuriated our rooster, Crosby, who believed himself the only protector the hens required.

Late one sunny morning, we left Pal at the coop and walked down to the beach. Two knives glinted in the basket that hung from my fist. Rei had recently given us a bottle of sesame oil and told us that it was delicious drizzled over cooked seaweed. As we walked down the path that cut into the cliff, I was happy to see that the rocks exposed by the retreating tide were covered with the deep-red fronds of grapestone.

We kicked off our shoes at the bottom of the path and made our way out to where the warm sand became wet and cold below our feet. Our knives cut easily through the gleaming tongues of seaweed. It was the sort of glorious, sun-soaked day that demanded I still my knife every few minutes and simply look around. From the top of the bluff you could see the curve of cliffs for miles in either direction, but down at the water's edge the only cliffs visible were the arms of the cove that stretched out on either side of us, carved by the pounding of the ocean so that they rose in a tenuous golden arc toward the sky. My father used to tell me that each touch from the sea, even one as soft as an exhaled breath, forever changed not only the land, but the shape of the sea itself. *True love's embrace,* my father called it. *Ever-changing. Eternal.*

When our basket was full, we stretched out on the warm, dry sand. Amir had taken off his shirt while we had worked. His brown shoulders were broad now but still bony, his torso narrow but strong. I knew his body as well as he knew mine. I was aware of how his body had changed, just as I knew he was aware of my own changes—namely, my breasts, which I caught his gaze lingering on from time to time. I knew the white flecks on his hands were nicks from his whittling knife. And I knew the trail of bruises on his upper arm were the exact thickness of Bear's fingers. He had grabbed Amir the night before, pulling him up from his seat and then shoving him to the ground.

You're disgusting, Bear had said, spitting and thankfully missing Amir. *Dad would be disgusted by the two of you.*

We had not been doing anything more than sitting on the steps of the back porch together. I was reading Mary Shelley's *Frankenstein* and Amir was bent over his geometry workbook. Still, even as I read, I felt acutely aware of every movement Amir made, no matter how small. Heat spread across my skin each time a part of his body grazed a part of mine. Our feelings for each other were changing along with our bodies. There were moments when he would look up from his notebook and smile almost shyly at me, and the question in his chocolate, black-rimmed eyes would make me aware of an answer that was buried deep within me.

We weren't smiling at each other when Bear stumbled out of the house. We were just sitting with our books on our laps. But I had recently begun to suspect that what existed between Amir and I was something the world could sense if not entirely believe, like the mysterious blur of a falling star in the corner of your eye. It turned out I was right.

Later, I wondered if Bear threw Amir to the ground at that moment because he saw that Amir did not have his knife in his hand. Perhaps my brother sensed the depths of anger quietly roiling within Amir, the untold lengths he would go to protect his place at Horseshoe Cliff.

You're disgusting. Dad would be disgusted by the two of you.

It had been years since I had cried; Bear had broken me of the habit. But that night I came as close to tears as I had in a long time. I felt my brother's words poisoning my feelings for Amir. I hated Bear for making me feel ashamed.

What if, I wondered for the first time, *the way I feel about*

Amir is less like a shooting star, bright with drama, and more like the strange glow of a distant planet, foreign and incomprehensible, a place where we are not meant to live?

I had tossed from side to side in my bed that night. We slept in separate rooms now—Bear had moved to my father's room, the biggest of the three, and Amir slept in Bear's old room. When at last I fell asleep, I dreamed of a red bird that peered down at me with a dry eye before turning and flying away.

ON THE BEACH, I gently touched the bruises on Amir's arm. He looked down at my hand and didn't speak. When I touched his arm, I felt a tremor run through me. I had never been kissed, but I wondered if this was a more intimate gesture, allowing someone to be so close that they touched your pain, shared it.

"We could run away," I said. "Hitchhike to San Francisco."

Amir's gaze shifted to the horizon. "I don't want to leave."

I sighed. We had had this conversation so many times. "Don't you want to get away from him?"

"This is our home. He can't chase us from it."

"He's not chasing us if we're running toward something. I love it here as much as you do. But there's so much more I want to experience. You've lived in India and New York. Rei lived in Japan. The farthest I've been is Osha. We could go anywhere together. There's no one to stop us."

"With what money? Where would we stay?"

"My father came to San Francisco from Nebraska with no plans and next to nothing in his wallet. My mother did the same from New York. We'll figure it out. You can sell your carvings. I can . . ." I thought about this. What could I do? I wasn't so naive as to believe that there was a market for my stories. After writing, my next best skill was that I was a quick reader. My shoulders sank. "I don't know. I don't know! But I want to see more than *this*." I gestured toward the ocean. Even as I said those words, my fickleness made me feel contrite. Horseshoe Cliff was my home and I loved it. Was I wrong to feel as I did?

Right then, as we both looked out at the ocean, a humpback whale rose from the water, its mouth gaping as it breached. It was close enough that we could see its teeth sparkling below the seawater that churned and poured from its mouth. And then it was gone. And then it returned. For nearly an hour we watched in silent awe as the whale surfaced and disappeared, surfaced and disappeared, until it had eaten its fill and moved on from our little cove.

AT THE TOP of the cliff path, when the noise of the waves faded, high-pitched yelping filled the air. I ran, the basket of seaweed banging against my leg. At the edge of the horse pasture, a coyote looked over his shoulder at me before loping away. The chickens in the coop darted and squawked. Feathers and dust filled the air. In front of the coop, Pal staggered and sunk onto a swath of dirt that was dark with blood and fur. His yelping abruptly quieted.

I dropped to the ground and pulled him onto my lap. "Oh, Pal." His blood poured out of his wounds in a dark, warm rush, drenching my clothes. He closed his eyes. The weight of his body was too heavy, as though the spirit that had always lightened it had already left.

Amir crouched beside us and stroked Pal's head with a shaking hand. "Pal," he murmured. "Sweet, brave Pal. We're here."

I curled my body over Pal's and felt his tongue lick my cheek. I pressed my face against his neck and sobbed, whispering his name over and over. "You did it, Pal," I said. "You kept the chickens safe. What a good boy." Amir's arm was around me, his cheek against my shoulder, his tears falling with mine. After a length of time I would never know, Pal sighed and became still in my arms.

I lifted my head and howled with grief and rage.

When I finally looked around, the chickens were quiet, as though dazed. Amir wiped his eyes.

"I'll get a blanket," he said, standing slowly.

I kept Pal on my lap, my head hanging, until Amir returned. Then we wrapped him in the blanket. Amir handed me the shovel he had also brought from the shed and hoisted Pal into his arms.

"The grove?" he asked.

I nodded.

We buried him just off our favorite path. I placed three long sticks of the type that he liked to chew on top of the grave. It was difficult to believe that he had been alive that morning and now was gone, but I knew by then that this was the nature of death. I thought that it had taken Bear a long time to steal Pal from me, but in the end, that was what he had managed to do.

It was as we walked out of the grove that I thought of the

sharp knife I had used to cut seaweed from the rocks. "Bear did this," I said, quickening my step. "Pal was trying to protect the chickens. He could have fought off that coyote if Bear hadn't hurt him." When I wiped at my eyes, the dirt on my hands stung them. "I hate him," I said. The words were hot in my mouth, and I spat them out.

When we reached the coop, the basket of seaweed was where I'd dropped it and bright sunlight reflected off the knife. Amir reached the basket first and picked it up. I could not stand to see how Pal's blood darkened the dirt in every direction. I kept my eyes instead on the knife. I reached for the basket, but Amir swung it away from me.

"Merrow," he said gently. "Let's change our clothes. I have an idea."

When my eyes met his, my anger gave way to sadness. I nodded mutely.

We changed our clothes and headed down the long dirt drive that led to the road. My body felt so heavy that I had the sensation I had stepped into someone else's—someone slower, older. I was lost in my memories of Pal. It took me a moment to realize that we were on the road walking toward Osha. When a car passed, Amir stuck out his thumb. The car sped by in a thrum of dampened music and dust. I pulled Amir onto the scrub grass off the pavement.

"What are you doing?"

"Getting us started," he answered. His dark hair fell in his eyes.

"Started on what?"

"Wait and see."

When the next car approached, I stepped up to the side of the road and stuck out my thumb. A man with gray hair that curled below the back of his faded cap drove the car, and a woman with a long gray braid sat beside him.

She rolled down her mud-flecked window. "Everything okay? Need a ride to town?" A Grateful Dead song was on the radio—I didn't know which one, but I recognized Jerry Garcia's voice from the radio station my father used to play. It was music from another time.

Amir nodded, and we climbed into the backseat. Rei took us to Osha every few months, but we had never been there by ourselves. The woman looked over her shoulder. She had a kind smile and the sight of it made me worry that tears would rise to my eyes.

"Seat belts, please," she said. Once we had buckled ourselves in, she nodded to the man beside her and he pulled the car back onto the road. No one spoke again after that. The music changed from one Grateful Dead song to another. The road south to Osha curved toward the ocean and then away from it toward the hills and then back toward the ocean again. Clouds sat up high in the bright blue sky, so perfectly white and still it was hard to imagine they would ever break apart. I watched this all numbly.

The car stopped in front of the Osha co-op. Amir and I opened the door and climbed out.

"Thank you," Amir said, as easily as if this were the sort of thing we did all the time.

"You got it," the driver said, speaking for the first time. The woman just nodded at us and offered up that smile one last time and then they were off.

I looked at Amir. "Now what?"

"Are you hungry?"

I nodded. Instead of heading into the co-op, he started up the street away from the ocean. The main street in Osha ended on one end at the ocean, and on the other it climbed up the hillside, eventually forking and then forking again, growing narrower with each turn. We were unusually quiet. I was lost in thoughts of Pal and hardly noticed how far we walked. In town, houses were set on small parcels close enough for one neighbor to stand on his porch and stretch out his hand to touch his neighbor's hand, but up on the hill the houses gathered distance between them, each one claiming a bit more land than the last. As we walked, Amir opened one house's mailbox and then another and another. We kept walking.

Amir stopped in front of a brown-shingled house with yellow roses lining its walkway. The driveway was empty. When he opened the mailbox at the fence, I saw that it was stuffed full of mail.

"It's not San Francisco," he said, looking back at me. "But you wanted to see somewhere other than Horseshoe Cliff." He headed down the driveway and disappeared behind the house. "Come on!" he called.

I was startled to hear how deep Amir's voice sounded. Years earlier, Rei had told us about puberty, and about sex. She'd warned me that I would be shocked by my blood when I had my first menstruation, but when that time came, I had not been shocked. Blood was not particularly frightening to me by then. I welcomed my period as though it were an end marker to my childhood; I was ready for something more.

The back door of the house was locked. Amir bent down and lifted the doormat and laughed when he saw the key. I picked up the key and slid it into the door lock as though I'd been unlocking doors my whole life.

Inside, we found ourselves in a large kitchen. The lights were off; the house was silent. Amir walked to the sink and gulped water straight from the faucet. When he stopped, he looked at me and smiled, his chin gleaming and wet. The kitchen floor was covered with beautiful pale blue tile. I wished I were wearing socks so that I could skate on it.

The refrigerator, sadly, was empty but for the rows of condiments that lined the door. I picked out a jar with a dark green and gold label that declared itself honey mustard and proved to be delicious—sweet and spicy, just as my father used to describe me. Amir and I sat on stools at the edge of the kitchen counter and sunk our fingers into the jar until we had wiped it clean. Then he rifled through the cabinets and returned with an unopened bag of pretzels. When we finished the pretzels, Amir rolled the crinkling bag into a ball and stuffed it in his pocket.

Something knocked against the kitchen window, making our eyes widen. It was only a branch. We smiled at each other, relieved. The smile felt funny on my face, but I didn't chase it away.

The living room had a thick gray carpet. I had never seen anything like it. I lay down and pressed my face against it, closing my eyes. I thought of Pal. When I stood, I saw that I'd left a smudge of dirt behind and felt a pang of regret.

Upstairs, we wandered silently through three bedrooms where beds were piled high with pillows and blankets. Pretty white drapes covered the windows. On a nightstand in the biggest bedroom there was a black-and-white photograph of a man and a woman on their wedding day. They were standing in front of a church, and the wind had pulled the bride's veil straight up in the air. They were both laughing. I bent down close to the picture and saw that the sleeves of the woman's gown were made of lace. She wore a diamond pendant on a chain so thin it was barely visible.

In one bathroom, when Amir flicked a switch, light seemed to glow from every surface, including the mirror that we made faces into. We didn't quite look like ourselves in that mirror. The whites of our eyes seemed very white, and our brown skin seemed luminous.

In a child's bedroom, a closet was full of colorful clothes. There was a red velvet dress that I imagined she wore only at Christmas, and a row of cotton dresses with delicately embroidered flowers and ribbon belts. On a shelf above the dresses, sweaters were neatly folded. On the floor of the closet, I saw a pair of silver sandals with small jewels on the straps. I tried to put them on, but my feet were too big; the girl who owned them was much younger than I was. I kept trying, though, pulling on the jeweled strap of the sandal until it broke. Amir had wandered off somewhere, but now he was returning; I heard his footsteps in the hall. When I looked over my shoulder, he was watching me. I ran my thumb over the jewels on the broken strap in my hand.

Amir crossed the room and sat beside me.

"I'm going to carve a new bird," said Amir. "For Pal. Will you paint it?"

I nodded. After Rei had discovered that we were sleeping in the shed, we'd moved the nests to a ledge high in the back of a cave in the face of the cliff. It was our best hiding place yet, far better than the tree pockets in the grove where I'd put my treasures as a kid. I liked to imagine that sometime in the future an adventurous child would find the cave and recognize our birds as priceless clues to a mysterious and indelible past.

"I think my mother killed herself," I said to Amir on the floor of that girl's room. "I used to think that she just fell, that it was an accident. But my father told me that she had dark moods. I think he was trying to tell me the truth about what she'd done."

Amir put his arm around me. I rested my head against his shoulder. His slow breath moved my hair. I did not worry about the owners of the house returning. I felt safe. We sat like that for a long time. Energy moved from his warm, lean body to mine, sinking into my skin like a balm.

"Imagine having all these clothes," I said, looking up at the closet.

Amir shifted. After a beat of time he said, "It's just a bunch of stuff."

But it wasn't just a bunch of *stuff*. Having that many beautiful things signified something. If you had enough beautiful things, they could never all be taken away from you. You might lose one or two, but the loss would never feel like much when you considered how much more you had. You could never be left with nothing.

I folded the broken, jeweled sandal strap and put it in my pocket.

I think I knew even then that a part of me would never be the same again. Something had shifted within me the moment I stepped into that house, grieving the loss of Pal, and saw that blue kitchen floor. A fissure of longing had opened and grew deeper by the day.

CHAPTER NINE

When I was fifteen, Rei handed me a thick workbook and told me I should begin studying for the GED.

"You have completed the required high school curriculum. I don't see why you should wait. You can take the GED and apply to college. You'll get a scholarship. I'm sure of it."

Her words thrilled me, but I thought immediately of Amir. Schoolwork had never come easily to him. Rei had brought only one GED workbook.

"What about Amir?"

Rei sighed. Her face was etched with lines that reminded me of the cobwebs that appeared in the corners of my bedroom overnight.

"You and Amir are not one person," Rei said. "He has his pace of learning and you have yours. He has his future and you have yours. Already, you spend too much time together."

Her reproach made my cheeks grow warm. I knew that she felt our bond was unnatural. *Siblings should not be so close,* she had told me recently. *But we aren't siblings,* I replied. This did not satisfy her. I remembered how Bear had said that our father would have thought that our relationship was disgusting. Amir and I were not supposed to have the feelings that we had for each other, feelings that I had become too ashamed to allow myself to linger on even in the privacy of my own mind. I longed for him in a way that made me self-conscious; I worried that my desire for him was visible on my skin.

Whenever I looked at Amir's lips and thought of kissing them, I felt a rush of humiliation that could be overcome only by convincing Amir to explore another house with me. Over the course of a year, we'd let ourselves into nearly a dozen houses. If anyone in Osha was aware that houses were being broken into, the news never reached us. And yet, though we never took anything more than snacks—and, that first time, a sandal strap—surely some owner along the way must have noticed something slightly off about his home upon his return. The half-eaten tub of ice cream? The throw blanket inexpertly refolded? The once delicately curved red lipstick now flattened within its golden tube after being pressed too hard to the lips of a girl who had never worn makeup? As far as we knew, no one was perturbed by these subtle trespasses.

In those houses, there were no consequences for our transgressions. And so, in those houses, I allowed myself to look at Amir with all the longing that I felt for him. I did not silently berate myself when he returned my gaze. In those strangers' homes, my attraction to Amir felt untethered from the mortification that accompanied it at Horseshoe Cliff. When his hand, on occasion, grazed my skin, or mine his, I enjoyed the thrum of pleasure that ran down my spine.

Our touches grew more frequent, and it was difficult to say what would have happened between us if we had not, that summer, stumbled upon the house at which everything changed.

THE HOUSE WAS so high in the hills that we were out of breath by the time we found it. On some outings we never found a house to explore, and I had been beginning to feel a needle of disappointment that it might be one of those days. When I saw the small dark house nestled within the fog and trees, a flutter of excitement moved through my chest. The driveway was steep and curved and lined with tall plants that were dotted with bursts of orange flowers. There were no cars parked in front, no dogs barking from within, no lights glowing through the fog, and no security company stickers warning us away.

The sliding door at the back of the house was locked. I cupped my hands around my eyes and peered through the glass. On a round white table there was a bowl of fat cherries with skin so shiny that I knew they were perfectly ripe. I imagined their taut skin bursting as easily as a strained seam.

When I pulled back from the glass door, I noticed a window at the far corner of the house. It slid open silently. Amir climbed through first. His hands held mine as I stepped through the window and then straightened. I felt his thumbs run over my skin. A presence beside me made me turn with a start, but it was only our reflection. We were in a bathroom: black tiled floor, bathtub surprisingly deep and round.

In the mirror: a line of dried blood above Amir's eyebrow from the wall that Bear had shoved him against that morning. As I'd helped Amir clean the cut, I'd felt as though it were my own skin that had split open, my own bright blood that ran down his face. His cut was my cut; his blood, mine.

Now, Amir studied the wound. Anger transformed his face, making his languid eyes glitter. He was always controlled around Bear, infuriating my brother with his measured voice and the detached expression that communicated that he was better than Bear. But I knew that Amir's hands tightened into fists when he saw Bear approaching. Amir seemed to get a little taller every day, and I wondered what would happen when he stopped having to look up at Bear and instead met his bleary gaze straight on.

"You know not to listen to him, right?" I put my hand on his. "You're not nobody. You're the opposite of nobody."

"I'm everybody?" Amir's smile was sad. I ached to run my fingers over his long black eyelashes, to cup his face in my hands.

"You are to me." I would do anything for him. And he would do anything for me. The intensity of this realization made me feel jittery. I looked around the room. "Check out the size of that tub. Whoever owns this house is a giant."

Amir smiled, and the anger in his face disappeared. "Giants eat a lot." He went off in search of the kitchen.

There was a bottle of something called rose water on the countertop beside a strange-looking toothbrush. I stuck my pinkie into the bottle and then dragged my pinkie up and down my arm. The scent was a thick floral smell that I loved. It made me think of Rei, who always smelled of sweet things. For a moment, I considered taking the bottle as a gift for Rei, but I knew I would never be able to explain how I came to have it.

In the bedroom, a large white bed seemed to float over the pale floor. A few photographs of the beach near Osha were framed on the walls, and a tall bookcase lined with books stood next to a large chest.

It was a quiet house. The boards below my feet did not creak and the sides of the house did not complain when the wind blew. I heard only the sounds of cabinets and drawers opening and closing as Amir looked for food. I remembered the cherries on the table that I'd seen through the window and was about to walk out of the bedroom when the chest caught my eye again. Inside, below a stack of neatly folded blankets, was a box.

It was big enough to hold a quilt and decorated with shells and thin gray stones. The beach at Horseshoe Cliff was rife with those stones, round as coins and veined with delicate white lines. Amir and I would have contests to see who could stack them higher and I always lost, stacking my stones too quickly so they wobbled and fell, while Amir took his time building a tower that reached his waist. I liked to sneak glances at Amir while he stacked those stones; his face grew still, the curves of his cheekbones hardening, his eyes steady with concentration. He held each stone in his palm as though warming it before placing it at the top of the stack. His long fingers never shook. I thought that Amir's hands, as calloused and scarred as they were, were easily the most elegant things at Horseshoe Cliff.

Whoever owned the box was careful, too. An artist. The stones formed a pattern of cresting waves. Sea froth was made from gold-flecked sand, a beach of perfect shells below. I ran my fingers over the pattern, wondering if I dared to take the box with me when I left, if its owner could possibly miss it as much as I would cherish it. My fingers found the small latch hidden in the waves.

Inside, there was money. Stack upon stack of hundred-dollar bills tied with red string. I stared. I reached out to touch the money and started when I realized Amir was calling my name. His voice had a strange catch in it.

"Mer—" he said, appearing in the doorway. His eyes widened when he saw the money. Quickly, before I could think better of it, I picked up a thick pad of bills. I looked at Amir. The sight of the cut curving above his black eyebrow caused my heart to pound.

"Amir," I said. I knew he already knew what I was thinking, that I didn't have to say a word more. A sort of breathless excitement took hold of me as I cradled that money. "We could leave. We could go anywhere we wanted. We could go to San Francisco! We could stay in a hotel and order room service." It was something I'd wanted to do since reading *Eloise* as a child. "We could buy luggage and fill it with new clothes. We could leave right now, just start hitching rides until we're far away from here."

I stopped talking only when I saw the funny look on Amir's face.

"We can't take that money," he said.

"But listen—"

"It's Rei's."

I stared at him, confused.

"This is Rei's house," Amir said. "She's in the photographs in the living room. There's a grocery list in her handwriting in the kitchen."

I sat back on my heels, gripping the money with both hands now. Rei had distinctive handwriting, as quietly precise as embroidery. I thought it was very sophisticated, and I had shaped my own handwriting after Rei's, tracing her letters for most of my life. We knew Rei's handwriting; we would recognize it anywhere.

This was Rei's house.

We knew she lived near Osha, but we had never been to her house. It was funny, but I wasn't sure I had even ever wondered about Rei's home . . . Rei's life outside of Horseshoe Cliff. I glanced at the closed closet door, knowing the colors and materials of the dresses that were hanging inside, the overalls that were folded within the bureau, the assortment of bracelets that would be stacked carefully somewhere, the collection of wide-brimmed hats. I breathed in and smelled Rei. I ran my fingers over the money. Rei's money.

"There's something else," Amir said.

I followed him out of the bedroom. Amir's brow furrowed, but I could not bring myself to leave the money behind.

On the shelves of the living room, amid photographs of Rei and my father and me and Amir and Bear and other people I did not know, were my father's houses, each and every one of the tiny wood houses that he had made over the course of so many years. Amir's animals, too, were there, sanded perfectly smooth.

We stood very still. The house echoed our stillness. It felt as though time were frozen, waiting for us to understand.

"There are no craft fairs," I said at last.

"I guess not."

"She just bought them all herself. Rei is rich."

Amir looked around the room. "Richer than us. That's for sure."

My father would never have accepted the money from Rei if he'd known it was charity. She had been very clever to find a way to help us without offending him. It was strange to feel our world shifting, to see everything in a different way. To know a truth that my father had never known. I felt no animosity toward Rei for her duplicity. I felt only gratitude. She had been watching over us, all of us, for so many years.

I looked around. I imagined Rei stretched on the cream-colored sofa, reading a book. The lovely scent on Rei's skin was rose water—now it had a name. I imagined Rei settling into her deep bathtub at night when she returned home from Horseshoe Cliff, how the bubbles might turn brown with the dirt she'd carried from her visit to the farm. I imagined her stepping out of the bath and pressing rose water to her newly clean wrists.

What if all those years ago when Rei had asked if Bear was hurting us, we had told her the truth? Would she have found a way to keep us together? Would she have brought us to this beautiful house where we might have grown up the way the kids on Bear's television grew up instead of the way we actually had, perpetually swinging from fear to our wild, wonderful kind of freedom to fear again? If I had ignored Amir's pleas in the shed that night and instead blurted out just once to Rei the extent of Bear's cruelty, everything might have been different.

But of course, there was no way to know just how different it would have been. My life was tied to Amir's, and if we had been separated, there was no amount of clean sheets and jeweled sandals that would have been worth his absence.

"We need to thank her," I said. "We need to thank her for everything she's done for us."

"How can we? She can't ever know that we were here."

Of course he was right—there was no way we could thank Rei without her learning that we'd broken into her home. This would be another secret we would have to keep.

I turned the stack of money in my hand sadly. The weight of it surprised me. It was so light, all that money. A soft wind could blow it far away. This was the image that for months would come to me at strange moments of my day: money that floated and looped through the air, forming first the lines of Rei's beautiful handwriting and then the thin outline of a path I could never reach, a road that narrowed and disappeared from view before I could set foot on it.

CHAPTER TEN

We felt chastened after breaking into Rei's home, and for a spell we stayed close to home. I missed the pleasure of trying on other people's lives and the sense of freedom Amir and I experienced when we were away from Horseshoe Cliff. So I felt a thrill when Amir suggested that we venture out to just one more house, one final press of our luck.

"Your pick," he said. I had passed the GED, and this was his gift to me.

Amir's eyes widened when I stopped in front of the house I'd chosen. Separated from the road by a stone wall, it was larger than any of the homes we'd previously explored. A locked gate—a rare sight in Osha—spanned the driveway.

"This one?" Amir shook his head. "There's no way we'll get inside."

"But wouldn't you love to see it?"

"I'd love to not get arrested. This place definitely has an alarm. Pick another."

I peered through the gate. The driveway was a long stretch of sleek black pavement, empty of cars. Though it was dusk, none of the lights in the house were lit.

I stuck out my hand and said, "I bet you a million bucks there's no alarm."

Amir looked skeptical, but he shook my hand. "A million bucks. Don't forget it. I'm going to need that money to buy toothpaste in prison."

I laughed. He helped me scramble to the top of the wall, and the feeling of his hands on my legs made my breath catch in my chest.

Amir, who was much taller than me and still as skinny as a sapling, managed to grab hold of the top of the wall and pull himself up beside me. The house was new but made to look old with a stone tower at one corner and thick black porch columns.

"How many bedrooms do you think it has?" I asked. "Ten?"

"It's ugly. It looks like an insane asylum."

"What are you talking about? It looks like a castle."

"You say potato, I say *po-tah-to*."

I smiled. "Well, I'm dying to see the inside of this potato."

We hopped down from the wall. The moment our feet hit the driveway, light flooded the air. We froze.

"Let's go," Amir said in a low voice. "Now."

He turned, but I stood still. The house was quiet. We were so close. The thought of giving up filled me with disappointment. "The lights are probably on motion sensors," I whispered. "I don't think anyone is home. I'm just going to peek in the window."

Amir's hand encircled my wrist. I felt a charge where his skin touched mine. I knew every shade of brown that existed within his irises and knew that they seemed to darken when he was worried.

"Merrow."

I gently shook my wrist free from his hand. "I'll be right back." I ran toward the house.

I'd only made it a few feet when enraged barking filled the air like a siren. I skidded to a stop and in that instant saw the dog that raced toward me in a blur of fur and teeth. I spun and ran, but the dog's nails clawed my back, knocking me to the pavement. His teeth ripped through my jeans and into my calf. I cried out at the pain that coursed through me. The dog held tight as I tried to kick free.

"Hey! No! Get off!" Amir hollered. I twisted to see him pulling at the dog's collar, but the dog would not loosen his grip on me.

I heard a woman's voice. "No, Tiger! No!"

And then the dog was gone. I rolled into a ball, moaning and clutching my leg. My hands came away from the wound covered in blood.

Amir was beside me. "Merrow—"

"Oh my god," said a man in a horrified voice.

I struggled to sit up. Behind Amir, a man and an older woman looked down at me with stunned expressions. The dog, still quivering with excitement, sat beside the woman and stared at me hungrily.

"Your dog bit me!" I managed to say. I couldn't quite believe it.

The man knelt in front of me. There was a golden light that

seemed to emanate from him, brightening the sky that was otherwise as matte and purple and gray as a dusty plum. I had never seen someone so beautiful in all my life. His blond hair curled gently at his forehead, and his eyes were a shade of blue that was soft and deeply comforting. The pain in my leg momentarily ebbed; the man's presence overwhelmed me.

"You're bleeding." His brows were knit with concern. I wondered if he was an actor from television. "Can you stand? We have a first aid kit in the house."

"*I'm* fine," I said. "But your dog could clearly use more to eat."

He sat back on his heels and laughed, surprised.

I looked over at Amir. "Let's go," I said shakily. I had no idea how I was going to move.

"Now, wait a minute," said the woman. "What were you doing, hopping over the fence like that?"

I tried to stand but putting weight on my injured leg triggered a stabbing sensation that made me stumble. Amir took my elbow and steadied me. And then, startling me, the blue-eyed man took my other elbow. Despite the pain I was in, I felt a shiver at his touch. So it wasn't just Amir who did this to me. His hand was very soft. His skin was a beautiful cream color. His hair was a golden blond. Even his eyebrows were blond. How must I have looked compared to what he saw in the mirror every day? *Filthy,* I thought. My eyes were a murky green brown, my skin a dusky shade of tan, my hair a mix of blond and brown, my eyebrows as dark as the dirt under my fingernails.

"Take it easy," the man said. "I think you're more hurt than you realize."

I had been trying to ignore the warm gush of blood that I felt trailing down my leg and pooling in my sneaker, but at his words, I looked down and then quickly away. Amir's grip tightened on my elbow.

"Merrow," he said, worried.

"Please, come inside and let me give you a bandage," the man said. "It's the least we can do."

"Is it?" the woman asked. "I'm wondering why I'm not on the phone with the police right now."

"Because *look* at her, Mom. Your dog is—"

"Deranged," I said, yanking my elbow from the man's hand.

"To be fair," the woman said coolly, "Tiger was only doing his job."

The man turned to her. "You're not helping."

"Is that the goal, William?"

"Yes."

"We should go," Amir said. He tugged at my elbow. "Come on, Merrow."

"Merrow? That's a lovely name. My name is Will Langford. This is my mother, Rosalie."

"We're leaving." Amir's voice was deeper than usual.

Will held up his hands, conceding. "Can I at least help you to your car?"

This made me laugh, and my laughter made the pain in my calf surge. I gritted my teeth and leaned into Amir, putting my weight on my uninjured leg. "We don't have a car."

"Oh." Will frowned. "I'd offer to drive you home, but we're stranded here without a car at the moment. We all drove from

San Francisco together, and now my father is off with the car on a fishing trip."

"You're bleeding quite a lot," said Rosalie. It was the first time I heard a note of concern in her voice.

I looked down again, and when I did, my balance faltered. In an instant, Will scooped me into his arms and began walking toward the house. I stared at his face, suddenly so close to my own.

"Please follow us," he called over his shoulder to Amir.

Since I'd learned that it hurt to laugh, I now tried not to, but it was actually very funny to be carried in the arms of this handsome stranger as though I were a damsel in distress, or one of the ladies in the soap operas I had loved so much for a time. I felt entirely unlike myself—my leg throbbed and my surroundings were looking more unfamiliar by the moment. I rested my chin on Will's shoulder. When I caught Amir's unhappy gaze, I fluttered my eyes and lolled my head as though I'd succumbed to womanly weakness. Amir looked away and did not smile.

Rosalie strode past us and opened the front door, that terrible dog at her heels. We stepped into a space that seemed to have no purpose except to be beautiful. Below Will's feet lay an Oriental carpet that did not seem like the kind you were supposed to wipe your shoes on.

"I don't want to bleed all over your rug," I said. My voice sounded strangely quiet. Something was making my chest feel tight. The throbbing pain in my calf. The beautiful house. The closeness of Will's face. He had no scent, I realized. If I climbed to the top of a mountain at daybreak and stuck my nose into a newly formed cloud, it would have smelled like Will Langford.

"I'm not worried about the rug," he said. He strode through the entry, and then we were in a big room that was a kitchen and living room in one. There was a stone fireplace with a couch and two gray armchairs surrounding it. Rosalie appeared with a towel that she spread across one of the armchairs. She gestured for Will to set me down and he did, gently. She rolled up my pants and wrapped another towel around my leg. With a third towel, she wiped the blood from my hands. I stared at her, unable to look away. Her white-blond hair was pulled into a high ponytail, revealing twin swirls of bright green stones that hung from her small earlobes.

Amir sat on the arm of my chair. "Are you okay?"

"Not really." The truth was that I wavered between regret at having gotten us into this situation, and a sneaky delight that I had managed to get us inside the house after all.

Amir put his hand on my shoulder and didn't move it when Will returned with a bucket of soapy water and a first aid kit. Rosalie unwound the towel, now stained with my blood, from my leg. The bleeding seemed to have slowed. Her dog was stationed beside her, his eyes pinned on me. When Rosalie pressed the soapy towel to the wound, I sucked in my breath.

"I'll try to find some pain medicine," Will said.

Rosalie put the towel back in the soapy water and then pressed it to the wound again. Her face was still, but her eyes flickered with thought.

I supposed that someone must have taken care of me like

this in my life—my father or my mother—but I had no memories of a moment like this one. I watched Rosalie, wanting to remember the experience. She wasn't particularly gentle in her movements, but still, something that felt worrisomely close to weepiness trembled within me. I refused to let the feeling grow.

After a couple of minutes, she sat back and looked up at me. "I don't really have any idea how to deal with a dog bite," she said. The water turned pink when she returned the towel to it.

"If I had the choice," I said, "I'd start by dealing with the dog that did the biting."

Rosalie had blue eyes like her son, but hers were a steely version. "Is that so?" She tore open a bandage wrapper and pressed the bandage to my leg. I winced but was determined not to cry. Amir gave my shoulder a sympathetic squeeze. "And what punishment would you deal my Tiger?"

I closed my eyes, but it only seemed to make the pain sharpen. When I opened them, I saw that Rosalie had begun to stroke the dog's head.

"In *The Accidental Tourist*," I said, "the biting dog is put into obedience classes. It's not exactly punishment, but at least the behavior is addressed and not encouraged." I glared pointedly at Rosalie's elegant hand and when I did, she stopped petting her dog.

"You've read Anne Tyler?" She did not bother to hide her surprise. She stood and resituated herself in the other armchair. The dog moved with her, curling himself at her feet. At long last, he seemed to lose interest in me.

"That's one of my mother's favorite books," Will said. I had not heard him return to the room.

I looked at Rosalie anew. How strange to have something as important as literary taste in common with this woman who outwardly could not have been more unlike me. As different as we were, we had read and gathered insight from the same thoughts, the same passages. I wondered if Rosalie had adored the romance between Macon and Muriel, how it seemed to rise from their grief like a wildflower from dirt, if she'd underlined the same passages that I—

"How old are you?" she asked, interrupting my thoughts.

"Sixteen."

"Is that all?" She looked at Amir. "And you?"

"Sixteen."

"You haven't told us your name."

"Amir."

"Do you attend that little school down in Osha?"

"No. We're homeschooled."

Rosalie glanced back and forth between us, confused. "Both of you? Together?"

"Yes," I said. "My father was Amir's guardian. We've lived together since we were eight years old."

"So Amir is your brother," Will said.

"No," Amir said.

He was not my brother. That was a role that belonged entirely to Bear in the way that a hive belonged to the bees that made it buzz with warning. Amir's place in my life was so much greater than that of a brother. I'd never settled on the right word for him. He was like a piece of myself that lived outside of myself. We were attached in a way that, even if I had wanted to, I could not easily explain.

"My father was his guardian," I repeated. "And now my father is dead, and my brother is our guardian. Amir is . . . We're best friends." It did not feel right to describe our connection this way; the phrase "best friends" was too common, too frivolous a phrase to encapsulate what we meant to each other. I regretted my choice of words the moment I spoke, though I told myself it was silly to feel so strongly. They were only words; they could not diminish us.

The room was quiet. I sensed Amir's unhappiness. When Rosalie spoke, the edge in her voice had softened. "So the two of you live with your older brother . . ." She trailed off, waiting for me to continue.

"Bear."

Her white-blond eyebrows shot up. "Bear! Bear and Merrow. And Amir. What remarkable names."

"Mom . . ." Will said. He seemed embarrassed by her.

She ignored him. "When was your last tetanus shot?"

"I . . . I'm not sure."

"I couldn't find any pain medicine," Will said. "I'm sorry. This isn't our house. Friends of ours let us borrow it for the week."

Rosalie studied me. The pain I was in must have showed in my face, because she walked over to a cabinet in the kitchen and returned with a bottle of whiskey and a glass. She poured out a splash and handed the glass to me.

"In a pinch," she said, "this counts as medicine."

I took the glass from her. The whiskey burned my throat, but it did, almost instantly, dull the pain I was feeling.

In my relief I felt a rush of goodwill. "You know," I said, "we were only curious to see what the house looked like. That's why we hopped over the wall."

"We're not thieves," Amir added. We both knew that it was surely what Rosalie had been thinking since the moment she'd set eyes on us.

"I never thought you were," Will said.

Rosalie studied us, her lips pressed together in a thin line. If she believed us, I could not tell. "What is your doctor's name?"

"Doctor Clark."

"I'll look him up. He needs to see that wound." When she left the room, I was relieved that Tiger followed her.

I suddenly longed to curl into the armchair and take a nap. I gave an involuntary shiver.

"You're cold," said Will. He flicked a switch on the side of the fireplace and blue-gold flames burst from the logs.

"We should go," Amir whispered. Seated on the arm of my chair, he looked uneasy. The stains on his blue jeans and ring of brown at the neck of his T-shirt seemed to stand out against the backdrop of the white kitchen. I knew that my own clothes had the same marks, that my hair surely had the same dull sheen as his. We did not belong in that beautiful house. Amir—both of us—had every reason to be nervous. We'd been caught trespassing. The longer we stayed, the closer we were to finding out the consequences of our actions. Will seemed forgiving, but it was impossible to guess what Rosalie was thinking. What if she hadn't left the room to call Doctor Clark, but the police?

I nodded my agreement to Amir, but when I tried to stand, it felt as though shards of glass were sinking into the meat of my calf. I sank back into the chair. Amir's expression grew more anxious.

"*Merrow.*"

"I'm *trying.*"

Rosalie returned holding a small phone. "Good news. Doctor Clark is on the way. He tried very hard not to reveal the details of your file to me, but I've cracked tougher nuts on Christmas Eve." She pointed the phone at me. "You are in need of a tetanus shot." She looked at Amir and then me again. Her head tilted to the side, her expression relaxing. "In the meantime, how about a little something to eat?"

At the mere mention of eating, my stomach, as it was prone to do, growled. I hoped the noise of the fire's flames was enough to cover it, but when I heard Amir's stomach make an echoing call, I knew that neither of us was fooling anyone. As Rosalie busied herself in the kitchen, I wondered what other details of our life Doctor Clark had revealed to her. Amir and I exchanged a look. I was relieved to see that his excitement mirrored my own. The promise of food always had a way of preempting our other feelings.

A GIRL WHO did not look older than ten appeared just as Amir was helping me to the table. She stared at us with open curiosity.

"Hello," she called, stopping in the doorway. Her hair was

as pale as Will's, and she wore it in two long, neat braids that fell in front of her shoulders. I felt a twinge of shame thrum within me. Bear's voice was in my head, telling me that my hair looked like seaweed. I trimmed the ends myself with our house scissors, but I knew my efforts did not improve the situation by much. When I touched my hair, it felt unclean below my fingers. This little girl's hair shone like silk. In the light of the room, it glowed, just as Will's had seemed to when he'd knelt before me in the driveway.

"Hello," I said.

Amir looked at the girl and nodded.

"This is Emma," said Will. "My sister. Emma, these are our guests. Merrow and Amir."

"Come sit by me, Emma," said Rosalie. I could not help but notice that she gestured to the seat that was the farthest from the end of the table where Amir and I sat.

Emma sat obediently beside her mother but stared in our direction with wide blue eyes. "Mommy told me that Tiger bit you," she said in a small voice.

"Yes."

The girl's eyes grew round and threatened tears.

Rosalie touched her daughter's shoulder. "Tiger was only doing what he's been taught to do," she said. "He would never hurt *you*, Emma. He knows you. You're family."

I had no right to be stung by this comment, so why did it bother me so? I took a bite of the sandwich that had been set before me and in an instant, my emotions swung from resentment to elation. The bread was thick but deliciously fluffy. As my stomach filled, I felt sleepy and energized all at once. Amir caught my gaze and the look on his face was so delighted that I laughed.

"What did I miss?" Will asked. He had a face that took to a happy expression easily, as though it were returning to a natural state.

I paused from eating long enough to tell him that the bread was delicious.

"We brought it with us from San Francisco," said Rosalie.

"It's my favorite," said Emma. "It's called Dutch Crunch."

Amir groaned with pleasure. His cheeks darkened when he realized we were all looking at him. Everyone laughed then, even Rosalie.

"That's where we live," Will explained. "In San Francisco. I'm in the Marina, and Mom and Dad and Emma are in Presidio Heights."

I nodded, though the neighborhood names meant nothing to me.

"We're here on vacation," Emma said.

"Why did you pick Osha?" Amir asked.

Did the others hear the hostility that I heard in his voice? He'd finished his sandwich. His plate gleamed in front of him. I hoped we would be given seconds.

"My husband considers himself a fisherman," Rosalie said. "When our friends offered us their house for the week, we took them up on it. It's nice to stretch out in a bit of countryside. Everyone needs a break from the city now and then."

"Believe it or not," Will said, "Mom was once a Girl Scout."

"We've been camping all over California!" Emma said.

"I do adore Osha," Rosalie said. She sounded surprisingly wistful. "This whole area is stuck in time, isn't it? The back-to-the-land hippie movement lives on up here. All of these artists and farmers and tree-hugger types. It seems like a simpler sort of life."

"I love swimming in the ocean," Emma added.

"That's true." The way that Rosalie smiled at her daughter made my throat tighten. "Emma is wild about the sea. I can't even get her to put on a wet suit—she just runs right into the freezing water. We think she might be a mermaid."

"That's what my name means," I said. "In Irish folklore, mermaids are called merrows."

Emma looked so excited that I wondered if she had misunderstood and believed that I was an actual mermaid. "Do you love the ocean, too?"

I nodded. "I swim every day. Our house is on top of a bluff that drops right down to the sea, so we have our own little beach. You can visit us if you'd like."

Before Emma could answer, Rosalie said, "So Merrow means mermaid. And Amir, what does that mean?"

We knew the answer to this because Rei had shown us a book of Hindi names and their meanings. "In Hindi," Amir said, "Amir means rich."

We had often wondered if his parents had settled on the name because they *were* rich, or if it was because they longed to *become* rich. We decided it must have been the latter; if they'd been rich, it didn't seem likely that Amir would have ended up in an orphanage. Surely if his parents had been wealthy and died, the money eventually would have been given to Amir. Of course there was always the possibility, Amir said once, that his parents hadn't named him at all. Maybe someone who worked at the orphanage, someone with an inclination toward irony or even cruelty, had selected his name. I tried to talk him out of believing in this version of events; it bothered me that I was given the memory of my parents choosing my name while Amir did not have even that small certainty.

"*Rich,*" Rosalie said. "Isn't that interesting."

"His parents must have seen what was in his heart," I said.

"Rich of heart," said Will with a level of warmth that made me like him more than I already did (which I was afraid was quite a lot).

"I'd like someone to tell me the name that's written in my heart someday," declared Emma.

This made us all smile. As silence fell over the table, a bell rang.

"The gate!" cried Emma.

"That must be Merrow's doctor." Rosalie stood and folded her napkin. "I'll get him."

I shifted uncomfortably in my seat. It was difficult to see Doctor Clark and not be brought back in time to my father's death. Amir offered my foot a gentle nudge under the table. I gave him a grateful look. It wasn't easy for either of us.

"Children," the doctor said as he walked into the room at Rosalie's side. It had been years since he'd last seen us, and I suspected he had no recollection of our names. "What trouble have you gotten yourselves into?"

"I'm afraid it's our dog that has caused the trouble," Will said, standing to introduce himself. "Tiger didn't offer our guests the finest of greetings."

"Your guests, eh?" Doctor Clark cast a doubtful glance in our direction. Then he shrugged. "I won't ask. Let me see that leg."

I turned in my seat and tried to keep my expression neutral as the doctor peeled off the bandage around my calf. He prodded at the wound and didn't stop until I released an agonized gasp. That seemed to satisfy him enough to turn toward Rosalie.

"Is your dog up to date on his rabies vaccine?"

"Of course."

Doctor Clark turned back to me. "You don't need stitches, but there's a high chance of infection with dog bites so I'm going to clean the wound and redress it. But first, your tetanus shot."

Emma and Will and Rosalie looked away in unison as Doctor Clark readied the needle, but neither Amir nor I could tear our eyes from the sight. We were as impressed as we were curious. I yelped in surprise when the needle sunk into my arm. Emma was at my side in an instant, grasping my hand.

"Poor Merrow!" she cried.

"Emma," said Rosalie sharply. I thought I heard revulsion in Rosalie's voice when she saw Emma's hand in mine. I shook my hand loose from the girl's, my cheeks warm.

"I'm fine," I told her, though I felt mortified. I managed to smile.

After the doctor spent a few minutes cleaning and redressing my leg, he straightened. "That's that," he said. "It's fine to wash it, just remember to reapply the ointment and a fresh bandage after you bathe." He looked me up and down and seemed to be on the cusp of saying something more. Instead, he asked Rosalie if he could have a word with her in the hall.

"Let's see if Doctor Clark can give us a ride home," Amir whispered once they'd left the room. I thought I sensed Will, on my other side, listening. I murmured agreement.

When the doctor and Rosalie returned, it became clear they had other plans.

"It's critical that you keep that wound clean," Doctor Clark said. "Dog bite infections are nasty business, and I'd like to see you avoid one. I've spoken with Mrs. Langford and we both agree . . ." He trailed off for a moment. "Well, *I* feel—quite strongly—that Horseshoe Cliff isn't the ideal spot to heal from an injury like this one. The risk of infection is simply too great."

"We'd like you to stay here, Merrow," Rosalie said. I stared at her. "At least for the night. It's already dark out and you must be exhausted. Give the wound a day to mend. Doctor Clark can swing by again tomorrow to check on you and drive you home. We'll take good care of you. It's . . . well, it's the least we can do, isn't it?"

I could not believe our luck. To stay in a place like this for a whole night? I wondered if we would be offered more to eat. Surely there would be breakfast!

"Thank you. We really appreciate it." I looked over at Amir, expecting to find him as excited as I was, but his expression was dark. *"Amir,"* I said. "We really appreciate it, don't we?"

When Rosalie leveled her eyes on Amir, something cool flickered within them. She cleared her throat. "Doctor Clark thought that he could give Amir a ride home so that Amir could let your brother know you're okay. Bear, wasn't it? Bear must be worried."

"No," I said. "Bear is not worried."

Doctor Clark peered at me. "Maybe not yet, but surely if you didn't return home . . ."

"I won't stay without Amir."

"Oh, please stay!" Emma said. Her blue eyes were bright with excitement.

Will put his hand on Emma's shoulder. "The point is for Merrow to be comfortable. If she's not comfortable here without Amir—"

"Actually," Rosalie interrupted, "the point is that Merrow should stay somewhere that is sanitary for the night while her leg heals."

Sanitary? I understood then what the doctor had said about us, and where and how we lived. And whatever the doctor had said had obviously not come as a surprise to Rosalie, who had been judging us from the moment she'd seen us. And now she'd mustered enough goodwill to extend to me, but not enough to include Amir. I wondered how the Langfords would have reacted if it had been Amir who had been bitten by their dog instead of me.

"I'll be fine at Horseshoe Cliff," I announced. "Can we go now?"

The doctor, irritated, began to stuff his ointments and bandage kit back into his bag. He stopped suddenly and faced Amir.

"Talk some sense into her," he said in a low voice. "She'll listen to you. It's safer for her to stay here. An infection would be very serious. Surely you don't want to see her in any more pain than she's already in?"

Amir chewed on his lip. I hated to see him look so unhappy; it bothered me more even than my aching leg. "Merrow, they're right," he said quietly. "You should stay here and let your leg recover."

"But Amir!" What would Bear do to him if they were alone for the night at Horseshoe Cliff?

"I'll be fine."

"If Bear—"

"I'll see you tomorrow," he said, cutting me off. He nodded at Doctor Clark. "Let's go now, if you don't mind. You're right; Bear will be worried."

I tried to stand and released a growl of frustration when pain shot through me. I grabbed Amir's shirt. I could feel everyone in the room watching us, but I did not care. I hated the thought of him alone with Bear. *"Please . . ."*

He took my hand. "Just rest." His eyes were so dark and soft they looked as though they were made of velvet. "Everything will be okay."

His expression implored me to not say anything. He squeezed

my hand again, and then let it go. I watched, stunned, as he left the room.

"Well, good," the doctor said, sounding somewhat uncertain now. He shook his head as though clearing it, and—after dispensing pain medication, antibiotic ointment, and extra bandages—he, too, strode out of the room and then the house, leaving me alone with the Langfords.

CHAPTER ELEVEN

I was grateful when Rosalie, perhaps sensing that I needed a moment to myself, asked if I would like to take a bath. She helped me to a bathroom with dark walls and a large white bathtub and proceeded to fill the tub with steaming-hot water. A stream of lavender-scented soap produced fluffy mounds of bubbles across the water's surface and an irrepressible murmur of delight from my throat. After setting a change of clothes, ointment, and a bandage on a small bench, Rosalie walked briskly out of the room.

Alone, I undressed and sucked in my breath as I peeled the bloodied bandage from my calf. I lowered myself into the bath, biting my cheek as the water stung my wound. The room fell quiet. As the ache subsided, I heard myself sigh deeply. I felt as though I were living inside one of the daydreams that I had when I walked through the bathrooms of the houses that Amir and I explored. I squeezed my eyes shut and opened them again and I was there still, alone in the most beautiful bathroom in the world.

Two hand towels hung over the edge of the tub. I scrubbed my body, turning first one and then the other towel brown. There was a strange little brush hanging from the bath spout and I used it to scrape below my nails. The soap smelled of a flower garden in the middle of July, a decadent, sun-kissed scent that made me consider, for just a second, what the soap might taste like if I bit into it. Instead, I sunk my entire head under the bubbles and held my breath for so long that when I surfaced the room was filled with stars. I washed my hair with handfuls of shampoo and conditioner, and it became so soft that it did not feel like my own. I drained the bath and filled it again with even more hot water and then I drained that, too, and stepped clumsily from the tub to dry myself.

I discovered that the pain medication was working; it was easier now to put weight on my leg. My thoughts were a dreamy, contented blur. I pressed a new bandage gently to my leg. When I lifted a folded blue dress from the bench where Rosalie had left it, I saw beneath it a pair of cream-colored silk underwear and a matching bra. I laughed in surprise. I had only the white cotton bras and underwear that Rei gave me on my birthday each year—a gift that I had always been thrilled to receive, but now saw had been a gift for a child. The silk undergarments Rosalie had left me were edged with soft lace. I slipped them on and felt shaky with delight. Would Rosalie let me keep them? I thought I might do anything to be allowed to call such beautiful things my own.

I lowered the dress over my head. My bath-pruned fingers fumbled over the slippery pearl-colored buttons. It was a blue cotton dress, plain but for the buttons that lined the front, but it swished and rippled below my knees in a fancy way. Rosalie had not left a pair of shoes, and my own sneakers were so filthy and bloodstained that I decided to remain barefoot. I pressed the plush towel against my long hair, drying it. There was a brush on the bathroom vanity. Thinking of Emma's pretty, neat hair, I plaited my own into a thick braid that fell over my shoulder.

When I cleared steam from a corner of the mirror, I hardly recognized myself. I looked older. Or perhaps younger. I could not decide which. I was a different version of myself.

I felt a pang of remorse thinking of Amir, home alone with Bear. I worried for him, but I also realized, guiltily, that it felt wonderful to pretend that I was someone who wore clothes like these, who took hot baths that brimmed with bubbles. If Amir were with me, I could not have pretended; his presence would have been a reminder of who I really was. I would have looked at him and seen myself, the person I had always been. This was usually a comfort.

Together, Amir and I were tethered to our childhood at Horseshoe Cliff, but alone, I felt suddenly, unsettlingly, feverishly free.

I turned away from my reflection and walked as steadily as I could manage from the bathroom.

"Well," Rosalie said, looking me over when I entered the great room, "aren't you lovely?"

I glanced down, self-conscious. "Thank you for the clothes," I said. "And the bath."

"The dress suits you. Keep it."

I felt my mouth hang open for a second. Maybe she thought I would refuse her generous offer, but it was all I could do to stop myself from hobbling out of the house right then and there before she could take it back. "Thank you. I love it."

She nodded and told me to sit by the fire while she fixed us something to eat. Emma was perched on the edge of the sofa, working on a puzzle. She'd managed to piece together a yellow sailboat, but the tempestuous sea on which it sailed was strewn in bits across the coffee table. I looked around but didn't see Will.

"Do you want to help?" Emma asked hopefully.

I nodded. I'd never done a puzzle before, but I started gathering the white pieces that formed the froth on top of the waves. We worked together in silence for a time.

"Will is studying," Emma said. I was embarrassed to realize she'd caught me gazing toward the door. How long had I been looking in that direction? The pain medication made me feel as though all of my thoughts and movements were at half-pace. "He's *always* studying," she added. "He's in law school."

How old did that make him? I wondered. Did people go to law school right after college? I had no idea. How strange to think that Will might be around the same age as Bear, who was twenty-six. Bear was dark, bristly, and bulky—fat now, really, with his ever-expanding belly full of beer. Just thinking of his glowering expression made me tremble involuntarily. Will, slim and smiling, with skin like the inside of a clean shell, looked years younger. And yet, it was possible that they'd been born in the same year, on the same day even, bursting into the same world with equal ignorance of their futures.

Rosalie walked toward us from the kitchen with a wooden platter. "Can we clear some space on the table?"

Emma and I swept the scattered puzzle pieces into a pile. The platter that Rosalie set down was covered with an array of cheeses and meats and olives, as well as sliced bread and a small pot of honey.

"Will!" Rosalie called, walking back toward the door and leaning out into the hall. "Come join us!" When she returned, she sat on the couch next to Emma. "We call this a fireside picnic, Merrow." She handed me a white plate that felt delicate in my hand. "Please help yourself and don't be shy. There's plenty more."

"I love fireside picnics," said Emma happily. She began to drizzle honey over a piece of bread, and once she started I wasn't sure she'd ever stop.

"Saving any for me?" Will asked as he walked in.

"You snooze, you lose," Emma replied, grinning.

"I was hardly snoozing." Will settled into the other armchair. "Though I was tempted." I was gratified to feel his eyes flick over my hair and dress. "How are you, Merrow? Feeling any better?"

"I think so. To be honest, the medicine is making me feel a little fuzzy."

"Too fuzzy to eat?"

I laughed at the thought. "No."

The little knife that Rosalie had set out was sharper than it looked, slipping easily into a block of blue-veined cheese. Within a few moments, my plate was covered with food. I sat back in the armchair and ate and ate and ate. I listened as Will and Emma and Rosalie teased one another with gentle affection. They smiled often. I tried not to stare, though I felt like an observer of another species. How would it be to live within such a family? They spoke with such easy generosity and listened with patience and good humor.

Full at last, still woozy from the medicine Doctor Clark had given me, I felt as though I were wrapped in a warm cocoon. Will turned on music—weightless piano music that seemed to float down softly toward us from the ceiling, filling the air like snow in the pages of a storybook. I did not know what we were listening to, but I loved it. The fire glowed. Through the window, the night sky was navy.

When Amir and I wandered through the homes of people we did not know, I tried to piece together a life from the clues that I found. As I looked at photographs, the contents of pantries, and bedside reading materials, the lives of strangers took shape. But it had never occurred to me to imagine this—this love that existed between Rosalie and Will and Emma Langford. A twinge of resentment momentarily pierced my contented fog. I dragged my finger through a puddle of honey on my plate and licked it clean.

My mind drifted away. I found myself thinking of the time years earlier when Amir and I had slept in the shed. We had tried our best to make it feel like this, cozy and warm and safe. And we had succeeded. It had been a place of love and beauty— even with so much less than what the Langfords had.

I blinked away tears, suddenly overwhelmed by a sense of melancholy, or perhaps loneliness. Who but Amir could understand how I felt in that moment, sitting by the fire with this family that loved each other so? The three of them had one another; they were bound by ties that felt to them like an embrace, like something that could be depended upon.

I should never have let Amir leave. What would Bear do to him when they were alone together? I set my empty plate on the table. My eyes landed on the sharp knife that was buried within a block of cheese. I thought of Amir's whittling knives; I thought of the knives in Bear's eyes. My stomach ached as though I hadn't eaten a bite.

Emma had been stretched out with Tiger on the rug by the fire, but she was suddenly at my knee, looking up at me.

"You have such pretty green eyes, Merrow," she said. "I've always wanted green eyes."

I could not imagine having everything that Emma had and still wishing for more. I leaned toward her and studied her heart-shaped face. It was clear and honest. Had Amir and I looked so young when we were ten, with our parents dead and Bear perpetually seeking out ways to hurt us? It was impossible for me to imagine harming someone so innocent, and yet Bear had managed it over and over again.

"I think your eyes are beautiful," I announced. Emma's eyes were identical to Will's: cornflower blue. "You should be grateful." These words arrived with sharper edges than I'd intended.

I felt the mood of the room shift. Rosalie exchanged a glance with Will. I worried that the tears that had threatened to fall earlier would now arrive. I felt disoriented, and not at all like myself. I blinked quickly and looked around the room, trying to find something to move my thoughts in a new direction. On the shelves that flanked the fireplace I noticed a collection of porcelain boxes.

"What are those?" I asked.

Will followed my gaze. "Mrs. Corrino must collect them." He stood and took one of the boxes from the shelf and set it in my hand.

"How beautiful." The box fit neatly on my palm. It was painted with an intricately detailed image of five ladies in long robes standing in front of a red pagoda. The women's robes were in blues and pinks and greens, patterned with gold. "The paintbrush couldn't have been thicker than a hair."

"That one is Japanese," Rosalie said from her spot on the sofa. "You can open it if you'd like."

The inside of the box was gilded. The bottom of the lid revealed another depiction of the red pagoda, but now a golden dragon stalked its steps and the ladies were gone. The dragon had scales like a fish. I ran my finger over them and found them smooth. I thought it remarkable to consider all the others who had held the box before me, those who had called the box their own, and those who had only dreamed of calling it their own. The pang of envy that I felt was so strong that it made my fingers tighten around the box.

"It's Satsuma ware," I said without looking up. "From the

Meiji period. Nineteenth century." I was showing off, but how could I not? It was a strange twist of fate that Will had handed me this particular box.

I felt Rosalie's stare.

"My teacher, Rei, was a professor of art in Japan before moving to the United States," I explained. "She rattles on a bit too long when Japan comes up in our lessons, but we try to be patient with her. Who could blame her for being nostalgic about things that remind her of home? Satsuma, ukiyo-e . . . Oh, don't even mention ukiyo-e to Rei unless you have a comfortable seat. She'll start listing the themes of woodblock painting and then move on to her theory of its influence on the Impressionists, and before you know it hours will have passed." I smiled, thinking of Rei. "Wait until I tell her about this collection."

The feeling of Will and Rosalie and Emma gazing at me in astonishment proved intoxicating. "Until now," I said, "I've only seen Satsuma in books. It's a whole different experience to see it in person. I've always loved the dragons. The geishas I could do without." Though I wanted more than anything to tuck the box below my leg and figure out a way to smuggle it home with me, I held it out to Rosalie with a smile.

"Well, aren't you full of surprises?" she said, shaking her head in wonder. She turned the Satsuma box in her hand, studying it as though seeing it for the first time. "Frankly, I, too, could do without the geishas."

Beside her, Emma yawned and stretched.

"It's late," Rosalie said, brushing Emma's hair from her face.

Her hand lingered on the side of her daughter's face and they smiled at each other. "Off to bed, you."

Emma groaned but rose and said good night to her brother, offering him both a hug and a kiss. When she reached me, she hesitated for a moment and then ducked her head toward my ear. "What are geishas?" she whispered.

"Female companions," I whispered back, "who begin training at a very young age—"

"Bed, Emma!" said Rosalie quickly.

I flushed. I'd been about to tell Emma that geishas were trained in art and dance and music—nothing more.

Emma was still rooted in front of me. "Will you sit next to me at breakfast?" she asked.

I nodded. I could see that she was curious about me, but the truth was that I was just as curious about her. To live in a family like this . . . I didn't want to envy a ten-year-old, but how could I not?

I wondered if Rosalie would help Emma to bed. Wasn't that what mothers did? I glanced at Will and thought I saw him look away from me just as I did. He stared into the fire. The curl of his blond hair against his forehead made something in my chest pull tight and begin to thrum. What if Rosalie left us alone? What would I do if he leaned over to kiss me? I'd been spending a lot of time recently wondering if I would ever kiss a boy. My thoughts on the topic centered, of course, on Amir. I'd awakened from strange dreams lately feeling unsettled, filled with longing and also a sour sense of shame.

Emma left the room and Rosalie remained. Will stood, announcing that he needed to return to his reading. He wished his mother a good night. "And good night, Merrow," he said politely. "I hope a night's rest makes all the difference."

And then he was gone.

"Have you ever been to San Francisco?" Rosalie asked. If she'd caught me watching her son leave the room, she didn't let on.

"I've never been anywhere but Osha. Amir and I sometimes talk about hitchhiking to San Francisco, but we always worry about what would happen if we were caught."

"If you were caught? By the police?"

"Well, I don't know . . . someone who was worried about our safety. If someone decided that my brother wasn't taking good enough care of us, we might be forced to leave Horseshoe Cliff. Amir and I might be separated."

Rosalie studied me. I could not tell what she was thinking.

"You're sixteen," she said at last. "I think you'd have a say about what happened to you."

"It's never felt worth the risk to us."

We both fell quiet then, listening to the music. I was almost asleep, and thinking of San Francisco, when I murmured, "What's it like?" I opened my eyes and looked at Rosalie.

"Hmm?"

"San Francisco," I said. "What's it like?"

She smiled. "Oh, I don't think I should describe it to you, Merrow. You'll see it yourself someday—someday soon, I hope—and when you do, I don't want my words to be the ones that come to your mind. You should have the experience of seeing it through your own eyes first."

I was disappointed. At that moment, it felt as though I might never live anywhere but Horseshoe Cliff. Rosalie was so sure I would go to San Francisco, but what if I didn't? If there was a life for me beyond Osha, I had trouble seeing it. Rosalie Langford didn't know anything about me. Homesickness overtook me again—I'd never faced a night away from Horseshoe Cliff.

"Maybe there are times when it's *better* to see something through the eyes of someone else first," I said. "For example, if you went to my home, you'd probably only be able to see a little shack groaning in the wind. You'd see a saggy front porch with peeling paint and a broken step. You'd smell an outhouse and wonder how someone could live with the stench. And when you walked far enough to stop smelling the outhouse, you'd start smelling the chickens. You'd pass a dry patch of garden and scrub grasses stretching to the horizon, where the edges of cliffs crumble straight into the ocean. That view, on the edge of the cliff, might impress you. But that's about it."

Rosalie watched me as I spoke. I closed my eyes and thought of home.

"But if you let *me* describe Horseshoe Cliff to you, then you'd know about the eucalyptus grove, which smells like heaven and is full of hiding spots and fog so thick you can open your mouth and drink it. You wouldn't know until I told you that we used to have horses, and that their hooves beat the path that leads down to the beach. You wouldn't know that when you sing in harmony with someone else in one of the caves that are carved into the cliff, the sound is more beautiful than any other sound in the world. You wouldn't know that if you really want to be unreachable and you're very brave, you can sit in the back of the deepest cave, the one that curves up to a ledge, and watch the tide roar toward you until it sweeps over your toes and then your ankles and then, just as you're getting really worried, it slouches away as though all it ever wanted of you was a taste. And the sunsets—it's just not possible that there is anywhere on earth that has more spectacular sunsets than the ones we see from our back porch. And the fog! It's like the whole world has been shrunk down to the size of the whitecap on a wave, and you're just hugged within it, the wash of white and gray, the bit of sun that filters through . . ."

I trailed off. I opened my eyes.

Rosalie's head was cocked, her lips set in a curious smile. "How beautiful," she said. "If I were half as eloquent as you, I'd attempt to describe San Francisco now, but I'm not. And frankly I'm more convinced than ever that you need to see it through your own eyes. Perhaps when you do, you'll tell me what you see. I'd love to hear what you make of it."

I smiled, basking in the glow of her compliment. *Eloquent.*

"Do you keep a journal?" Rosalie asked. "Do you write these sorts of descriptions down?"

I nodded.

"Maybe you'll study writing in college. Or art history. Your teacher seems to have given you quite a head start."

"I don't think I'll go to college."

Her eyebrows shot up. "But you have to go to college! You're clearly very smart, Merrow. I bet you could take the GED to-morrow and pass."

"Oh, I already passed the GED."

Rosalie leaned toward me. "Have you applied to any colleges? I don't want to be presumptuous, but I hope you realize that there are many organizations that could help fund your education."

Rei often spoke to me about college, too. I listened as Rosalie listed a few of the scholarships that she thought I might be eligible for. She didn't know, as Rei did, that I would never leave Amir behind at Horseshoe Cliff. Like an echo of my heart, my leg throbbed.

"I think I might need another one of those pills Doctor Clark gave me," I said, interrupting her.

Rosalie looked surprised. "I'm sorry. I hope I haven't upset you . . ."

"No, no. It's just that my leg is starting to hurt again."

Rosalie retrieved the pills from the kitchen counter and handed me one along with a glass of water. "Would you like me to help you to your room?"

She held my elbow and guided me down a hall that was lined with beach photography. She stopped and opened a door. "Here you are." We looked into the room. The bed was huge and white, and I felt a little thrill just seeing it. "I've put some pajamas in the bathroom that's just through that door, and you should find everything else you might need in there as well."

"Thank you." I was tempted to say more—something about how much nicer she was than I'd expected her to be, perhaps nicer even than I deserved, considering how I'd trespassed into her life. But before I could speak, the strangest thing happened. Ever so briefly, Rosalie lifted her hand to the side of my face just as she had done with Emma.

"Good night, Merrow," she said.

"Good night," I said quietly. As she turned and walked away, I touched my face and swallowed away the lump that had formed in my throat.

Alone in the bedroom, I stood still and listened but could not hear any sound except my own breathing. The carpet was thick below my bare feet. I limped into the bathroom and shut the door. I lifted the blue dress over my head and carefully folded it. The pajamas Rosalie had left for me were made of white flannel and trimmed with blue silk. On the counter there was a toothbrush still in its packaging and a bar of face soap. Three jars of lotion sat in a pretty row on the vanity. I dipped the tips of my fingers in each of them and rubbed the lotions onto my face and neck. I loosened my hair from its plait and brushed it with a large-toothed comb that I found in one of the drawers of the vanity.

When I finally slipped into the cool white sheets, my thoughts turned again to Amir. I hated not knowing exactly where he was at that moment in time. Was he in his room? Had Bear forced him out to the shed again? Was he hurt? Worried for Amir, I was sure I would toss and turn all night.

Instead, I fell into a restless sleep that I awoke from with a start. The sheets were wet and cold; in my dream, I'd been drowning in a freezing sea, my own limbs unfamiliar and weak. It was a terrible dream, with my oldest friend, the sea, betraying me. I sat up, shivering and shaken, and tried to remember where I was, but for a long, fearful moment I could not. I blinked against the black room, searching for something familiar. I heard a noise.

Someone was in the room with me. I was sure of it. My tongue was thick in my throat, choking me. When the figure moved in the darkness, I began to scream.

CHAPTER TWELVE

I t's me, Merrow," a woman's voice said.

I twisted away from the light that suddenly flooded the room.

"You called out, and I . . ." I felt a cold hand on the side of my face. "You're burning."

When I tried to open my eyes, the light stung them. The bedsheets felt like ice and the tears on my cheeks were hot.

A wet cloth was pressed to my head. I could not stop shivering.

"I want to go home," I managed to whisper.

The voice that answered me was so tender that my trembling body stilled.

"I know, dear. We'll bring you home very soon. But for now, just rest and let us take care of you."

It was my own mother standing over me. It was Marigold Shawe. She'd returned, just as my father had always said she would. I felt a rush of warmth spread through my body, a sense of peace and security, my mother's love enveloping me for the first time in so many years. *This is what it feels like,* I thought. *This is it.*

WHEN I AWAKENED, sunlight was streaming into the room. Rosalie was asleep in a chair. There was a cup of water on my bedside table and I drank it greedily, my mind racing. Something had happened in the night, but I could not remember it clearly. When I set down the cup, Rosalie stirred.

"Hello," she said. "You developed an infection in the night, and a fever. How are you feeling now?"

My leg throbbed, and I felt groggy, but I didn't think I had a fever. "I'm okay." I thought back over the night, trying to remember. "Did the doctor come again?"

"No. I called him, and he talked me through bringing your fever down with wet washcloths and ibuprofen. He'll be here later to take another look at the wound."

I glanced toward the window. The sunlight did not seem like the thin light of morning. "What time is it?"

Rosalie checked her watch. "It's nearly noon."

I had never slept so late. At Horseshoe Cliff, Amir would have been awake for hours by now, wondering where I was. I moved to push the sheets aside, but Rosalie stood.

"Rest a bit longer." She smoothed the sheets over me. She wore pale gray cashmere pants and a top. I could not tell if they were pajamas. Her hair was pulled back in a loose ponytail and white-blond strands framed her face, which was long and as pale as her children's, her eyes a bright blue. Everything about her seemed softer than it had the day before. I was amazed to think of her sleeping in the chair at the foot of my bed.

"Are you hungry?" she asked. "What would you like? Scrambled eggs—"

I must have pulled a face because she laughed.

"Not a fan of eggs?"

"We have chickens at Horseshoe Cliff. A *lot* of chickens. So . . ."

"A lot of eggs. I see. Well, we did bring a box of chocolate croissants from the city. If Emma hasn't already eaten them all, would you like one?"

I grinned. I'd never had a chocolate croissant—or even a plain croissant, for that matter. "Yes, please."

When Rosalie left, I sunk down below the covers and pressed my face against the soft pillow. I would need to remember this feeling, to etch it into memory.

Rosalie returned with a tray that held two croissants and a glass of orange juice. The croissant was warm in my hand and when I bit into it, chocolate dripped from the other end of the pastry and landed on the white plate below. I didn't pay any attention to Rosalie while I ate, and by the time I finished both croissants and she came into focus again, her expression was troubled. I felt embarrassed for eating so quickly, but not so embarrassed that I didn't lick each of my fingers clean. I was debating licking the plate when Rosalie spoke.

"You were very upset last night. You screamed in your sleep."

My face grew warm. "I'm sorry that I woke you. I don't think I knew where I was."

"There's no need to apologize." Rosalie hesitated before speaking again. "You were screaming your brother's name over and over. Bear."

I looked down at the plate on my lap. The smears of chocolate were as dark as mud.

Rosalie spoke softly. "You were scared."

I did not look up. What if I just told her how worried I was for Amir's safety? What if I told her how Bear treated us? Rosalie was not who I'd thought she was when I first met her—I could see now that she was someone who would try to help us. My heart began to race. What a relief it would be to finally tell someone!

"Bear . . ." I began.

Her face was set in an encouraging expression.

I thought of the aloof way she had looked at Amir. I had made a promise to him in the shed on that night years earlier—a promise not to tell anyone how Bear treated us. Yes, we were sixteen now, but we were not adults. Amir could still be taken from Horseshoe Cliff. We could still be separated.

I forced a laugh. "I remember now. I was dreaming that a bear was chasing me. It was one of those awful dreams that felt real. It must have been the fever."

Rosalie sat back in her chair and folded her hands in her lap. "Well," she said slowly. "I'm glad it was just a dream."

I could tell that she did not believe me, and I was grateful that she didn't push me on the subject.

That afternoon, I sat with Will on the patio, awaiting the doctor's arrival. A lawn sloped steeply away from us, ending in a neat row of bright hedges. The woods beyond the lawn had been cleared just enough to catch glimpses of the ocean, but it seemed very far away, much farther than it actually was. It was odd to see the ocean but not smell it or hear it. The view was like a backdrop for that neat lawn; it seemed more like a drawing of the sea than the sea itself. Even so, the glimpse of blue was a comfort, a touchstone that put me more at ease. The air was cool, and I shivered within the sweater that Rosalie had given me. I wore her jeans, too, and a pair of black rubber boots that were at least a size too large for me.

Emma, in a long red sweater and leggings and sequin-covered sneakers that made my inner ten-year-old writhe with envy, turned cartwheels down the sloped lawn, gaining speed until she collided with the hedge and released a squeal of surprised laughter.

Will and I sat at a table, reading. I had borrowed Hemingway's *A Moveable Feast* from the bookshelf in the living room. Will read a thick textbook with pages that fluttered in the breeze. I watched his eyes scan back and forth down the length of one page and then another. He was a fast reader. He did not take notes, but he paused every so often to consider something he'd read, his expression serious. He looked out toward the view in those moments, but I did not think he was aware of what his eyes saw; he seemed lost entirely in his own thoughts. I caught his eye during one of these ruminations and smiled. He blinked before offering a polite smile in return. I had the sense that he'd forgotten I was there.

"How's the book?" he asked.

"I like the descriptions of Paris. I like books that are set in places I've never been." Then I laughed. "Which is everywhere but Osha."

His expression relaxed into a more natural smile. "That must make picking out your next read easy."

"Yes. The world of books is my oyster."

Will laughed. "Mine, too."

"But I bet you've been to Paris. You've seen it in person."

He nodded. "I went as a kid with my parents, and then again a few years ago when I was in college. Some friends and I took the train from Paris to the French Riviera." He grew enthusiastic as he told me about the trip, his eyes brightening. He laughed telling me how his poor French had landed his group on a two-hour train ride in the wrong direction during one leg of their journey. But they were helped by an older couple who invited them to spend the night at their flat in Nice. Will was still in touch with this couple and had taken their grandson out to dinner in San Francisco when he was in town.

"It's the people you meet when traveling," he said, "that I love the most. Well, and the history. And the architecture. The cafés. The food! Who am I kidding? I love it all—I even love the trains themselves."

I was leaning toward him, taking in every word. Rosalie had given me a thick wool blanket to spread across my knees, and when it slipped from its place, Will reached down and scooped it off the ground. My stomach fluttered at the possibility that he might spread the blanket over my knees, but instead he handed it to me.

"I've never been on a train," I said.

Before Will could respond, Rosalie and Doctor Clark stepped onto the patio from the house. Just seeing the doctor made me think of Amir and Horseshoe Cliff. I felt ashamed of how enthralled I was of Will, when I should have spent the day worrying about Amir.

"How are you feeling?" Doctor Clark asked me. "I heard you had an exciting night."

"Yes," I said. "My first fireside picnic."

Rosalie smiled. "I think he means your fever."

"But my experience of the fever wasn't actually very exciting. And it's gone now."

"Can I take a look?" Doctor Clark said, gesturing toward my leg.

I nodded. Will tucked his textbook below his arm, gave me a sympathetic smile, and then walked toward the house. Rosalie asked if I'd like her to stay and I said yes. It was only my leg, after all. Will had raced off as though I were about to undress.

After rolling up my pant leg to check the wound, Doctor Clark recommended a course of oral antibiotics to stave off an infection.

"I stopped at Horseshoe Cliff this morning," he added. "Bear agreed that if the Langfords will have you, it would be best for you to stay here another night."

I stared at him, wondering what it was that Bear had really said, because there was no way that he had actually expressed interest in doing what was best for me. "What about Amir?" I asked. "Did you see him?"

Doctor Clark nodded and reached into his pocket. He pulled out a smooth gray stone of the sort that Amir and I spent hours stacking on the beach. "Amir asked me to give you this. He thought you might want a piece of home while you stay here. He said it might help you to believe that he doesn't think you should travel until your infection is fully under control. I don't know why a stone would convince you to take your health seriously, but there you have it."

I turned the stone in my hand. It was warm from the doctor's pocket, but I imagined the warmth that I felt was from Amir's hand.

"Why don't you at least stay until my husband returns from his fishing trip later today?" Rosalie asked. "We'll have a car then and if you still want to leave, I'll drive you myself."

I nodded. Once Doctor Clark left, Rosalie took the seat across from me. Emma returned from wherever she had wandered off to and dropped herself with a sigh in the chair beside mine.

"Are you staying?" she asked.

"Just for the day."

"Do we have time for a game of Monopoly?"

Rosalie gave a wry laugh. "Watch out," she warned. "Emma is a Monopoly shark."

I told Emma that she would have to teach me.

She nodded eagerly and sprang from her seat. "I'll go set it up by the fire." She hurried into the house.

The day seemed to be growing colder rather than warmer. I wondered whether Rosalie had any hot chocolate. I still held in my hand the stone from Amir. There were two lines that criss-crossed the gray surface. I traced them with my finger.

"Is that a stone from your property?" Rosalie asked.

I nodded. "It's from our beach. Well, it's not really *our* beach. We don't own it. But we're the only ones who are ever there because the only access is from our land. I guess you could arrive by sea, but so far no one has."

"No other merrows?"

I smiled and shook my head.

"It seems magical," Rosalie said, "this Horseshoe Cliff."

Horseshoe Cliff felt as much a part of me as my own mind, so for elegant Rosalie Langford to say that it was magical . . . it felt as though she were saying that *I* was magical.

"I guess it *is* magical," I said. "So much is hidden in plain sight."

"What do you mean?"

"Well, take the beach. It's beautiful when the tide is high, but if you wait for the tide to retreat, you discover an entire garden—an entire secret world—exists below. The sea looks blue or green or gray, but hidden within it are sea anemone in every color of the sunset, and dark red grapestone seaweed, and pink Haliclona sea sponge, sunflower sea stars, black snails . . ." I trailed off, lost in the memories of Amir and me barefoot, crouched beside a tide pool, silently exploring small, hidden worlds.

"Can I ask you something?"

I blinked at Rosalie, working to orient myself back at the table on the patio and not on the beach at Horseshoe Cliff. The look on her face made me nervous. I was sure that she was going to ask me again about Bear. I knew that she did not believe my explanation of the screams that had sent her running to my room in the middle of the night.

"Why did you and Amir really come here?" she asked.

"Oh." My relief was quickly displaced by embarrassment. "We weren't going to steal anything."

"No?"

My ears burned. "No!" My anger was unjustified, but I could not subdue it. "We were only curious."

"You were . . . 'curious'?"

"I'd never seen a house as big as this one, with that huge gate. I just wanted to see what it looked like. I wasn't going to take anything."

"So . . . you were going to look in the windows?"

I hesitated. Would she understand if I told her what Amir and I had been doing for years? How we'd entered people's homes, wandered around, let our imaginations run, and then left without taking anything more than a nibble of something to eat? We did not cause anyone harm. We were like spirits, I thought, seeing but never seen.

Rosalie would not understand. How could she? I did not think that you could be very curious about other people's lives when your own life was perfect.

"Yes," I said. "I wanted to peek inside. We would never have tried if we'd realized someone was home. We didn't want to upset anyone. It's just something we do for fun. Something we *used* to do for fun. I don't think we'll be doing it anymore." I gestured toward my leg.

Rosalie put her hand on my arm. "I'm sorry that Tiger attacked you. That must have been very scary."

I felt a wave of guilt. Again, she was being kinder to me than I deserved. "Oh, I'll survive." I adjusted my arm below hers so that she pulled her hand away. "Anyway, how mad can I be? I only wanted to peek inside, and look what I got instead. A vacation at a luxurious resort, complete with Dutch Crunch, chocolate croissants, and a fireside picnic."

Rosalie laughed.

A breeze traveled up the lawn toward us and I caught, at last, a hint of brine in the air. When I looked over at Rosalie, I realized that she had closed her eyes and seemed to be breathing the air in deeply, a smile lingering on her face. When she opened her eyes and looked at me, her eyes shone with emotion.

"Do you ever feel aware of being within one of the moments of your life when everything changes?" she asked. "As though you can feel the shift happening?"

I was astonished. It was just how I had felt in a few key moments of my life. I thought of my fifth birthday, when Bear had pinned me down in the woods. I thought of holding Amir's hand on his first night at Horseshoe Cliff. I thought of standing in the bathroom the day before, hardly recognizing myself in the mirror.

"Yes," I said. "I know just what you mean."

Rosalie nodded as though she'd known this was how I would answer. "I didn't always have a happy family," she said. "My father did things to me that no father should do to his daughter, that no adult should do to a child. My mother pretended these things did not happen. She chose him over me. I have not spoken to either of them in thirty-seven years."

I listened, startled, with no idea how to respond.

"When I was your age, I could never have guessed how my life would turn out," she continued in a clear, steady voice. "That I would marry a kind man—Will's father—who would die at too young an age. That as a widow I would fall in love again and marry a wonderful, equally kind man and that we would have a daughter, completing our family. There were years when I could not imagine the turns my journey would take. There were times in my life that I didn't believe in myself and I couldn't see a way forward. I was lucky in those moments to have other people step in and do the believing for me.

"You see, I carry my past with me, but it no longer defines me. This"—she waved her hand toward the house—"is me: the love that I feel for my husband and children. It turns out that the past can fit into a very small box."

She pressed her lips together, thinking. Then she leaned toward me and said quickly, "Merrow, whatever you think is keeping you here in Osha isn't. You can be whoever you wish to be. You have your GED, and I could—"

The door to the patio was thrown open. "Mom!" came Emma's high, happy voice. "Dad's home!"

Rosalie offered me an apologetic smile. "Well, more on this later," she said, standing. "Let's go tell Wayne that you showed up on our doorstep, claiming to be his daughter from some long-forgotten tryst."

I stared at her. "What? No!"

She laughed. "The look on your face! I'm only kidding." She offered her hand, and, without hesitation, I took it. "Stay for dinner," she said. "Monopoly with Emma will last at least that long."

I nodded, leaning on her as I limped inside, feeling confused and exhilarated. No one had ever spoken to me as Rosalie had—and yet, what exactly had she been trying to tell me? Her words were a gift that I could hold but not yet unwrap.

AFTER DINNER WITH Rosalie, Will, Emma, and Wayne Langford—a cheerful man bursting with self-deprecating stories of his attempts at salmon fishing—Rosalie offered to drive me home. She gave me a cotton grocery bag to pack my things in, telling me to keep all the clothes she had given to me over my stay, including the white pajamas I'd worn to bed and the rubber boots I'd been wearing all day. When I returned from gathering together my old and new clothes, I felt a thrill to see Will standing in the hall beside his mother.

"All packed?" he asked, taking my bag from me. "I'll drive you home."

"Apparently I'm a terrible night driver," Rosalie said. "Which was news to me." There was an edge to her voice that I did not understand.

I waited for her to say more, to continue her line of thought from earlier in the day, but Emma and Wayne appeared from the kitchen to wish me goodbye, and then Rosalie put her hands on my elbows and kissed my cheek and told me that she would not forget me. I looked around the grand hallway, sure that I would never see the house again.

In the car, I gave Will directions to Horseshoe Cliff. Once I spoke, I could not seem to stop. When we passed a field of grazing horses, I told him the story of how Bear had sold our horses without my permission, and when we passed Little Earth I told him how Teacher Julie had given me the first notebook I'd ever owned and encouraged me to write down my stories. Will kept his eyes on the darkening road the entire time. It was only as we neared Horseshoe Cliff that I grew quiet. Will had not said more than a few words during the drive. I felt a flood of embarrassment for how long I had rambled without any encouragement from him, for how silly my stories must have seemed to someone like him, for what he would think when he saw where and how I lived. I wished I had kept my mouth shut. I wished I had left him with the memory of me dressed in a fancy sweater and boots, with my hair brushed, my face set in a thoughtful, intelligent, mature expression as I gazed at the passing countryside.

Will slowed the car to a crawl as he maneuvered it over the bumps and ruts of our long dirt driveway. I watched him from the corner of my eye, but he hid his thoughts well and I was grateful for it. I wasn't sure I could have taken it if he had flinched at the sight of our rotting clapboard and broken kitchen window.

The car headlights moved over the porch as we pulled up to the house. Bear sat on my father's old chair. He took a long swig from a can of beer, squinting, but otherwise he didn't move. I could not see Amir, but I knew that he would not be anywhere near Bear.

Will stopped the car and turned off its lights. He lifted his hand in a wave and nodded in Bear's direction. Bear took another swig of his beer.

"That's Bear's version of a greeting," I said. "It's efficient—he says hello and quenches his thirst at the same time."

Will didn't smile. He turned off the car's engine.

"Don't get out," I said sharply. Then I tried to laugh. "If you think Tiger was rough on my leg, you don't want to see what our chickens do to strangers."

Will looked at me. My face burned when I saw the pity in his eyes. He reached for something on the car's backseat. "This is for you," he said, handing me the copy of *A Moveable Feast* that I'd borrowed earlier. "You should finish it."

I took the book and pressed it to my chest. "Thank you."

"At least let me help you up the stairs. I can carry your bag."

"This little thing?" I patted the bag on my lap. "I'm fine. Really. Thank you for the ride, Will. And the book. Thank you for . . . everything." And then, before I could lose my nerve, I leaned over and kissed his cheek. When I opened the car door and stepped out, the air smelled of the sea, of home. The sound of the waves crashing against the cliffs filled the air. As I limped up the steps to the porch, I heard the car engine spring to life behind me. Lights slid over the boarded-up kitchen window. Wheels crunched against the dirt.

I stopped at the top of the stairs and closed my eyes. I waited until I couldn't hear the car anymore. *Goodbye,* I thought when the sound of the ocean again filled the night. With Will gone, my connection to the Langfords was officially severed. In a moment, the experience moved from the present to the past, and something within me ached at the change.

"Fancy car," Bear slurred. He muttered something else, but I could not understand him.

I opened my eyes. Bear had a spectrum of drunkenness and I could pinpoint his place on it the moment I heard him speak. When he fumbled to enunciate his words, he was drunk but aware. This was when his tongue was sharpest—it was when he referred to us as "the cunt and the runt" or spat at me and told me I smelled like chickenshit. When he stopped even attempting to speak clearly, and his words whooshed and churned like boiling water, I knew he was very drunk. When he was very drunk, he focused his attacks on Amir.

Right now, he was very drunk.

I dropped the bag I was holding. "Where is he?"

Bear shrugged.

"Where is he?" I shouted.

His bloodshot eyes roamed my face but could not settle in one place. "In his room." I didn't like the smirk that flickered across his lips.

I threw open the door to the cottage, calling Amir's name. It was quiet. His room was empty. His pillow still held the indentation from his head. I put my hand on it. *Amir,* I thought, *where are you?*

Where is he?

In his room . . . in his room . . . in his room . . .

The shed.

CHAPTER THIRTEEN

A shovel was wedged through the door handles of the shed. I pulled it out and opened the doors. From the darkness inside, Amir blinked up at me.

I rushed to him as he stood and brushed the dirt from his jeans. "I'm fine," he said. He sounded hoarse but didn't appear injured.

I hugged him. If Will smelled like nothing, Amir smelled of everything—the earth, the sea, everything I loved.

"I'm so sorry." I whispered the words into his neck. I felt acutely aware of how my body fit against his, the soft movement of his breath at my temple. All I had to do was lift my chin and my lips would find his. His hand moved over my hair. When his thumb grazed my earlobe a thousand sparks of light danced across my closed eyes.

Disgusting. Bear's voice tore through my thoughts. I shifted away from Amir, shame burning in my chest.

There was a crashing sound and then a jumbled shout from the direction of the cottage. My body went stiff with fear, but a moment later the unmistakable sound of the screen door slamming told me that Bear had gone into the cottage for the night.

My heartbeat steadied. "You sent the stone with Doctor Clark," I said, looking up at Amir. "I thought it meant you were okay."

"Bear locked me in here after the doctor left." His eyes darkened and skidded away from mine. For a moment, fury transformed his face. At his temple, his pulse skittered. I ached for him, for the fear and isolation and sense of powerlessness he must have experienced while I was gone. A violent storm spun behind his eyes.

"Amir." Worry choked my voice.

He looked down at the hand I'd placed on his arm and released a long, ragged breath. When his eyes found mine again, his gaze had softened. He shook his head as though clearing away whatever vengeful thoughts had run through his mind.

"It's you I've been worried about," he said. "How's your leg? The doctor said it was infected."

"It's better now. I should have come earlier. You must be hungry." I thought about the meals I'd had with the Langfords. Why hadn't I thought to bring something home for Amir?

He gave me a sideways smile and sunk a hand into the pocket of his sweatshirt, pulling out the end of a Dutch Crunch roll.

I laughed. "You took it from the Langfords'?"

His eyes glinted with mischief. He bit into the roll and shrugged. "I did what was expected of me."

"What do you mean?"

"You saw how they looked at me. They thought I was a thief."

"They thought we were *both* thieves. Their dog had just attacked me for jumping over the wall."

"Yes, but they forgave you almost immediately."

I understood what he meant. He thought the Langfords were racist. The possibility had occurred to me, too, while we'd sat together in their den. I'd wondered how differently they would have treated Amir if he had been the one whom Tiger had bitten instead of me. Would Will have insisted he come inside? Would Rosalie have bandaged his leg?

"They ended up being nice," I said quietly. "Rosalie surprised me. She was generous."

Amir reached out and rubbed the cuff of my new, soft sweater between his fingers. "I think," he said, "that her generosity extends to smart blond orphans and ends there."

I had no basis to disagree, but still the urge to defend Rosalie sprang within me. She'd told me that I reminded her of herself. Was it so awful to feel a connection to the familiar?

"Maybe," I said, "it's easier for some people to have sympathy for people who look like them, whose lives they can imagine more easily."

"Why would she be able to imagine your life any better than mine? Because you have the same skin color?"

"I don't know. Maybe. Or maybe because I'm a girl. I think I make her think of her own childhood." I thought for a moment. "If she'd had time to get to know you, it would have been different. With a little time, I think you would have felt differently about each other."

"You want *me* to forgive *her* for looking at me the way she did." I felt Amir's gaze travel through me, below my skin, through my veins, quickening the pace of my heart. "You think *I* should have empathy for her . . . because it's too much work for her to feel sympathy for a boy with brown skin." He shook his head. "That's bullshit, Merrow. People like that need to try harder. It's on them. Not me."

Amir was angry, but I had always seen his anger as the way he expressed feeling hurt. He had been treated as though he were less than whole by so many people—by the head of the orphanage, by his adoptive mother's father, by Bear, and now by Rosalie Langford. I felt sick with remorse. Why hadn't I understood how insulted he had been by the Langfords? I had meant to always be there for him, to stand up for him in the way that he had always stood up for me, and I had failed him.

"You're right." I put my hand on his arm. "I'm sorry. You're right."

He nodded. The clouds in his expression slowly parted.

When we left the shed, we instinctively walked toward the ocean. The peace sign my mother had painted on the lean-to in the paddock glowed in the moonlight. Amir glanced at my leg.

"Can you make it up?"

I nodded. We climbed to the top of the split-rail fence and pulled ourselves onto the lean-to's slanted roof. My calf throbbed, but I tried to ignore it, happy just to be near Amir. We sat huddled together on the roof, his arm around my shoulders, mine around his waist. The line where the bluff fell to the sea glinted like silver filament in the dark. Beyond, the ocean seemed still, but the sounds of its waves tumbling against the sand told the true story. My heart swelled with the beauty of this vast, wild place, my home, and the connection I felt to the boy who sat beside me.

"Soon we're going to look out at this same view, beneath these same stars," Amir said, "and everything is going to be different." His dark hair hung over his forehead, hiding the scar that I knew curved over his eyebrow.

"What do you mean?"

"In two years we'll be eighteen. Two-thirds of Horseshoe Cliff will be ours. We can build a house on the other end of the property. If Bear lays a hand on either of us, we can have him arrested. Once we're eighteen, we won't ever have to worry about being separated or taken away from here."

I rested my head on Amir's shoulder, afraid that if he saw my face he would know how conflicted I felt about his vision for our future. I loved Horseshoe Cliff and I never wanted to be apart from Amir, but I ached to be free of Bear and to experience more of the world. If anything, my stay with the Langfords had made these contradictory desires—to stay at Horseshoe Cliff and to get as far away as possible—only grow in intensity. How could I equally long for two different futures? How could I love a place and also wish to leave it?

Amir's earthy, familiar scent was a comfort, but I was not sure I had ever felt so confused.

"I'm glad you're home," he said. I heard in his voice that he was worried by my silence.

"I am, too." I closed my eyes. Even with them shut I saw the silver thread of the cliffs unspooling against a dark sky.

Amir cupped my chin and turned my face toward his. I opened my eyes. His sable eyes roamed my face. The way he looked at me made me feel as though I were the most important, most cherished person in the world. Warmth moved through my body. He lifted his hand to my hair, touching the thick, soft braid that hung in front of my shoulder. "Did you cut your hair?"

"No. It's just clean. I took a bath. A really hot bubble bath. And Rosalie told me I could keep these clothes. Even the boots." Amir didn't care about fashion, but I knew he would appreciate the practicality of a pair of rubber boots that did not have a single crack.

"They're nice," he admitted. "What else did I miss?"

I told him that the woman who owned the house had a collection of Satsuma ware, and I'd held one in my hand. "You should have seen the look on the Langfords' faces when I told them we'd studied Satsuma with Rei. If I'd sprouted another head, they wouldn't have looked more surprised."

Amir smiled. "Rei will be proud."

"Oh, and I did a puzzle and played Monopoly. And Will gave me a book—Hemingway's *A Moveable Feast*."

"The *food*, Merrow. Tell me about the food."

I grinned. "Cheese and bread and lots of honey." I closed my eyes, remembering. "Salami. Prosciutto, I think? I'm not sure. Orange juice and chocolate croissants—"

Amir groaned.

"I'm sorry! I'll stop," I said, laughing, but Amir shook his head and smiled.

"No. Don't stop. I want to hear about every last crumb."

I leaned my head on his shoulder again, sighing happily. We were both quiet for a moment, and I knew without looking at him that he was smiling, as I was. "I really am glad to be home," I said, and this time I meant it.

Days went by, and my leg slowly healed. I could not manage to forget the Langfords, but I was sure that they had forgotten me.

And then one day while Amir and I worked in the garden, I heard my name being called. I straightened. The sun was bright and high in the sky, but it was cold, and every so often the wind would rise off the sea and hurtle toward us. Rosalie Langford strode down the garden path in corduroy pants and a pair of gleaming black boots that were similar but not identical to the ones that she had given me. She wore sunglasses and a wide-brimmed hat that cast the sharp edges of her face in shadow. Her coat was navy blue and waxy, similar to a raincoat but with a corduroy collar. This was her "farm visit" outfit, I realized. I tried not to love it and failed.

"Hello!" she called as she tromped toward us, pulling off her sunglasses and waving them in the air. "I'm dropping by unannounced, but in my defense, you did it first." She smiled.

I felt excited—relieved even—to see her, though I tried not to show it in front of Amir. "What are you doing here?"

The wind picked up and she held the brim of her hat to keep it from blowing away. "Will gave me directions. I wanted to check on you. How is your leg?"

"Much better. Thank you."

I felt acutely how she kept her eyes on me. I was glad that

I'd tucked my hair into a baseball cap that morning and she couldn't see how it had returned to its seaweed state. She could not have helped noting that I still wore her sweater. It had been cold all week and there'd been no reason to take it off.

She barely glanced in Amir's direction.

"You remember Amir, don't you?" I asked.

"Yes, of course." If she heard the rebuke in my tone, she hid it. "How are you, Amir?"

"Peachy."

Rosalie smiled but Amir had already turned away. She put her sunglasses back on. "We're leaving to go back to the city tomorrow," she told me. "I've been wanting to check on you all week, but since you don't have a phone . . . Anyway, I thought perhaps you might have needed some time to think . . ." She trailed off, looking around, still holding her hat as she gazed out toward the blue curve of the sea. Her eyes widened. "This is quite a piece of property." She glanced down the rows of our garden. "And quite a bit of work, I imagine."

I knelt to help Amir drape a long swath of fabric—white once, now gray after many winters of use—over the hoops we'd staked over a row of lettuces. There was the possibility of frost that night and even though the heartier winter vegetables like the broccoli and cauliflower wouldn't mind the chill, the spinach and mesclun would.

Rosalie watched us. "Will you sell these when they're ready?"

"About half. The rest, we split with the chickens. Come spring, we're all sick to death of salad."

"Even the chickens?"

I laughed. "No, they'll eat nearly anything." I straightened and put my hands on my hips. "Do you want a tour?"

"I'd love one." She added, "If you're not too busy."

I shrugged. "There's always something to do, but most of it can wait."

Amir had moved farther down the row. He suddenly knelt, plucked what I knew was a snail from the dirt, and sent it flying in a high arc out of the garden, toward the sea. He could always send snails farther than I could, which he insisted was due to his perfect form, and I insisted was due to the fact that his joints appeared to be made of rubber bands.

"Are you coming?" I called.

Without looking back, he shook his head.

"It was nice to see you, Amir," called Rosalie.

He didn't turn.

As we walked away, Rosalie admitted that she knew nothing about gardening.

"Everything I know, I learned from Amir," I told her. "And everything he knows, he learned from my father. There were years when I was too wrapped up in reading to pay attention to learning how to farm, but luckily Amir has been interested in it since the moment he set foot on Horseshoe Cliff eight years ago. He only had a couple of years to learn from my father, but he picked it up almost immediately. From the beginning, he felt connected to the work."

"He enjoys it."

I thought about this. "Yes, but it's more than that. He *needs* it. He needs to work in the earth every day. And not just any earth—it has to be this earth, here at Horseshoe Cliff. This is *his* land. He belongs to it, and it belongs to him."

"And you? Is that how you feel about Horseshoe Cliff, too?"

I studied the ground, feeling my cheeks warm. "Yes. Of course."

We walked through the orchard and peered into the eucalyptus grove before heading back past the garden. I circumvented the cluster of buildings that were the cottage, the outhouse, and the shed. I wanted to show Horseshoe Cliff at its best angles, and those did not include the obvious disrepair of our rotting structures. Anyway, Rosalie had already seen them—she'd parked in front of the cottage. She didn't need a closer view. I walked with her along the path to the chicken coop. Our arrival—or Rosalie's, really; they did not care for strangers—caused the hens to scramble and trill.

"This is Rosalie," I cooed. "She won't hurt you."

"Not unless you have some barbecue sauce in there," Rosalie murmured in a soothing voice.

I laughed.

I pointed out the paddock and lean-to that used to hold our horses but now stood empty, sprouting more weeds with each passing year. The bluff was brown but soon the rains would come and turn all the land bright and varied shades of green. We kept walking until we reached the cliff. I walked right to the edge. The ocean was quiet for a moment, as though listening. It was as close as I could be to my mother, standing on that cliff.

I inched forward and sent a rush of pebbles skittering over the edge. Behind me, Rosalie sucked in her breath.

"Merrow! Be careful!"

A wave crashed on the sand below. I stepped back. Rosalie held her hand over her heart.

I smiled. "Do you want to walk down to the beach?" It was low tide, and the beach was wide and inviting. I pointed out the path to her.

She followed the line of my finger, her expression shaken. Her hand still covered her heart, but she nodded. When we reached the beach, she opened her arms wide and turned around in a circle. "I can't believe this is all yours."

"Mine and Amir's and Bear's. But Bear never comes down here. He hates the cliffs. And the beach."

"Why does he live here if he hates it?"

I'd never asked myself this question. "I don't know." Then I thought of the only time I'd seen Bear at the beach—walking out into the water with my father's ashes—and I thought that maybe I did know why. This place was all we had left of our parents. It was hard to imagine Bear's feelings, but that did not mean he didn't have them.

"Can we sit for a moment?" Rosalie asked.

I led her to the area near the back of the beach where Amir and I had long ago arranged some large rocks into seats. Rosalie looked surprisingly comfortable on those rocks, even in her nice clothes. Maybe she really was an avid camper, as Emma had claimed. For a few minutes we sat in silence and took in the view. I hoped to impress Rosalie with a sighting of one of the gray whales that traveled from Alaska to Baja, but it was early in the season for that journey and I knew the chances were slim. The sun sparkled against the water, making it look like an unending expanse of glistening ice. No whales appeared.

"It's gorgeous here," Rosalie said, looking out at the sea. I wondered if she was going to tell me what had really spurred her visit. "It's so . . . untamed. I can see why you and Amir love it."

She removed her hat and pushed her sunglasses up into her blond hair. When she turned toward me I was surprised to see that her face, suddenly exposed, was etched with concern. Her blue eyes held mine.

"I know you love it here," she said again. "But, Merrow, you're sixteen. You're allowed to have big plans for your life. And I think that you do. I think that sometimes you dream about a future that is very different from your past. That's why you wanted to look in our windows, wasn't it? And that's why when you described Horseshoe Cliff to me—even though the words you used were beautiful—you sounded so sad.

"This is your home," she continued. "You are a part of this place, and it will always be a part of you. But sometimes home is the place you have to leave in order to discover who you truly are."

I realized that my hands had begun to tremble only when Rosalie covered them with her own.

"We don't know each other well, but I meant what I said last weekend. I believe there are moments when your whole life changes, and I felt that sort of change when you stayed with us. I think I'm meant to help you. I think I *can* help you. I hope you'll allow me."

"I don't understand."

"I think you should apply to college. Now. Today. What reason is there to wait? I don't know the exact details of your life here, but I know enough to think that you would be better, maybe even safer, somewhere else."

"I don't know if he'll let me." My face burned.

Rosalie leveled her eyes on mine. "Bear."

I nodded. If Bear thought leaving would make me happy, he would do everything in his power to make me stay.

"Then we'll file emancipation papers. You have your GED. We can use that to establish your maturity." Rosalie squeezed my hand. "I know how to do this, Merrow. I did it myself. And you don't need to worry about the financial aspect. Between any number of scholarships and my own contributions, you'll be okay."

I understood then that she *had* spent the week thinking about me, that her words were not empty promises. But I would not leave unless Amir left with me. Why should we wait out the two years before we became adults in a place where Bear would continue to hurt us when we could be together somewhere else? In two years, the land would be ours. We could return to Horseshoe Cliff as adults.

"I can't leave without Amir."

"Does he have his GED?"

"No. But I won't go without him. You have to help him, too."

Rosalie patted my hand and at the same time, without any hesitation at all, she said the words that would make me love her forever. "We will."

AFTER ROSALIE DROVE away, promising to return soon, I checked the garden for Amir but could not find him. I figured he was working in the orchard. I wanted him to be in a good mood when I told him the news that Rosalie had agreed to help us leave Horseshoe Cliff, and since both of our moods were tied to our stomachs, I decided to make him a sandwich. The television blared from Bear's room, and I felt so exhilarated that I almost considered knocking on his door and asking if he wanted me to make him a sandwich, too. Then I realized that my happiness would only make him suspicious. The less Bear knew about my plan, the better.

I'd put two boiled-egg-and-lettuce sandwiches on a plate and was adding the last of our fall carrot harvest when I heard a car in the driveway. I set the plate on the counter and walked outside.

Rei stepped from her car. "Where've you been?" I called down to her from the porch. We hadn't seen her all week.

She blinked up at me and shook her head. It was her favored response when she thought I was being rude. The bracelets that lined her arms shook, *tsking* against each other. Amir had made her a wooden bangle engraved with stars for Christmas the previous year, and I hadn't seen her without it since.

"Hello, Merrow. I've been on a baking tear. Help me bring some of this inside, please."

I headed down the steps to help her. Though my limp was almost gone, she stopped and narrowed her eyes at me. "What happened?"

"It's a long story. Let's get this food inside first."

We set down the tinfoil-wrapped bread loaves and tubs of muffins on the dining table.

"Where's Amir?" she asked.

"I'm not sure. Maybe the orchard? I was just going to bring him a sandwich."

"Why bother? He'll be here any second. That boy can smell fresh-baked bread from two miles away."

She poured us each a mug of tea from the thermos she'd brought, and I pulled a blueberry muffin from one of the tubs. We sat on the back porch. I told her that a dog had bitten my leg and that the dog's owners had turned out to be visiting the area from San Francisco. Thankfully, Rei seemed more concerned about the dog bite than why I'd been bitten. I told her that Doctor Clark had given me antibiotics and that I was feeling better.

"Doctor Clark saw you? Why didn't he tell me?"

"You saw him this week?"

"He came to my house." She caught my worried look and waved me away. "It was nothing serious." She looked over her shoulder toward the house. "Bear should have driven over to let me know you'd been injured."

I bit into the blueberry muffin. It was no surprise to me that Bear hadn't let Rei know what had happened. He only left Horseshoe Cliff to drive to the co-op, and when he returned, he inevitably brought with him only half the things on the list I gave him and a truck cab full of the cheapest beer that the co-op stocked.

"It doesn't matter," I told Rei. "I'm fine now. And," I said, leaning toward her, "the most amazing thing happened! Rosalie Langford—that's the woman whose dog bit me—wants to help me go to college." I was glad that Bear's television was so loud that there was no way he would hear me—I was too excited to speak softly.

When Rei set her mug of tea in her lap, her thin fingers shook slightly. "What do you mean?"

"She wants to help pay for everything. She'll even help me file for emancipation if I need to. She did it herself when she was my age."

"Well!" Rei leaned so far back in her chair that she seemed to grow smaller by the moment. Then she released a wide smile. "Isn't that wonderful?"

I wasn't sure I had ever seen her look so tiny. I certainly hadn't seen her look so happy since my father was alive. She used to smile like that when she saw him, as though just the sight of him amazed her, making her little corner of the world brighter. It occurred to me suddenly what a burden we had been on her over the many years that she had worried about us, supporting us. We were Jacob's children, and she would never have let any of us down, but I thought I saw now the price she had paid for taking us on. Released for a moment from the stoic burden of worrying about my future, she looked frail.

"You're leaving," she said, her eyes shining.

"But I'll write to you all the time. I'll write you letters from all over the world . . ."

"The world!" Rei's face crinkled with delight.

"Why not? I want to see everything! Maybe I'll be able to

study abroad." I was excited, and carried away, but for the first time my most extravagant fantasies felt possible. *You're allowed to have big plans,* Rosalie had said. I wanted to hold on to the moment, and Rei's shared excitement, for as long as I could. "I'll send you something from Japan!"

Rei laughed. There was a sound then, as loud as a person walking through dry grass, at the side of the house. My heart jumped. I worried that it was Bear, eavesdropping, but immediately dismissed the thought; it would have taken too much work for him to have walked out the front door and crept around the side of the house when he could have just stood in the kitchen and listened.

Rei and I had both turned our heads toward the noise. For a moment, all was quiet, and then a red bird landed on the railing. It was smaller than a cardinal, as bright as a ripe strawberry.

"Oh!" I should have remained still, but instead I sprang to my feet.

The bird flew away.

I felt exultant. It was a sign. I was right to embrace Rosalie's offer. It was time to leave Horseshoe Cliff. I looked back at Rei. "My father always said that a red bird represents a visiting spirit."

Rei gave me a puzzled look.

"The red bird! Didn't you see it? It landed right there on the railing."

She sighed. "My eyesight has never been as sharp as my mind. The gap seems to be widening."

"But it was right there!"

"If you saw it, it was there, Merrow, and it was there for you."
As I sat down again, her expression narrowed into the worried
look I knew best. "What about Amir?"

"Rosalie said she would help him, too."

"He doesn't have his GED."

"I know, but we'll think of something. Maybe he can find
work for a year and try for his GED again."

"He's sixteen. Where is he going to work?"

"I don't know, but Rosalie said she would help him. She
promised."

Rei looked skeptical.

I was beginning to feel agitated. "I won't leave without Amir."

"It might be best if you went without him. You are ready
for something more than this life. You have been given an
opportunity—a gift. You should be free to accept it, wholly,
without anything, or anyone, holding you back."

"Amir's not—"

"Listen to me, Merrow. I will look after him. You know how
I care for Amir."

"You don't understand." I leaped from my seat and paced the
length of the porch. My words rushed from me, a familiar sense
of shame heating my body as they did. "I won't leave without
Amir. I can't. It would be like leaving a part of myself behind, a
part of myself that I need to survive, to breathe. I'm in love with
him, Rei!" I stopped and faced her, my cheeks burning with the
confession, a secret thrill spinning within my chest. I'd said it!
I'd said it. I was in love with Amir. There was nothing that could

have made me take the words back. "I'm in love with him! I won't leave him."

I would never forget how Rei looked at me in that moment— her expression shocked, her skin drained of color. My declaration left me raw; I could not stand to feel her stunned eyes on me. I ran into the house, slamming the back door behind me. Inside, I grabbed the sandwiches I'd made and ran out the front door toward the orchard.

But Amir was not there.

I wandered through first the orchard and then the grove, calling his name. Eventually I left the sandwiches nestled in the roots of a tree and ran to the shed. Its door swung open easily. He wasn't inside. I walked through the garden, around the chicken coop, and through the horse paddock. I peered up at the empty roof of the lean-to. I scanned the bluffs and down the coast, the wind roaring in my ears. I stood at the edge of the cliff and looked out. I walked down the path to the beach and called Amir's name into the caves. My own voice returned to me, a solitary sound.

When I trudged back to the cottage, Rei was gone. I sat on the back porch and looked out at the sea. There were countless places at Horseshoe Cliff to hide, and I knew them all. Where was he?

The television fell silent. I heard the fridge door open and close. Bear walked out on the porch.

"I can't find Amir," I told him.

"Good riddance," Bear said, but if I hadn't known better I would have sworn he scanned the land around the cottage before he took a slug of his beer and walked back inside. I wondered why he'd come to that side of the cottage at all. He hated the back porch, with its view of the cliffs.

I looked out toward the sea until the sun began to lower. Still, even then for a time, I looked to the horizon, waiting. Finally, when the sun was so low that it threatened to blind me, I closed my eyes.

IT WAS DARK when I awoke. I looked around the porch, disoriented and hungry. I straightened, rubbing my eyes so hard that red spots appeared behind my eyelids.

I thought of the red bird I'd seen. Rei had said it was just for me. I thought that it was a sign that I was doing the right thing. But what if it had been a sign of something else? I remembered the sounds I'd heard just before I saw the bird, when I'd wondered if Bear had crept around the side of the house.

Amir. Had he stood just out of view, listening?

I thought back, trying to remember what he would have heard. At the point when I heard the noises on the side of the house, I was telling Rei how Rosalie wanted to help me go to college. If Amir had been listening, would he have thought that I planned to leave without him? If he had left then, he would not have heard me tell Rei that I loved him.

I needed Rei. She would help me find Amir.

I hurried inside. The house was empty. On the front porch, Bear drank a beer and tore fist-sized hunks of bread from the loaf that Rei had brought. He didn't turn to look in my direction even when the screen door slammed.

"Can you take me to Rei's?" I asked.

He took a drink of his beer and wiped his lips with the back of his hand before tearing off another piece of bread.

"Please," I said. "It's important. I'm worried about Amir. It's getting darker and I don't know where he is."

"Did you check the shed?" Bear's laugh was hard and mean. He had a glint in his eye that told me he was itching for a fight. He hadn't really hurt me since Amir had arrived, but now Amir was gone, and it was just the two of us.

I turned and went inside. I waited a beat, ready to sprint for the back door if Bear followed me. He didn't. I looked around the kitchen, trying to decide what to do, and saw that Bear's jacket hung from the back of a chair. I sunk my hand into its pockets and fished out the keys to the truck. I hadn't driven since my father used to give me lessons on our long driveway. I hoped I remembered enough to get me to Rei's house.

I went out the back door and snuck around the side of the house. The truck was parked in plain view of Bear. There was nothing to do but run.

I had my hand on the door handle when Bear grabbed me around my waist. I managed to wriggle free and shove him away. I was stronger than I'd ever been when we used to fight, and he was drunker. I was halfway into the cab when he grabbed my leg. He fingers dug into the wound on my calf. I screamed, kicking at him again and again. I managed to get him far enough away from me that I could slam the door shut. I locked it.

He pounded on the window. "Merrow!" he roared. "Get out of my truck!"

I jammed the key in the ignition and turned it. The truck sped down the driveway toward the road, and I didn't lift my foot from the gas pedal until Bear was finally small in the rear-view mirror.

CHAPTER FOURTEEN

When I arrived at Rei's house, I was relieved to see that her car was in the driveway. There was a glow of light beyond the living room curtains.

But when I knocked on the door, she did not answer. I knocked again and called her name. I waited a few moments and tried again. I picked my way through the plants in front of her house and knocked on the living room window. I cupped my hands around my mouth and yelled her name.

I walked around to the back of the house. Her bathroom window was dark. I knocked on it but heard no response. The window was once again unlocked, and I felt a pang of guilt for not warning Rei, years earlier, of how easy it was to break into her house.

"Rei?" I stepped into the bathroom. An inexplicable sensation of dread passed over my skin like a cold wind. "It's me, Merrow!"

I walked from the bathroom into the bedroom and flipped on the light. Rei lay on top of her covers, asleep.

My relief quickly changed as I ran to the bed. Rei did not move, and she was not asleep. Her eyes were open. Her face was frozen in an expression I had never seen her wear—she looked as though she were staring at something that terrified her. Her lips formed a thin, immovable circle. Her black eyes were still and unseeing. Nausea roiled my stomach. I sunk to my knees at the side of the bed. "Rei," I cried. My voice did not sound like my own. "Rei!"

I would never know how much time passed as I knelt beside her. The bones in my body dissolved in response to my grief; I could not move.

I had just seen her. We had just spoken. It was not possible that she was gone.

I thought of how tired she had seemed as we sat together on the porch. I thought of how dismayed she'd become when I expressed my love for Amir. I had run away from her, leaving her alone and frail with shock.

Had I done this to her?

I lowered my forehead to the bed and sobbed. Rei was more than my father's friend. She was more than my teacher, more than my thankless benefactor. I loved her. After so many years of laughing when she worried over me, now I cried at the thought of my life without her in it. Would I have longed to see the world without Rei's stories of her childhood in Japan? Would I have loved art the way that I did? She had affected me in ways for which I rarely paused to give her credit.

I cried for her forgiveness.

Through the window, the moon was a bright eye watching

me. What was I supposed to do? I decided I should find Doctor Clark and tell him how I'd come to discover Rei.

As I stood shakily to my feet, my gaze fell on the trunk across the room. It was open. On the floor, Rei's box—the beautiful box covered in shells from our beach—lay ajar. I walked over to it, my heart hammering in my ears.

It was empty.

I looked back at Rei, my understanding shifting. Had someone done this to her? Had someone killed her and stolen her money?

The pillow beside her was indented, as though an invisible hand pressed it. I thought of spirits, of the red bird on the porch railing, of Amir believing that I planned to leave Horseshoe Cliff without him.

The last time I had left Amir alone with Bear, he had ended up locked in the shed.

But Amir would not do this to Rei.

I thought of the way his face had transformed that day when I returned from my stay with the Langfords, how I had hardly recognized the Amir whom I loved within the storm of violence that had spun in his eyes.

I did not want to think what I was thinking.

I did not want to do what I did, but I did it anyway: I closed the empty box and returned it to the trunk.

"Forgive me," I whispered to Rei.

I remembered the light that was on in the living room. I hurried down the hall and there, on the shelf that held the carvings that my father and Amir had made, one carving was missing. I remembered the one that had been in that spot. It was the first tiny house that Amir had created. My father had helped him with it, teaching him; they'd made it together.

I thought suddenly of Rosalie's words, how there were moments in life when you realize that everything has changed.

I stared at the empty spot, feeling my world shift.

Amir was gone.

PART TWO

CHAPTER FIFTEEN

Finally! Someone who knows the value of a dollar," said the girl as she slid into the seat beside me. I was startled. In nearly a year of classes at San Francisco State University, few of my classmates had spoken to me. The girl registered my confused look and gestured toward the students who were filling in the rows of the lecture hall behind us. "It's like no one has explained to them that the best seats in the house cost the same as the worst ones."

She had a point. In many classes, I found that I was the only student who sat in the front row. I preferred it this way. When I raised my hand to speak, which was frequently, it was easy for me to pretend that I was simply conversing with my professor, and not being silently judged and scowled at by my less-eager peers. I had not made any friends, but I told myself it didn't matter. I was there to learn.

I was acutely aware of how different I was from my classmates. I was younger than everyone I met, I had only a passing knowledge of pop culture, and I had little experience with making new friends. I knew that my classmates thought me strange. A toxic mixture of guilt and grief and homesickness roiled within me—but I did not cry. I was skittish, half expecting that at any moment I would hear Bear's voice in my ear and turn to see him looming over me with knives in his eyes. Fear had turned me into a dry-eyed recluse.

College was not what I'd thought it would be. *I* was not who I'd thought I'd be.

I had thrown myself into my studies. I wrote stories, and in them the sea always appeared. It was perpetually on my mind, tugging at me as insistently as an actual tide. I was sure that I could hear the sea even when it was miles away. I held the stone Amir had sent to me at the Langfords' in my left hand as I wrote, longhand, in my notebook.

"Veronica Quilici," the girl beside me said.

I set down my pencil and shook her hand. "Merrow Shawe."

"Merrow? That's pretty." Veronica had shoulder-length brown hair that she'd pulled back in a twisted red bandanna. Her face was round, her cheeks dimpled, and her front teeth were crowded and bulging as though elbowing each other out of the way. "You can call me Ronnie," she said. I had the distinct sense it was the first time she was trying out this nickname. "Did you start any of the books?"

I nodded.

The class was Contemporary Women Writers, and the reading list that the professor had circulated two weeks prior to the start of the semester was comprised of seven novels. I had immediately signed all seven books out of the library and had finished reading the last one on the list the night before the first class.

"I read them all," Ronnie announced. "I couldn't wait."

I could not help but smile. "I read them all, too."

She looked at me in surprise and, I thought, relief. I guessed that she was thinking what I was thinking: Here, at last, was a kindred spirit. A fervent reader of books. An unapologetic front-row seat taker. Someone who looked in need of a friend.

As the professor opened the classroom door and headed toward the lectern, Ronnie leaned toward me and asked if I wanted to get coffee after class. I answered, as casually as I could, "Sure." I was seventeen years old and I had never had a cup of coffee.

It was hard to concentrate on the lecture. Ronnie's offer of friendship was not a small thing for me. I had spent the last year so immersed in grief that I could not imagine my way out. Rosalie had fulfilled her promise to me, helping me file for emancipation and supporting me financially as I applied for and received various scholarships. Still, I felt alone. For the first time in many years, I remembered how lonely I had been before Amir had arrived at Horseshoe Cliff. I felt returned to that place of friendlessness, except now it was exacerbated by Rei's death, Amir's disappearance, and how disorienting it felt to be so far from anyone or anything familiar. I walked along San Francisco's beaches as often as I could and let the sound of the waves calm me. I had what I'd always wanted—the chance to go to college, to live in a big city, to see more of the world than one crumbling cliff—but it was not at all how I'd envisioned it.

I was not sleeping well. In my dreams, Amir and Rei stared at me and would not speak. I could not read their expressions.

I had not gone to the police or even to Doctor Clark that night a year earlier when I found Rei dead and her money gone. I drove Bear's truck home. His bedroom door was shut when I arrived. I put his keys back in the pocket of his jacket that still hung from a chair. I went to my room and lay awake all night. The next day, Bear didn't say anything about how I had taken his truck. I guessed alcohol had made his memory of the night hazy—or perhaps that he would rather forget the embarrassment of his little sister stealing his truck. I did not say a word all morning. There was work to be done around the farm, but I did not do it. I sat on the porch and watched the driveway, hoping that Amir would return and knowing in my heart that he would not.

Late in the afternoon, Doctor Clark arrived. I supposed I'd been waiting for him, too. Bear came out to the porch.

The doctor asked if Amir was around. "I'm afraid I have news that he should hear, too."

"He's working in the orchard." The lie came easily, but I looked off into the distance to avoid meeting his eye.

Doctor Clark gave a weary sigh. "Well, you'll tell him then, when you see him." He explained that after Rei had not answered his calls all day, he'd checked on her and discovered that she had died in her sleep over the night.

"She wasn't in pain, Merrow. She fell asleep and didn't wake up. It was peaceful."

I pressed my lips together to keep myself from crying out the truth. I had seen Rei's face. She had not died in peace. She had died in terror.

Doctor Clark went on. It seemed to me he was speaking as much to himself as he was to us. "When I ran into her at the co-op earlier in the week, she mentioned she'd been feeling short of breath. Dizzy. She didn't look particularly well. I told her to go to the hospital, but she waved me off. She said it was age, pure and simple. I called on her a couple of days ago, just to check. She said she was feeling better." He looked off in the direction of the orchard and his hangdog eyes swam. "I should have driven her to the hospital myself."

His anguish pained me. "You did what you could," I whispered, my voice catching on the words.

Doctor Clark returned to his car. Beside me, Bear smelled like he hadn't bathed in a week. When the doctor's car was halfway to the road, my brother's fingers squeezed my wrist.

"So Rei is dead and Amir is nowhere to be found, but you're in a big hurry to tell Doctor Clark that Amir is working in the orchard."

I wrenched my arm from his grip and went inside without responding.

Days went by. I hoped that Bear had decided to let go of the subject, but then Doctor Clark returned with a lawyer. Rei had a will. Years earlier, she had inherited money from her parents when they died. She had no living relatives. Her house was to be sold, and the money from the sale would be given to the Osha Conservation Fund. Her savings were to be divided among Bear and Amir and me. Amir and I would inherit the money when we were eighteen. Bear could collect his inheritance at intervals over the next couple of years so long as he was taking "good care" of us.

The lawyer frowned at Bear. "That's a tricky thing, that part about taking 'good care' of your sister and your . . . ward. Rei didn't specify what she meant by that."

My heart hammered in my ears. I stole a glance at Bear. His face was impassive. I could not tell if he even understood what the lawyer was saying.

"But here's where things get even trickier, I'm afraid," the man continued. "There's a small bank account with a bit of money in it, but her will states that she kept most of her inheritance at home in a box in her bedroom. When we checked the box, we found it empty." He looked at Bear, waiting for his response. I was waiting for it, too, waiting for Bear to tell them that Amir had gone missing the very night Rei had died.

But my brother just gnashed his molars together and stared off into the distance.

"Money doesn't disappear," Doctor Clark said. "It will turn up as the house gets cleared out for the sale."

I listened, afraid that if I spoke or even moved, Bear would break his silence.

"You keep looking," Bear said. "We could use that money."

The lawyer nodded. "Meantime, I'll get your share of the money from the savings account over to you as soon as the estate has settled."

Doctor Clark had me sit in the kitchen so he could take a look at my calf before he left. "Just about good as new," he said, rolling my pant leg back down. "Amir's out working again?"

I nodded. As he gathered his coat and left, I stared at the floor, wondering how long I could keep pretending that Amir was at Horseshoe Cliff. Where *was* he, anyway? For a moment, I entertained an elaborate fantasy of Amir and Rei strolling through the front door, laughing off my worst fears as a ridiculous misunderstanding.

Instead, as soon as the doctor's car pulled away, Bear stormed into the kitchen. Before I knew what was happening, he upended my chair and I fell to the floor.

"Amir killed her, didn't he?" Bear said, standing over me, his chest heaving.

My pulse immediately thundered in my ears. "No. *No.* Of course not."

"'*Of course not,*'" Bear mimicked, sneering. "I bet you never thought Amir would run away and leave you here all alone, did you? Looks like you didn't know him as well as you thought you did. *I* knew who he was the second I saw him. Now you do, too. Wake up, Merrow. Amir is *gone*. Rei is *dead*. He killed her, and he took her money, and he ran."

I opened my mouth to defend Amir, but my mind churned in darkness so thick I could not find the words. Had my actions pushed Amir to do something he never would have done in other circumstances? I had known that deep emotions boiled within him; in the face of Bear's treatment he had grown angrier with each passing day. When I spent the night with the Langfords,

Amir had to face Bear alone, and I'd returned to find him locked in the shed. What had that done to him? If he believed that I planned to leave Horseshoe Cliff without him, and that Rei encouraged me to do so, could his anger have pivoted toward her? Had I driven him to steal from her? To murder her? I did not want to believe this was possible, but I could not erase the memory of what I had seen that night at Rei's house. The empty box. Rei's awful, frozen fear.

Bear was watching me. His eyes narrowed. "You were there, weren't you?"

I shook my head. I did not trust myself to speak.

"I need that money, Merrow. We need it. It's ours." Bear's expression shifted, darkening. The air between us crackled with warning.

I crab-crawled away from him until my back hit the kitchen cabinet. "They'll find the money. You heard Doctor Clark. It'll turn up."

"He also said Rei died in her sleep, and we both know that's bullshit."

He seemed as though he was going to walk away, but instead he suddenly crouched down and wrapped my shins in his huge hands. As he squeezed, I felt his fingernails through my pants.

"Stop," I gasped. "Let go of me!" I thrashed on the ground and tried to push him away, to kick him away, but his hands were clamped tight. It was like the eight years when Amir had been the focus of his violence had never even happened; his rage winnowed on me. I'd nearly forgotten how it felt to be so terrified. This was how Amir had felt, alone with Bear while I had slept in comfort with the Langfords.

My hands were free. Bear's hands were tight around my legs.

I stuck my thumbs into his eyes. He howled, but when his hand rose to hit me it froze in the air. I scrambled into the corner. He came after me.

I kicked out wildly. He threw my legs to the side. He could do anything he wanted—there was no one for miles in any direction. This was how it would be from now on.

"I hate you!" I screamed.

His face was inches from mine. When he spoke, spittle flew at me. "You better not run," he said. "If you run, I'll know you're meeting him. I'll know you helped him do it, and I'll tell."

Then he stood. His shoulders heaved; he was out of breath. He grabbed a six-pack of beer from the fridge and slammed his bedroom door behind him.

I stared after him. The only reason he hadn't hit me in the face was that he wanted Rei's money and the lawyer had said he was going to check on us. But it didn't matter whether or not I stayed; the most Bear would ever see of Rei's money was the amount in her bank account. Amir had taken the rest. Bear's rage would only grow.

I stood, shakily, and packed the bag that Rosalie had given me. I walked out the front door. I kept walking all the way down the driveway. When I reached the road, I looked over my shoulder. From a distance, our little cottage was a solitary light in a sea of black, a home at the edge of the world.

If I left, how would Amir ever find me?

The sea was invisible in the night, but I could hear it still. I could not imagine a life without this sound, its murmur and its roar, its perpetual reminder of everything I feared and everything I loved.

I turned onto the road and kept walking. Eventually a truck approached and I hitched a ride into town. I used the phone in the café to call the number Rosalie had given me. When she picked up, I felt a rush of relief at the sound of her voice.

"Please help me," I said.

RONNIE WAS THE only true friend that I made in college. She was more than enough. We became roommates and, with Ronnie leading the way, I began to embrace San Francisco, exploring its neighborhoods, trying cuisines from around the world at new restaurants, dancing on sticky floors to live bands, and huddling together, laughing, on overcrowded buses that sped too quickly over the city's steep hills. At night, the sky was a dull gray haze pierced by the lights of office buildings. After many months of anxiously wondering when Bear would follow through on his threat to tell someone that Amir and I had played a role in Rei's death, I slowly began to allow myself to enjoy my new life.

Ronnie and I studied together, we went to coffee shops and art museums and movies, and even—rarely, but sometimes—went on double dates. To her exasperation, I could never bring myself to go on more than one date with the same boy. Each boy, however different from Amir, would reveal some small trait that made me think of him. One held his fork tightly as though it might jump from his hand. Another widened his eyes when he listened to me. A fellow English major's living room contained neat piles of hardcover novels, and I could think only of the stones that Amir had always managed to stack so high on the beach.

"Whoever he was," Ronnie announced one morning after I'd described another miserable date, "you need to forget him."

"Who?"

"The guy who broke your heart."

I was surprised, but of course she was right. Amir *had* broken my heart. I could not believe that he had left me, that he had disappeared without a word. Most of the time, I could not bring myself to believe that he'd had anything to do with Rei's death. But there were nights when I lay awake and thought of the indented pillow I'd seen beside Rei. The look of terror on her face. The empty box on the floor. The many years of violence and humiliation that Amir had experienced at the hands of Bear.

What frightened me perhaps most of all was that in those moments when I forced myself to consider what Amir might have done to Rei, I loved him anyway.

RONNIE VOLUNTEERED WITH Learning Together, a nonprofit organization that offered a free after-school enrichment program for elementary school children. Many of the children lived in low-income housing, and some lived in shelters. I joined Ronnie one afternoon and was assigned to help two second-grade girls with their homework. One of the girls, Keira, was amiable and talkative. The other, Marty, did not say a word to me. She pushed out her lips and glared at me each time I tried to talk to her about her homework.

"You know what?" I told her. "I'm going to wait for you to ask for help if you need it. I'm working on being patient. It's hard for me. But I'm going to try, okay? At the end of our time together, you can let me know how I did."

For a moment, surprise registered on Marty's face. Then she shrugged and hunched over her worksheet, shielding it from me.

Keira talked enough for both of them. She told me about her friends, her favorite teacher, her school's awful lunches. I had to bring her focus back to her homework repeatedly, but her openness charmed me. Though Marty was silent on my other side, I sensed her listening to our conversation. After twenty minutes, she tapped my arm and asked me how to spell the word *daughter*. I told her, and she returned to her work. I saw that her letters were small and neat. When another volunteer came to collect the girls for an art project in the studio, Marty stopped on her way out of the room. She turned to me with a very serious expression and said, "Ms. Shawe, you're doing fine."

Her words caused me to experience a rush of joy that I had not felt in years.

I signed up to volunteer three afternoons each week. I never missed a day; I wanted those students to know that they could depend on me. Sometimes I read to them, but more often I told them stories. I told them about children who turned into butterflies each time they entered a forest thick with fog. I told them about the adventures of a family of whales traveling from Alaska to Baja. I told them the story of a boy who crawled deep into a cave and heard the voices of his ancestors. I told them about a mermaid who was so powerful that her songs caused the ocean to crash against the land and change its shape forever.

For all its flaws, what I remembered most from my childhood was the abundance of magic; it was a gift that I longed to share.

WHEN I FIRST left Horseshoe Cliff, Rosalie Langford had given me a phone, and every so often she would call and invite me to lunch. Sometimes we ate at a restaurant and sometimes at her home, which I preferred because it allowed me to imagine, for a couple of hours, that I was a member of the family. It also meant that I would see Emma, who was just as sweet as she entered her teenage years as she had been at ten years old. Emma and I also swam together every few weeks at Baker Beach. Afterward we would wrap ourselves in huge towels and stare out at the sea. Neither of us liked to go too long without putting our feet in the sand.

These were my closest friends: a fourteen-year-old girl and a twenty-two-year-old college classmate and a woman in her fifties.

Rosalie frequently asked me about my work with Learning Together. One day, I walked into the center and learned from my boss that she had donated such a large sum to the organization that they would be able to double the number of children it served.

When I graduated from college, I was offered a full-time role at the center. Rosalie insisted on throwing a dinner party to celebrate. It would just be the family, she said, but if I wanted to invite a friend, I could. I invited Ronnie, who was curious to finally meet the famous Langfords, whom she enjoyed referring to as "the Benefactors" in an overarticulated English accent. She knew bits and pieces of how we had met—but not, of course, the entire story.

When we rang the doorbell at the Langfords' home, a caterer greeted us with glasses of champagne and told us we were expected in the living room.

"Fancy," Ronnie whispered, excited.

I was surprised to see Will Langford sitting in the living room alone. Rosalie *had* said the family would attend, but I had not seen Will once in the four years that I'd been visiting Rosalie and Emma and Wayne, and it had not occurred to me that he might be there. He traveled frequently, Rosalie had told me, for business and for pleasure. *He's become something of an* adventurer, she'd said, and the way she'd emphasized the word had let me know that she approved.

It was possible that he was even more handsome than I'd remembered. I felt myself blush deeply, and when I managed to greet him my voice sounded strange.

"It's nice to see you, Will. This is my friend, Ronnie."

"Hello," Ronnie said. She turned to me with eyes that brimmed with delight and mouthed the words *hubba hubba* in plain view of Will.

I shook my head sharply, but it was impossible not to laugh.

Will smiled. "Nice to meet you, Ronnie. And it's good to see you, Merrow. How is your leg after all these years?"

I wore a green silk dress that Rosalie had given me on my last birthday and gold leather sandals I had found at Goodwill. I turned and showed him my bare calf. A series of small, pale scars formed a rough circle. Since they were on the back of my leg, I almost never thought of them, but there were times when, out of the blue, my calf would throb. I always thought of my brother, not Rosalie's dog, when this happened. I felt Bear's hand encircling my leg, his fingers clawing at the wound on that last day I'd spent at Horseshoe Cliff. I would shiver then and feel glad to be far away from him. In four years, he had not contacted me, but it did not mean that I felt free.

"Well," Will said. He seemed uncertain how to respond. "I'm glad it healed."

"Well," I said, "I'm glad your parents put me through college."

He burst into a surprised laugh. "I suppose it was the least they could do."

At the sound of his laughter, I felt myself relax. "Where are they, anyway?"

"Emma is in the kitchen—"

"She loves to cook."

"Yes, she does. Wayne is running late, as usual. And Mom—last time I saw her, she was working on a toast."

"A toast?"

"You don't know? Rosalie Langford is famous for her toasts. Emma's middle school graduation was really something special. And I've been the honoree a few times myself." I knew from Rosalie that Will had graduated from law school and was working downtown.

"She takes no prisoners with these toasts," he continued, warning me. "There won't be a dry eye in the house."

"Oh boy," said Ronnie. "I didn't wear waterproof mascara."

"Shame," said Will, catching my eye and smiling.

LATER, AFTER ROSALIE and Wayne and Emma made their entrances and I introduced them to Ronnie, I walked my friend over to the window to show her the impressive view of the Golden Gate Bridge and the Bay. Neither of us could keep our gaze in the direction of the windows for long.

"Ugh," Ronnie whispered. "Underneath all that . . ."—she nodded in Will's direction—"*hotness,* he must be awful." She was on her second glass of champagne, and her cheeks were pink. "I bet he's totally full of himself. I bet he doesn't read novels . . . or *ever* eat dessert before dinner . . . or date short women. No one that handsome is a good person."

"I think he is, actually," I said. I had never forgotten that he had been the one who convinced his mother to invite me inside their home after her dog had bitten me. Rosalie had become a sort of fairy godmother in my life, but it was Will who had persuaded her to feel that first pang of empathy. I remembered, quite suddenly, how Will had lifted me into his arms and carried me inside. "I think he's very kind and a little reserved and—"

"Oh my god." Ronnie's left dimple deepened to the point that you could have rested a tack in it without injuring her. "That's

him, isn't it? That's the guy you've been pining for all these years?"

"What?" I said. "No." I was saved from saying anything more by Rosalie's announcement that dinner was ready.

"When I met Merrow she was a girl—a rather terrifyingly scrappy and articulate sixteen-year-old girl," said Rosalie, standing at the head of the table with a champagne glass in her hand. "She stood fearlessly on the edge of soaring cliffs, she killed chickens with her bare hands when duty called, and she scaled very, very high walls around strangers' private property because she was curious about how other people lived." Rosalie raised her eyebrows in my direction.

"She also loved reading novels. And she was a writer. She spoke of the sea, of her home, in the way that a poet writes about love. She had a bright light within her, and she was unafraid to let it shine."

Rosalie paused, glancing at the slip of paper in her hand. I was astonished to see that her eyes glistened. I had known her to be compassionate, protective, and frequently droll, but I had never seen her as sentimental.

Don't cry, Bear growled in my ear.

I clenched my teeth together. *He's not here,* I reminded myself. My memory of him loomed so large that it cast me, momentarily, in shadow.

"The light within Merrow," Rosalie continued, "has only grown brighter as she has become an adult. She has chosen to shine this light on others. As she continues to embrace her position as a role model and friend to our city's youth, I am comforted to know that so many lives will change for the better, as mine has, thanks to her unique spirit." Rosalie held up her glass. "Merrow, as you graduate from college and embark on the start of a new and exciting time in your life, I want to say congratulations on all your hard work. I am so very proud of you."

No one had ever told me that they were proud of me. I looked around the table at the faces of my friends and felt their kindness envelop me. I longed to stay in that moment.

Still, my eyes brimmed with tears that refused to fall.

Later, while Emma was giving Ronnie a tour of the house, I stepped onto the balcony. The night was cool but there was no wind. The sun had almost set. The Langfords' view was of the Bay and the bridge, but a sliver of ocean was visible, too. Its presence in the distance always reminded me that my father had once thought of the ocean as an enormous, sleeping animal. I leaned against the railing and looked out toward it.

Within moments I was overcome by the sense that I was being watched. It was not a bad feeling, but on the contrary left me comforted. I thought of how after I learned that my mother had died falling from the cliff, I always felt her watching me when I stood on the beach. The feeling that I experienced in that moment on the Langfords' balcony was similar: I was watched by someone who cared deeply for me.

I turned when I heard the door to the balcony open. It was Will, and he had a white blanket in his hand.

"I thought you might be cold."

"Thank you." He placed the blanket on my shoulders and then began to walk back inside. "Stay," I said. "I've had enough of my own thoughts."

He nodded and stood beside me. For a few moments we both looked out at the view.

"Did you ever finish *A Moveable Feast?*"

I turned to him in surprise. "Yes." He had given me the book when he'd driven me back to Horseshoe Cliff, and I had it still. "I can't believe you remember."

"We had a conversation about Paris. I told you how I traveled with my friends around Europe." He looked down at his hands, his expression suddenly pained. "I can't tell you how many times I went over that conversation in my head afterward."

"Really? Why?" I'd gone over it in my own mind countless times, but it had never once occurred to me that he might have done the same.

"Later, after I drove you home, I thought of how I must have sounded, talking to you about traveling through Europe when . . . when . . ."

I remembered studying his expression when he drove up to our cottage. I remembered how Bear had sat on the porch with his beer and barely moved, a dark mountain of resentment, of silent fury. Now that I had been away from Horseshoe Cliff for four years, I had a sense of how it must have appeared to Will. Run-down. Bleak. Battered by coastal winds and rain and the unrealized dreams of our sad, hopeful parents.

Fancy car, Bear had said as Will drove away.

"It's been years," I said. "All this time you've been upset with yourself for telling me that you traveled in college?"

"I wish I were as proud of my finest moments as I am ashamed of my mistakes."

He gazed out into night, the lights of the houses below us, the Bay beyond. I liked how serious he appeared. Even when he wasn't speaking, I sensed his mind at work.

"For what it's worth," I said, "I wouldn't call that conversation a mistake. I enjoyed it. I've thought about it since then, too. And never in the way that you're thinking. You made me wonder what my life could be like if I went to college. You inspired me. I wasn't listening with closed ears. I knew you were speaking from a place of kindness. Right from the beginning, you were only kind to me."

He turned toward me. "'Closed ears,'" he echoed. "My mother is right about you. You speak like someone who loves words."

Four years earlier, he had been nice to me, but distant. Now, he seemed more open. I thought that perhaps it was because I was older. I was a college graduate, and I had a job and an apartment. I was an adult.

"You know," he said, taking a step closer to me, "that weekend was surprising in a lot of ways. I've never forgotten it. I hope you won't mind me saying this, but meeting you made me realize how little I really knew of life. I'd been so immersed in my studies, and you . . . you were like a breath of fresh air." My expression must have revealed my surprise because he looked momentarily stricken, then laughed. "Oh no. Did I just create a new moment to feel mortified about for the next four years?"

"No, no. It's just I don't think 'breath of fresh air' is how most people would have described me then. There wasn't a big emphasis on oral hygiene in my childhood."

His smile flashed and then was gone. "Oh, Merrow," he said quietly, "you have no idea how lovely you were, do you?"

I looked out at the water. *You're disgusting,* Bear whispered in my ear. I shivered. What would my brother say to me now, I wondered, in my green silk dress and golden heels, my hair as tame as it had ever been, the Langfords' soft blanket draped over my shoulders?

Will cleared his throat. "It's a beautiful night." He rested his hands on the railing. "I've always loved the hills across the Bay at sunset. The way they seem to turn purple."

I smiled. "'The golden day is dying beyond the purple hill.'"

"Yeats?"

"No, it's an old folk song. My father taught it to me when I was a child. This time of day reminds me of it."

"Will you sing it?"

I had never been shy about singing. My voice was not beautiful, but it was mine, and my father had always told me that he loved to hear me sing.

"The golden day is dying beyond the purple hill," I sang. *"The lark that sang at dawning, in dusky wood is still."*

I closed my eyes and felt the salt wind of Horseshoe Cliff against my face as I sang. My father had taught me the song as a round. Years later, Amir and I had sung it together, echoing each other in a solemn, contented loop as we lay on the bluff at night with a canopy of stars overhead.

A tremble entered my voice on the last stanza.

"And soon above the meadow, the silver moon will swing. And where the wood is darkest, the whip-poor-will will sing."

When I opened my eyes, Will was watching me, rapt.

"That was beautiful," he said.

"Thanks." I laughed. "I guess? I didn't write it."

He put his hand on mine and gave me a gentle smile. "You won't let my compliments stick, will you?"

I was startled by his words but even more so by the electric sensation caused by his hand on mine. His eyes were a blue that made me think of a cloudless sky.

"I've never met anyone like you, Merrow," he said then. "I haven't been able to get you out of my mind."

There was an urgency in his voice that drew me toward him. The wind rose off the Bay, swirling around us. I lifted my chin and pressed my lips to his. The blanket slipped from my bare shoulders, but it didn't matter; Will's arms were warm around mine.

CHAPTER SIXTEEN

That summer, Will took me on a two-week vacation to Italy.
We had been dating for a little over two months, seeing each
other mostly on weekends. Ronnie was surprised when I told
her of our travel plans. She thought we were moving quickly.
But I felt that I had known him for years. No matter how my
time in the city had smoothed my rough edges, it could never
cut away the gnarled parts of me that were rooted at Horseshoe
Cliff. It comforted me that Will knew where I had come from,
and that we had met in Osha.

It also comforted me that Will and Amir were nothing alike.
Amir loved what was most familiar; Will was curious about
the world and craved new experiences. Amir made art from
instinct; Will admired art through the lens of a scholar. I had
learned that I could not trust Amir, who had hidden within
him a capacity for violence that I could hardly bear to think
about. Will was upstanding and dependable.

But of course Amir had known so much trouble, while Will
had known only peace.

"Who is paying for this trip?" Ronnie had asked, watching me pack.

She already knew the answer, so I didn't respond.

"Merrow."

I zipped my swimsuits into an inner pocket of my bag.

"Merrow!"

I looked up at her. "Listen," I said. "I know you don't like Will. But I do. What does it matter if he pays for our trip? He knows I've always wanted to travel. We talked about it when we first met, years ago. It makes him happy to be able to do something nice for me."

"I bet it does. I'm sure it's a heady feeling to have so much money that you can make someone's dreams come true."

"Ronnie, I'm excited to go away with him." This was an understatement. I had been looking forward to the trip so much that I had hardly been able to sleep. It hurt me that Ronnie was not happy for me. "Please don't ruin it."

Her face softened. "I'm sorry. It's not that I don't like Will. He's nice. The whole family is nice. And the way he looks at you . . ."

"Yes?"

She hesitated. "It's clear he really cares for you."

I laughed. "So why do you sound so skeptical?"

"I don't know. I'm not." She ran her hand over a sundress that I had laid out on the bed and then stood. "Hang on." She left the room, returning with one of her own dresses, a white one I had always loved. "Take this. It looks great on you."

I thanked her, promising to take good care of it. Ronnie claimed that she didn't know why she was skeptical of Will, but

I thought I knew the answer. Since Will and I had started seeing each other, I was spending less and less time with her, and
she did not like the growing distance between us.

Will had many friends, and my weekends had become filled
with events at museums and restaurants and carefully decorated
homes. When, at a dinner party several weeks earlier, Will had
introduced me as a writer, I had felt a wave of pleasure move
through me. I found myself telling the table memories from my
earliest years at Horseshoe Cliff, when I'd had little for company
but the sea, the land, and my father's stories. Will's friends' attention dazzled me; I went on too long. Will watched me, his
expression amused and—I thought—proud. But when at last I
fell quiet, I was filled with regret. What would they think of me?
At best, they would decide I was eccentric—at worst, downright
odd. Within moments, though, Will put my fears to rest.

No one in this room has ever met anyone like you, he said, his
hand low on my back as he whispered in my ear. *And you've just
made each one of them fall in love with you.*

In Italy, our favorite thing to do was to get lost. In Rome, we
wandered through the shadows cast by the ancient arches of the
Colosseum. We walked the old streets and admired the stone
buildings, the way the sun hit the red roofs at dusk. In Flor-
ence, we returned each afternoon to drink red wine in the most
perfect little café that we would have missed if we had not happened to have wandered down one narrow, winding street and
then, instead of turning back, wandered farther along another.
In Venice, whenever we crossed a bridge, the light on the water

compelled us to stop and take in the view. I felt in awe of the beauty that we saw everywhere we went.

The world was so large, and I had only seen such a small part of it. I had understood this the moment our plane had lifted into the air and the coast of California, which had always felt so powerfully large, fell quickly away from view. I had never felt so distant from Horseshoe Cliff, but for the first time in years, I did not feel homesick. In fact, I felt almost as though I were someone else entirely. In a foreign country, I stood apart from the young Merrow who had lived that peculiar, wild childhood with Amir and her vicious brother and the lonesome beauty of Horseshoe Cliff. It felt natural to evolve, to take on a new shape and outlook while traveling. It was not a shameful or even a particularly intentional shift. It felt like growing up.

Will had been to Italy many times before that trip, but he looked around with the same wide-eyed excitement that I felt. When we grew hungry, he never steered us in the direction of a particular restaurant unless I asked him to. He made me feel as though he were seeing Italy through fresh eyes, each turn a new discovery.

We were discovering each other as well, of course. Traveling was an aphrodisiac. We made love in the morning and again at night, falling asleep naked with the bedsheets twisted at our feet.

One morning, my happiness vanished when I awoke to find Will's side of the bed empty. I listened for sounds from the bathroom but heard only the noises of Venice beyond the open window: a man calling to someone in Italian, water lapping against stone, the flap of wings. I sat upright.

"Will?"

There was no answer.

Panic swelled within me. For the first time in days, I thought of Bear and remembered how fragile happiness was, how easily stolen. I remembered then that the man who had checked us into the hotel had warned us of a rash of burglaries, advising us to store our passports and valuables in the safe. We were not to leave the window open.

We had left the window open all night! And now Will was gone. In my panic, these two events seemed connected. I ran to the window, but before I managed to shut it, I caught sight of Will strolling toward the hotel. He held a bouquet of flowers in his hands, a burst of pinks and oranges so bright that I was sure that even someone flying in an airplane far overhead would have spotted it and thought, *What beautiful flowers!*

"Will!" I was so relieved that I could not stop myself from yelling to him though I was naked and he was not alone on the walkway below.

He looked up, surprised, and when he saw me, he grinned and began to jog. I shut the window and locked it. When Will reached our room, he wrapped me in his arms and we toppled back onto the bed. I buried my face in his neck. Seeing my expression, he grew still, his brow furrowing.

"What is it?" he asked. "What's wrong?"

"I thought you'd left. Or . . . that something had happened to you." I heard how odd this sounded and flushed. "The hotel clerk mentioned those robberies, and I just thought . . ." I trailed off. Really, what had I thought? Why had I panicked at the sight of the empty bed?

Will smiled. "I'm not going anywhere."

I traced his jaw with my finger. I began to tell him how I had collected things when I was a child. My treasures, I had called them. They were only scraps of driftwood, stones with odd shapes or striations, sometimes an old button or a bit of string I'd found long buried in the dirt. Though I'd hidden my collections, storing them like an animal mindful of future hunger, they were always gone when I returned. For years, I thought I'd simply forgotten my hiding spots. I blamed myself for my losses. They were such little things, but I loved them so. And then, as I grew older, it was my books that went missing. I could not seem to keep track of them. And then my father died, and Bear sold the horses that had brought me such happiness. And then Bear kicked Pal, my dog, and I was convinced that the injury had led him to die in a fight with a coyote years later.

Will lay very still beside me, listening. "Your brother took those things that you loved."

"He could not stand to see me happy. If something brought me happiness, he destroyed it."

I did not mention Amir, and how Bear had treated him. It didn't feel right to bring up Amir as I lay in bed beside Will, but this story was about him, too: because I had treasured him, Bear had hated him. Amir was always in my thoughts. I was sure that Will sensed this.

Will's eyes moved back and forth between mine. How could someone who had grown up the way he had, loved by a family like his, understand? His arms enveloped me, but I felt alone. My heart sunk.

"I'm not going anywhere," he said again.

It wasn't enough. He didn't understand. And how could he when I barely understood myself? I felt myself pulling away from him.

"Merrow," he said quietly. "Bear isn't here. He can't take me from you . . . unless you let him."

This was true. I felt Bear's presence so deeply that it was nearly impossible to convince myself he wasn't in the room with us, that he had not followed me across the globe to steal my good fortune. I could not let my memory of things he had done to me as a child pull me away from Will.

This was my happiness, and I had a right to it.

Will brushed my hair off my forehead. I kissed him. I slipped my hand under his shirt and felt the warmth of his skin. He moved his hands down my body, pulling me closer to him. I felt a new sense of desperation as I kissed him, a need to *feel* more than *think*. His shirt was off and then his pants and I rocked against him, losing myself to those moments with him when our bodies were connected, my cries ones of pleasure.

Later, when we stumbled blearily from the hotel room and found a café that offered a late breakfast, I told Will that the strange thing was that Bear hated to see me happy, but he also hated to see me sad.

"Or at least, he hated to see me cry," I said. "It made him angry."

Will put down his fork. He reached across the table and took my hand. "What do you mean, 'angry'?"

I blinked. I had never told anyone, but why? For the first

time, I felt I understood what a disservice Amir and I had done to ourselves to keep Bear's treatment a secret for all those years. What good had it done us? In the end, we had still wound up separated, and far from home. It had been four years since Amir had disappeared.

"He hit me, sometimes. Or pushed me. But mostly he found other ways to punish me." I thought for a moment. "The really terrible thing, more than how he hurt me, was the fear I lived with even when he wasn't hurting me. I rarely felt safe. It was always more psychological than it seemed at the time. Nothing felt stable. I loved my home and I hated it. I even loved Bear at the same moment that I hated him. It was confusing." I cleared my throat. "And it was always worse for Amir. Always."

"Oh, Merrow. I'm so sorry. Didn't anyone see what was happening? I wish I could go back in time. I wish I'd known."

"I wouldn't have told you. Amir and I—we made a pact. We didn't want to be separated. We didn't want to leave, as crazy as that sounds. Horseshoe Cliff . . . the farm . . . the sea . . . we loved it there. It was our whole world. Even Bear couldn't destroy our love for it. Or at least we tried not to let him."

Will nodded, but I knew he could not really understand.

"But eventually Amir ran away, didn't he?" he asked.

I nodded. "I never heard from him again. And I left, too, with the help of your mother. So Bear managed to get rid of us after all. I guess in the end he won."

"No," Will said. He had not let go of my hand. "I don't think he did."

WILL CHARTERED A yacht to take us from Portofino to Monterosso al Mare, one of the towns of Cinque Terre. There, our pace slowed. We took long naps under colorful umbrellas on the beach and swam in the ocean. The Ligurian Sea was shockingly warm—an entirely different swimming experience than the one offered by the Pacific Ocean off the coast of Northern California. When I swam in California, I was always moving. I rarely allowed myself to simply bob in the water; it was too cold. The Mediterranean encouraged floating, and we obliged. I learned that Will, like his sister, Emma, was a strong swimmer. Still, while I would happily float about for an hour or longer, Will would head back to shore much sooner. He would kiss me before swimming away, teasing that he feared if I stayed out much longer, I would turn into my namesake and slip away from him forever.

If the sea encouraged floating, the town encouraged eating. A boat pulled up to the beach and offered plump anchovies and mussels in paper cups piled high with slices of lemon. For lunch, we had dry white wine and focaccia slathered with pesto.

In the afternoons, we retreated to our hotel room's shaded balcony overlooking the sun-soaked coastline. We sat in our bathing suits and let the breeze from the sea wash over us. Will read while I wrote. I had not really decided what I was working on. I wrote descriptions of the Italian landscape, snippets of dialogue. I lost myself in a world that was half real, half imagined.

It was there, on the balcony in Cinque Terre, that the sensation of being watched overcame me again for the first time since Will and I had shared that kiss months earlier in San Francisco. On a path below our balcony, a dark-haired man paused and then walked toward the sea. His bare torso was lanky; his skin brown. My heart raced. I leaned forward in my seat, Amir's name on my tongue—

The man called out in a merry torrent of Italian to someone farther down the path.

I sank back, my face flushed.

I squinted at the sparkling water, the boats bobbing offshore. How could I not think of Amir in a place like Monterosso? The cliffs around me were crowded with pastel buildings and darker than the golden bluffs of my home, but the sea that crashed against them sounded the same. The air was warmer but held the same primal scent, the half struggle, half embrace where land meets sea.

"Beautiful, isn't it?" Will asked.

I looked over at him. He sat back in his chair, shirtless, his arms speckled with the ghostly kisses of Ligurian sea salt. His hair was turning blonder and more disheveled by the hour. He looked relaxed, his smile vaguely suggestive.

"You know," I said, "this place suits you. The water brings out the blue of your eyes. I didn't think it was possible for your eyes to be bluer than they already were, but the Ligurian Sea has proved me wrong."

He clapped his book shut. "Well, that's it then." He stood and walked around the table and pulled me up, laughing, into his arms. "We'll just have to stay forever."

WE FLEW FIRST class back to San Francisco, just as we had on the way to Italy. Our seats were even the same, 1A and 1B. I wondered if it was the same plane. I had never in my life experienced two weeks that had passed so quickly. I wasn't sure I liked the feeling. Our time in Italy already seemed like a beautiful dream. I was glad that I had written so much of it down in my journal. I drank the glass of champagne that was offered to me and it helped to steady the fluttery feeling in my stomach. Will held my hand and listened as the flight attendant detailed our strategy for survival in case of emergency. I rested my head on Will's shoulder, overcome by a rush of love for him.

I wondered if life went by more quickly when it was easy, if that was the trade-off you accepted.

THE LETTER HAD arrived while I was away.

When Ronnie mentioned that I had received mail, for some reason, I immediately thought of being on the balcony in Monterosso, the sensation that I was being watched, the man who had looked so much like Amir.

A thorny sensation spread across my throat when I saw Bear's scraggly handwriting on the envelope. I opened the letter with shaking hands. There was no polite buffer of "Dear Merrow" on which to hang any hope. He simply said what he had to say, and in so doing, yanked me back in time.

> *I know what you did to Rei. You and him.*
> *I want my money. You don't get to run off with it.*
> *I know what you did, Merrow Shawe. All that you have, I can take away.*

CHAPTER SEVENTEEN

Rei's bank account must have finally run dry. Though I did
not have much money to spare, I began to send Bear a little
each month. I hoped it would be enough to keep him from
ruining the pleasure I had found in my work with Learning
Together, my friendships with Rosalie and Emma and Ronnie,
my relationship with Will. What would they say if Bear told
them that he believed that Amir and I had killed Rei and stolen
her money? I lived in fear of him showing up at my work. At
night, I felt his grip around my calf, his fingers pressing an old
wound.

The money I sent was not enough for Bear. He threatened
to come to San Francisco. I hid his letters in a box at the back
of my closet. I kept the stone that Amir had given to me in
that box as well, and so every time I received a letter from
Bear, I also thought of Amir. But I was always thinking of
Amir, really. Amir lived inside of me. He lived in the stories
I wrote, in the characters that had a connection to the earth,
the children without parents, the men who loved and hated

with equal passion. I saw him in each child whom I sat beside at Learning Together. I did not know where Amir was, but I knew that he was alive. I felt his presence when I went for icy swims in the ocean. I continued to feel that I was being watched, and I preferred to think that it was Amir doing the watching, or the spirit of my mother or my father or even Rei, rather than Bear circling ever closer.

WITH WILL BY my side over the following years, I saw parts of the world that as a girl I had hardly dared to hope I might someday see. Brazil. Alaska. Japan. France. Egypt. The more we traveled, the more I understood how uncomfortable I felt when I was not near a coast. When we visited places that were inland, away from a body of water, I felt unsettled. No matter where I was, my thoughts traveled to Horseshoe Cliff. When I was a teenager, each home I had broken into had left me longing for a new life; now, each new place I visited left me longing for a home to which I could not return. This feeling did not erase when I returned to San Francisco. There was something within me that held itself apart from the city; untouched for years, it began to ache. On buses, the windows shut against the wind, the ache worsened. When I walked, I was aware, always, of the pavement below me. I missed the soft yield of dirt below my feet. The golden glow of the cliffs at sunset. The black velvet night sky strewn with an extravagance of stars. Horseshoe Cliff was mine by then—I'd inherited a third of the land on my eighteenth birthday—but I wondered if I would ever see it again.

Once each month, Will and I had dinner with his family. If it had been up to me, we would have seen them more often. I adored the Langfords, and I did not like when too much time passed between visits. Will thought my love for his family was sweet, but he preferred to maintain a bit more space from them. I continued to swim with Emma, and I snuck in lunches with Rosalie between our monthly dinners.

During these meetings, Rosalie and I spoke of my work at the tutoring center, and my writing. We talked about the latest art exhibits and plays that she had seen. We rarely spoke about Will, or my relationship with him. I did not know whether to think that was odd or normal. One day I simply asked her.

"Don't you want to know how Will and I are doing?"

She glanced up from the leek soup she had ordered, her spoon paused midair. "Aren't you doing well? Everything seemed fine at our last dinner." Her expression grew concerned. "What happened? Did you have a fight?"

"No, no. But you never ask me about him, and I don't know if that's because you don't want to pry . . . or if you . . ." I trailed off.

"If I don't approve of you dating my son?" When Rosalie set down her spoon it made a surprisingly loud clatter. "Merrow Shawe. How could you even begin to think that? You are a lovely couple. You're perfect together, really. I've never seen either of you as happy as you seem to be when you're together."

Even as I felt relieved, I wondered if her assessment was true. Was I happier than I'd ever been? In so many ways, I was. And yet there was a void inside of me that throbbed even at that very moment as I sat so calmly across from Rosalie.

Her smile wavered. She seemed to be considering saying more, and then she did. "If I'm being honest, the only thing that worries me is the possibility that the hesitation you sense isn't mine, but your own. Will is in love with you. I believe that when he looks at you, he sees his future."

I found that I was holding my breath as I listened to her. She noticed and reached across the table to give my hand a sympathetic pat.

"If I were your mother," she said, "I would tell you that you should not run from joy. I would remind you that you deserve love. I would say that just because something is easy doesn't mean it is wrong." She pulled her hand back and rested it in her lap. "I would tell you not to live in the past when there are people right here in your present who love you so very much."

I swallowed. It had been nearly eight years since I had last seen Amir. "It's hard to let go."

"Oh, Merrow. You don't need to let go. Just free up one hand so you can hold on to someone else, too."

SIX MONTHS LATER, Will gave me a large blue sapphire ring and asked me to marry him. When I said yes, he slipped the ring onto my finger. It was the most beautiful piece of jewelry I'd ever seen.

"Is it okay that it's not a diamond?" he asked. "I thought you might like this better. It's an antique. The stone reminded me of you—well, of us, really. It made me think of our time in Italy."

I looked at him, feeling overwhelmed with love. "The Ligurian Sea."

Will nodded. He was right; the stone looked like the Ligurian Sea, which was the very color of his eyes. I loved that ring with a ferocity that sometimes confused me. I had never had a ring before, and I felt different with one on my finger. *What a strange comfort a circle is,* I thought, *with no beginning or end but only that smooth, eternal curve.*

What I soon learned—what we both learned—was that, for me, that ring was enough. Having an actual wedding ceremony did not strike me as particularly important. When we were first engaged, Will and I spoke, vaguely, about the idea of a spring wedding, but the spring quickly came and went. Instead of planning a wedding, we spent much of our time looking at houses. The prices were astounding to me, but Will had plenty of money. My own salary barely covered my living expenses and my portion of the rent for the apartment I shared with Ronnie. I had always known that the Langfords were rich, but it was only as Will and I were house hunting, and our realtor continually flashed her big, excited smile at me and cooed over my engagement ring, that I realized I was rich now, too.

I longed for a home by the sea. Will preferred a house that was on the Bay, closer to his office. But one day the realtor showed us a house in Sea Cliff with a small balcony off the master bedroom that overlooked the ocean, and when we stepped out onto it, I could see immediately how much Will liked it. The water below was not the jewellike blue of the Ligurian Sea, and the sandy crescent of Baker Beach was not dotted with bright umbrellas, and of course the view of the Golden Gate Bridge left no question as to our location, but still, there was something about that balcony that was undeniably reminiscent of the balcony off our hotel room in Monterosso. There was even a small bistro table with two chairs angled in an inviting way.

Will grinned at me. He gestured toward the table. "Did you set this up?"

I laughed and shook my head in wonder. "It's amazing, isn't it?"

The realtor looked back and forth between the two of us, her expression equally baffled and delighted. She backed toward the bedroom door. "I'll leave you two to discuss," she said, and disappeared inside.

It seemed like fate that this house had come on the market just as Will and I were searching. I leaned against the railing and looked out. I breathed in the sea air and felt a sense of peace. I already knew how this house would feel when the fog rolled in, buffering it from the world. It would become a fortress, safe and glowing with warmth amid a silver sky. I knew how the ocean would sound at night from the bed when the door to the balcony was left open, and I knew that the cold, wet air would creep in and wash over everything, leaving a hint of salt on my lips. I knew how it would feel to walk on the beach that lay below early in the morning before anyone else was awake, and how the green sea glass that would wash up onshore would feel in my hand, something once sharp now softened by the grip of the sea.

In the distance, across the mouth of the Bay, mountains rose from the ocean. My mother had taken my father to the beach on the day they met and pointed at the same view that I was looking at now. My father had said that the idea of living by the sea had seemed like the most wonderful sort of dream.

Even without turning around, I could feel Will watching me.

He walked to me and put his arms around me. "I love it, too."

"But it's so far from your office."

He looked over my shoulder, taking in the view. "It's perfect. It's ruined any other house for me."

The thing about Will was that, as much as he did love that house's balcony—and he did, I could see that—he was saying the house was perfect because he knew that I thought it was perfect. His kindness moved me. I rested my head on his chest and tried to breathe in his particular no-smell smell, but I smelled only the sea.

It was on that balcony a few months later that we first discussed the idea of eloping. There was a larger patio on the first floor of the house, but we found ourselves gravitating to that little balcony nearly every weekend. I wrote and Will read. There was so much that I loved about Will, but his devotion to reading was near the top of the list. He read as quickly as I did, and we had already made plans to install floor-to-ceiling bookshelves in the living room downstairs as well as in our bedroom to house our ever-growing collection.

It was funny, though, how differently we treated our books. *I see your books like to swim as much as you do,* Will had said, smiling, as he helped me unpack the boxes that I'd brought from the apartment I'd shared with Ronnie. The novels in his hands were bloated with salt air from trips to the beach, their pages dog-eared and marked by my pen. Will's books, I realized, were pristine. He treated them with a reverence that I supposed I understood but did not quite share. I thought that perhaps Will thought of books as possessions while I thought of them as sustenance. His relationship with books lacked the messiness and the hunger and the desperate sort of joy that mine held.

While Will read on the balcony that day, I worked on a story inspired by a coyote that I had seen recently while walking down our street toward the beach for my swim. After Pal's death, I hated coyotes. But for some reason my bitterness did not flare at the sight of this one in the city; on the contrary, wonder spilled over me like water. The coyote had seemed both ephemeral and eternal, like a reminder of a not-so-distant other world, or another point in time that might be in the future as easily as in the past.

"You always look peaceful when you're writing," Will said.

I looked up blearily. "Do I?" I laughed. "No, that can't be true." I could feel my forehead smoothing as I spoke; it was always furrowed when I wrote, I was sure of it, and I spent as much time chewing on the end of my pencil as I did writing.

"Well," Will admitted, "maybe *peaceful* is the wrong word. Transported? Wherever you go when you're writing, you like it there." He closed the book he was reading. "You know, if you ever want more time to write . . . I hope you know you can have it."

"Are you telling me you have the power to make the days

longer?" I teased. "Why have you never shared this with me before?"

He smiled. "I just mean that if you ever decide that you want to leave your job—or take a break from it—so that you have more time to write, I'd support you."

I knew he was only trying to be sweet, but I was surprised that he thought that leaving Learning Together would be something I wanted. "I like spending time with those kids. I like helping them."

A crease formed between his eyebrows. "I know you do. And you *are* helping them. I just know how much your stories are going to help kids, too—bringing them happiness, inspiring them. I'm thinking of your future readers. It's funny, but when we first saw this house, I immediately pictured you sitting at this table, just as you are now, looking so gorgeous and full of thought, gazing out at the water and writing."

It was a lovely image. So why did my throat tighten as he spoke? Did a part of Will think of me as he thought of his books, as something curious and beautiful and fragile, deserving of admiration and careful handling? I did not want to be a well-kept possession.

Perhaps I was being too hard on him. It was simply easier for Will to understand my relationship with writing than my relationship with children who had nowhere to go when school let out. But I could not think of writing without thinking of Horseshoe Cliff—and children who needed stories, yes, but so much else, too.

When I thought of Horseshoe Cliff, I felt very distant from

Will. It wasn't a feeling that I liked. There was nothing for me at my childhood home—only Bear, scratching out letters to me that were full of threats. This was my home now, the one I'd made with the man I loved.

"We should get married," I said.

He laughed, surprised. "I thought we'd already reached that conclusion."

"But soon, I mean. Let's go to city hall. And then let's take a honeymoon somewhere far away, somewhere even you have never been."

Will thought about it. "But *some* sort of celebration would be nice, wouldn't it? To mark the beginning of a new chapter in our lives? My parents would appreciate it. We could do it here, at home."

"A wedding party?"

"Or an engagement party. We never had one. It really doesn't matter what we call it. I just think it would be nice to celebrate with our family and friends."

While I was satisfied to have just Will, his family, and Ronnie in my life, Will's network of friends continued to grow. Being surrounded by people made him happy, and it felt selfish to deny him this pleasure.

And so I agreed, swallowing the knot that formed in my throat as I did so.

PART THREE

CHAPTER EIGHTEEN

A month later, when Amir emerged from the shadows outside the home that Will and I shared, my world went still for a beat of time that was as fragile as a shell, as vast as an ocean. I thought of Rosalie telling me that there are moments in your life when you can feel everything change. I thought of my mother standing on the edge of a cliff, the land below her feet crumbling. I thought of my father taking in his first breath of salt air, feeling his chest swell with new life.

"Merrow," Amir said. Everything about him was different, and yet the same. His voice hooked something deep inside of me, pulling me toward him. His arms were around me then, holding me tightly. It was Amir, solid and strong and *real*. I buried my face in his neck. The city was silent. I felt the sensation of wings beating within my chest and remembered the red bird I had swallowed in my dream the night before.

"I thought I might never see you again," I whispered.

Energy roiled from him, and this I recognized. He was always coiled tightly, his anger crouched and poised and quivering. Waiting. He was so much bigger than he'd been at sixteen. The arms hugging me were roped with muscle, the chest to which I pressed my cheek was broad. How different things might have been if Amir had had this strength when we were children. I looked up at him and touched my thumb to the scar over his eyebrow. His dark hair was clipped so short that I could see the smooth shape of his scalp. His eyes were both mournful and yearning; they roamed my face. I remembered this feeling—this feeling of being known, of being beloved.

"What happened?" I asked. Relief and anger and fear each threatened to choke my words before I could release them. "How could you have left—"

"Merrow?"

Amir's eyes lifted away from mine, moving over my shoulder, and a veil dropped over his expression. I turned, letting him go. Will stood beside Emma near the open garage door. Music spilled out of the house. Our engagement party. In the moments that my arms had been around Amir, I had forgotten it.

"Will . . ." There was a high, breathless quality to my voice.

Will squinted. "Amir?"

"In the flesh," said Amir.

Will and Emma moved to stand beside me.

"What a surprise. It's nice to see you," Will said. The two men shook hands.

After a moment, I said, "We're having a party."

Amir's gaze moved over my face, my dress. "I see."

I could not pull my eyes from him. "Emma," I said, without looking at her. "Do you remember Amir? You were very young when you met." I spoke in a daze. There was so much I wanted to ask Amir, and I couldn't bear that we'd been interrupted. I stared at him, unabashed. If he turned and walked away right then, I wanted to have him memorized, this new Amir. He did not take his eyes from mine, either. The smallest hint of a smile tugged at his lips.

"I remember. I'm not *that* young!" Emma said. "But do you remember me, Amir?" The question held a note of flirtation, and I remembered how tipsy Emma had been earlier in the evening. It felt like a lifetime had passed since we'd spoken on the patio.

Amir slowly moved his eyes from mine to look at Emma. His teeth were still as white as shells and rounded in a way that softened the forced smile he gave her.

"You're Will's sister. And you've grown up to be beautiful. That's no surprise." Amir's voice was suddenly flat. I realized that he'd managed to compliment Emma and withdraw the compliment in practically the same breath, implying her beauty was predictable, and unaffecting.

But Emma blushed. "Really?" She looked down at her dress and then clasped and unclasped her long fingers. "That's, well . . . thank you."

Will slipped his arm around my waist.

"I don't want to keep you all from the party," Amir said.

"Don't be ridiculous," I said.

"Oh, but you have to come in!" said Emma. "You'll stay, won't you?"

"If the lady of the house will have me."

My laughter sounded strange. "'The lady of the house.' When did you start speaking like that? Of course you should come in." I hoped he didn't hear my hesitation. I couldn't stand the thought of Amir leaving, but the idea of him in the home that I shared with Will . . .

"Fantastic," Emma said, looking back and forth between the three of us. "It's settled then."

"I'm underdressed," said Amir. He wore a black sweater and a neat pair of jeans, both of which fit him well but didn't appear particularly expensive.

"You look great!" Emma gushed. She ducked her head and laughed then, embarrassed.

A spark of humor played in Amir's eye when he glanced at me. That fluttering feeling rose in my chest again.

I watched as Emma linked her arm through Amir's. Did I imagine that he cringed at her touch? I must have, because he gazed down at Emma thoughtfully, as though seeing her for the first time, and in response to his study Emma seemed to pull him closer. As they walked away, I watched Emma tilt her chin up toward Amir and say something I could not hear. With my pulse pounding in my ears, I took Will's arm and followed them.

"Merrow?" Will called from bed.

I stood at the sink in our bathroom, washing my face. In the mirror, my skin looked raw, the makeup I'd worn for the party wiped away. But I continued splashing water against my cheeks. My mind raced. I longed to go for a swim. I could not imagine how I would ever fall asleep. I yanked a towel from the hook beside the sink and patted my face dry.

"Hmm?" I said, standing at the doorway between the bathroom and bedroom.

Will offered a wary smile. "I was saying that I thought Amir looked well, didn't he?"

I stretched beside him under the covers and rested my head on his chest. "He looked different."

"Yes. But the same, too. His expression is the same."

I murmured my agreement.

"What has he been doing all this time? Were you able to catch up with him?"

"Not really," I said. To my surprise and frustration, Emma had not left Amir's side all night, and she had not picked up on any of my hints to give us time alone. Even when my hints had grown less subtle and more forthright, she had ignored them—either willingly or simply drunkenly, I wasn't sure. As a result, every word Amir and I had exchanged at the party was in front of Emma. I learned only that Amir was living in California, working at a farm in a northern corner of the state.

Eventually we were the only four left in the house, save for the caterers wiping down the counters in the kitchen. Amir looked toward the windows. The ocean was a silky expanse glittering darkly below the moon. His eyes met mine.

"I should go."

My stomach twisted. "Don't," I said. "There's no reason to leave."

"I'm not at all tired," Emma announced.

We turned to Will at the very moment he lifted his hand to cover a yawn. He gave a sheepish laugh. "And I was just about to say that I'm not tired, either."

"It's late," Amir said. He walked toward the door and all three of us trailed after him.

"Where will you go?" I asked.

"I have a hotel room downtown."

"Let's share a car!" said Emma. "I'm staying at my parents' house tonight."

"I thought you were spending the night here, Emma," I said. "There's plenty of room."

She laughed. "It's practically your wedding night! I wouldn't dream of it."

"It's not our wedding night." I knew how annoyed I sounded. Will reached for my hand. I stared at the floor. My emotions made me feel as though I were carrying an enormous bowl that at any moment might fall from my hands, sending shards in the direction of anyone unlucky enough to find himself near me.

"I'll take you home," I heard Amir say to Emma. I lifted my eyes from the ground to stare at him.

"Oh! Really? Okay, um, great!" With her pink cheeks, Emma looked like a beautiful doll. "I'll get my coat." She hurried down the hall, away from us.

"Get her home safely, will you, Amir?" Will asked quietly once Emma was out of sight.

Amir nodded.

"Tomorrow, Amir," I said. The realization that he was moments from walking out our door filled me with anguish. "Tomorrow morning. Can we have breakfast? There's so much to catch up on."

Emma returned before Amir could respond. I watched as he helped her into her coat. At last, he turned to me. "Yes. I'll get your number from Emma."

And then, with a flutter of kisses and waves from Emma and nothing more than a nod from Amir, they were gone.

I LAY IN bed beside Will and tried not to think of what Amir and Emma might be doing at that very moment. Surely, he had simply dropped her off at her parents' house and then returned, alone, to his hotel room?

And if he hadn't? If they were in each other's arms just as Will and I were at that very moment? The jealousy that roared in my chest, lapping at my heart with its searing tongue, was a feeling that I had never experienced. For every stab of jealousy came one of guilt. What right had I to feel jealous? I was engaged to Will. We were getting married in a few weeks.

Unable to lie still, I hurried from the bed to the window. I opened it and breathed in the cold ocean air. The waves offered their usual whispers, and for one moment I was a young girl again at Horseshoe Cliff, alone with my only friend, the sea.

When Will spoke, I started. "Can't sleep?" he asked. I looked back at him. Our white bedspread seemed to glow in the moonlight.

I nodded.

"It's a shock, I'm sure. Seeing him again. The relief must be overwhelming."

"Yes." My emotions did feel overwhelming. Either I would drown in them, or I would pick a direction and begin to swim.

"Come here." Will's voice was gentle. "Leave the window open if you're hot. I don't mind."

He lifted the covers and I crawled into bed beside him.

"Oh, Merrow," he said, touching my cheek.

It was the first time in nine years I'd let anyone see me cry.

CHAPTER NINETEEN

The next morning, Amir knocked on the door without calling first. He looked as I did—as though he'd hardly slept. I ignored the sharp twist in my stomach—had he been with Emma?—and embraced him. He smelled exactly as he always had, earthy and warm and something else that was mysteriously, entirely him.

"Let's go for a walk," he said.

I nodded and asked him to give me a moment. In the kitchen, Will looked up at me expectantly. A mug of steaming coffee and an unopened book sat on the table in front of him. The light in the kitchen was soft; the sun was still working its way into the sky. We had shared many quiet mornings at that table.

"Amir's here?"

I nodded. I walked over to him and sat on his lap. It wasn't something that I normally did, but I felt drawn to him. There was a heaviness inside of me that I could not shake. Will wrapped me in his arms.

"He wants to go on a walk."

Will was quiet for a moment before nodding. "That's a good idea. It's a beautiful morning."

"We won't be long."

He kissed me. I leaned into him, remembering, suddenly, our first kiss on the balcony of his parents' house, and how I had initiated it. I had so wanted him to love me, and even now it surprised me to know that he did.

I HAD BARELY closed the front door behind me when I told Amir about Bear's letters.

"He's been writing for years," I said in an urgent rush. "Threatening to tell Will that we killed Rei and stole her money." It was both terrifying and a relief to finally say these words out loud.

"A threat sent by letter," Amir said drily. "How civilized. I wouldn't have guessed Bear had it in him."

"Amir."

When he looked at me, the amusement drained from his expression. His eyes darkened. "So I killed Rei. That's what you believe."

I felt my hands begin to shake. It was as though time fell away and I was standing in Rei's room. The sight of her unnaturally still body, the terrible expression on her face—a look of panic and fright and pain that she had never worn in life. The indented pillow beside her. The empty box that had once held so much money.

"I never wanted to believe that." My voice quivered with emotion. "But what choice did you leave me? Rei died and you went missing on the same day. Her money—the money that we discovered together—was gone. I have fought for nine years not to think of you as a murderer. That you could do that to Rei . . . it's not possible. But I also didn't think it was possible for you to leave me. And you did."

Amir raised his eyebrows. "*I* left *you*? You were the one who fell in love with the Langfords and decided they were your ticket out of Horseshoe Cliff."

His words were cold, but his delivery was not. He spoke in a voice that was thick with a pain that burned with equal measure within me.

"I would never have left without you," I said as we stepped onto the beach. "Rosalie Langford was going to help you. I made her promise that she would. She was going to help *both* of us get away from Bear. I wanted us to leave together."

A complicated series of expressions washed over Amir's face. He ran his hand over his shorn head, and when he did, I felt the nerve endings in my own hand come alive, imagining that his hand was mine, imagining the feel of his cropped hair against my skin. I had never experienced such an intense longing as I did in that moment. I gripped my hands together so that I wouldn't reach for him.

"I didn't know," he said. "I only heard you tell Rei that you were leaving." His eyes flickered with hurt and anger. "You were so excited. So happy. You couldn't wait to get away."

"That's true. I wanted to get as far away from Bear as I could. I wanted to go to college. I wanted to see more, to do more. But I always wanted to do it with you, Amir. I would never have left you the way that you left me. I trusted you. I thought you trusted me."

When he didn't immediately respond, I began walking faster, heading toward the ocean. I had not made it far when his hand encircled mine.

"I'm sorry," he said. His words were weighted with sadness. "I'm sorry that I left you. I made a terrible mistake. Not a day has passed that I have not thought of you and wished I had done things differently."

A current of desire swept through me. When I hugged Amir, it was difficult to let go. Our bodies remembered each other. We sat side by side in the sand and looked out at the sea, our arms touching as though forming a seal. I was aware of every breath he took. I was even aware, I was certain, of the restless beating of his heart. My attraction to him brought with it a wave of shame, as it always had. I was not allowed to love him as I did. Not then, and certainly not now, when I was engaged to Will.

"I heard you talking to Rei that day after you came back from the Langfords' house," he said. "I thought you were planning to leave without me. I felt frantic. I couldn't think clearly. I thought I was angry, but now I think I was more confused than anything. When you came home, you didn't look like the Merrow that I knew. You dressed differently. It seemed like you were looking at everything at Horseshoe Cliff in a new way. When I overheard you talking to Rei, you didn't even sound like you. I couldn't believe that you would go off without me. I told myself that maybe I'd just been imagining this relationship that didn't actually exist. We never talked about it . . . about us. Everything that I'd ever thought had passed between us, I suddenly doubted. It made me feel crazy."

He hung his head. "And then I remembered the money. Rei's money. I was going to ask her if I could borrow some to buy new equipment for the farm, and then I was going to use the money to run away. When I got to her house, it looked like she was home, but she didn't answer the door. I was worried. I climbed in through her bathroom window and . . . she was in her bed, and she wasn't breathing. I tried to wake her, but her skin was cold. She looked scared. I hated that she had died like that, alone. I didn't know what to do."

His voice was so thin and strained that I knew this memory of Rei had haunted his dreams just as it had haunted mine. All these years, we had been kept awake at night by the same memory, the same recurring nightmare. Our beloved Rei, frightened and alone as she faced death. Amir had not killed Rei. He had loved her. He had not run to her in anger, but in sadness.

"I couldn't imagine living at Horseshoe Cliff without you and without Rei," Amir said. "I just . . . I made a decision."

"You took the money."

He nodded. It seemed he could not bring himself to look at me.

"And the tiny house that you made with my father. That first one you carved together."

Now he turned to me, surprised. "How did you—?"

"I was there. Later. I wanted Rei to help me find you."

"So you saw her."

I nodded.

"I didn't kill her."

"I know. I believe you. Of course I believe you." I swallowed. "I was devastated when you left. Everything you just said . . . about feeling as though your world was ripped away from you, doubting everyone and everything . . . I felt that, too."

"Oh, Merrow."

I looked into his brown eyes and felt all the emotions of those years well within me. "You broke my heart."

His face twisted. He put his arms around me. "I wish I could go back. I wish I'd known."

For a moment, I felt myself sinking into his embrace. Though I longed to remain there, I pulled back. If Will stepped onto our bedroom's balcony and looked down toward the beach, he would see us. I hated the thought of hurting him.

"Where did you go?" I asked.

"I hitchhiked north. I'd sleep in the woods and wake up and hope for another ride. I kept going until I found a farm that needed an extra hand."

"And that's where you've been for all this time?"

"Yes and no. After a few years, another farm up north—a school, actually—offered me a job."

"A school?"

He nodded. "A farm school. They teach farming skills to people of all ages. They heard that I knew about dry farming and asked me to speak to their students. Next thing I knew, I was living there full-time, teaching in their program. I've snuck some whittling into the curriculum, too."

"Amir. My dad would be so proud of you."

He blinked, ducking his head. "I hope so."

"I know so." I was aware still of our arms, touching.

"I never spent Rei's money, you know. Well, I spent some of it. Just at the beginning. But eventually I opened a bank account and the money has been sitting in it for years. I don't know what to do with it now."

I realized that he had never learned about Rei's will. "A third of that money is yours. She gave her house to the Osha Conservation Fund, but she left all of her money to you, Bear, and me. In a way, you took the money from Bear and me, not from Rei."

As Amir listened, I could see surprise and relief wash over him. I realized how heavily, and for how long, taking that money from Rei had weighed on him.

"You know, I visited Japan a few years ago," he told me. "I took a cooking class there from a woman who spoke English with Rei's voice."

"Japan? How did you end up there?"

"The farm school has a cross-cultural mission. Teachers come from all over the world and travel all over the world."

I was astonished. "Where else did you go?"

"Costa Rica. Ireland. France."

Amir, who had never wanted to leave Horseshoe Cliff! "Well?" I prodded.

His grin was bound by invisible thread to my heart. "It was wonderful. The history, the stories . . . everywhere I traveled, I thought of you."

After a moment, I pulled my eyes from his. "I've been teaching, too." I told him about the children with whom I worked.

"Many of them come from families that are struggling. We give the kids food, a safe place to spend their after-school hours, academic tutoring, art classes, the consistency of a familiar face."

"You're their Rei."

I leaned my head on Amir's shoulder. No one had ever known me as deeply as he had known me. "I suppose so. Yes." I remembered Will and shifted away again. "Do you think I should go up to Horseshoe Cliff? Maybe if we give Bear the money that Rei left him and we tell him the truth—that neither of us had anything to do with Rei's death—he'll finally leave me alone."

Amir's expression darkened. "You don't need to worry about Bear."

"What do you mean? Have you been up there?"

He looked out toward the horizon. "The farm school was a good place for me, but it was never my true home. Horseshoe Cliff is my home. I finally went back last week. Bear is a drunk. He always was, but it's worse now. You would hardly recognize him. The cottage is ruined. He's living in a trailer near the road. The garden and the orchard haven't been tended in years. I don't think anything has grown there since we left. When he's sober enough, he does odd jobs for people in town who have good memories of Jacob, but they're really just giving Bear handouts."

I felt sick. All three of our lives—mine, Amir's, Bear's—had changed the moment I met the Langfords. The thought that Bear was now someone I would not recognize wrenched something inside of me. I was surprised to find myself worried about him. I had tried to stop loving him, but I had never succeeded.

"I should go up there," I said.

"Don't feel sorry for him. He did this to himself."

"But still—"

"He hurt us. He was supposed to take care of us but instead he hurt us. I still have trouble sleeping—I wake up with the weight of Bear on my chest, pinning me down. In my sleep, I'm a little boy who doesn't have the strength to fight back. I wake up swinging my arms at the air, relieved that I can move them, that if I needed to I could finally stop him from hurting us. But what does that matter now?" Amir's expression was so haunted that I longed to take him in my arms. "Have you forgotten what it was like, Merrow? Bear doesn't deserve your kindness."

"I haven't forgotten. Even if I wanted to forget, his letters keep his voice in my ear."

Amir was silent for a moment. His eyes narrowed as he looked out at the water. "Rei had a pulmonary embolism. There was an autopsy. A friend of mine looked into it for me years ago. Bear knows how she died. He knows that we didn't have anything to do with it. He's been blackmailing you over nothing. He knows exactly what his letters do to you."

My heart thudded in my ears. Time would never diminish Bear's cruelty.

Still, when I felt for it, the sliver of love that I felt for my brother needled me.

"When Doctor Clark and Rei's lawyer came to our house to let us know that the money Rei had left us was missing," I told Amir, "Bear didn't tell them that you had disappeared on the same night. He could have had the police chasing you, but he didn't. After all those years of hating you, in the end, he kept you safe."

Confusion flickered in Amir's gaze. He looked away from me. "Even if you go up there, you won't find him. I told him he needed to get off my property."

I stared at him. "What do you mean?"

"It's mine now. His share of Horseshoe Cliff. I won it from him in a few games of poker."

"Amir!"

"Don't look at me like that. Bear forced me to sleep in a shed when I was a kid. We lived in the most beautiful place on earth, and he managed to give me nightmares. Believe me, taking that land was the most peaceful of the retributions I've considered."

"But you said he's a drunk—"

"He wasn't drunk when he signed this contract." He pulled a folded paper from his pocket. Bear's signature was scratched at the bottom. "I made him sign it when he was in the middle of painting someone's house in town. He was sober enough to know what he was doing. He didn't even argue with me. So now I own two shares, and you own the third. Horseshoe Cliff is yours and mine."

I hardly knew how to respond. "Was he drunk when you won the card game?"

He slipped the contract back into his pocket. "It wasn't just one card game. I stayed there for three nights, and every night he wanted to gamble another piece of his land. He kept losing, but he insisted we keep playing. He knew what he was doing. He could have stopped the whole thing, and he didn't."

If time had mellowed my hatred of my brother, I could not expect that Amir's feelings would always match my own. We were not the same person, no matter how often it had felt like we had shared our thoughts when we were children.

"So this is why you came back," I said. "For revenge."

Amir held my gaze with his velvet, dark-rimmed eyes. "No. I'd like to never think about Bear again. I'd like to find a way to move past the way he treated us. No, Merrow, revenge is not the reason I came back."

"Then why?" I asked, though of course he did not need to respond. I could feel his words traveling through me even before he spoke them.

"I came back because I want my body to be where my heart has always been." He reached for my hand.

"But Amir," I said gently, and with some trouble. "I'm with Will. We're engaged."

"You're not married yet. You've known him a long time. What have you been waiting for?"

I didn't have an answer. "Why do you want Horseshoe Cliff? Everything Bear put you through . . . didn't it poison the place for you?"

Amir gave me a sad smile. "No. I had you, my antidote to every poison."

Tears stung my eyes. "How is that possible?" I asked. "How can we feel that way when it was always so hard? When there was never enough to eat? For so many years, we were alone with Bear and his rage. There was no one to look after us or love us the way a parent would."

I watched, almost as though in a trance, as Amir lifted my hand. He pressed his lips to my skin. "It's possible because we had each other."

Yes. Without Amir, I would have looked back on my childhood and seen the gaping loss where love should have been. Instead, I thought of how we built towers made of smooth gray stones. I thought of running through a veil of fog in the eucalyptus grove. I thought of swimming beside him in the icy sea, each of us daring the other to go farther, to be stronger. I thought of lying on the dirt floor of the shed, under the gaze of the red birds we had made, laughing and sharing stories. I thought of us singing together in a cave that glowed at sunset.

Who would I have been without Amir? I had no interest in knowing. My love for him was as surprising and nourishing and true as the plants that broke through the soil my father was told could never sustain a garden. Our love was a sprout of green, a burst of wild and unexpected beauty.

And yet—this knowledge pained me. What could I do with my love for Amir, and his love for me, when I also loved Will? I pulled my hand from Amir's.

"You'll pay Bear for his share of the land, won't you?"

Amir's face clouded. He released a sharp laugh. "You don't pay for things that you win."

"But where will he go?"

"I don't care. As long as he's not at Horseshoe Cliff."

It was as hard to think of Horseshoe Cliff without thinking of Bear as it was to think of Horseshoe Cliff without thinking of Amir.

"Drive up there with me," he said. "It's our land now. You must want to see it."

He was right. I longed for Horseshoe Cliff. I wasn't sure if I could have faced it again without Amir by my side, but with him . . . I wasn't sure there was anything that could have kept me away.

In the house I shared with Will, nothing looked quite as it had before my walk with Amir. Usually when I opened the front door and stepped inside, I felt contentment wash over me, but now I felt only unease. The smooth walnut table that held an oversized book of photographs of the Great Barrier Reef, the painted ceramic wine carafe that Will and I had bought together in Rab, an island off the coast of Croatia, even the framed photographs of the two of us that dotted the mantel, all took on a disconcertingly unfamiliar sheen. I paused in the entryway, peering into the rooms that surrounded me. I had a feeling of time folding over itself. I was fifteen years old, walking through a stranger's house, studying her life. The jeans I wore were too big—boys' jeans, once Bear's—and tattered at every hem. The backs of my hands were sun-darkened, my nails dirty and gnawed short. But my heart was buoyant with the understanding that I was not alone in this life. *I love,* thumped its steady beat. *And I am loved.*

"Merrow?"

I blinked. Will walked toward me from the doorway to the kitchen.

"Are you all right? Did something happen?"

"No." I shook my head. "I mean, yes, I'm fine."

He led me to the den. I had come to love that room more than I'd thought I would, considering it offered no view of the ocean. It was smaller than most of the rooms in the house, but it was always warm and dark, the perfect spot to curl against my fiancé and watch a movie.

Now, though, something in the room seemed wrong. It was the rug, I thought. I'd shopped for it with Rosalie. We'd chosen a burgundy color that now struck me as ugly. It wasn't Rosalie's fault; we'd both fallen in love with it at the store, running our hands over it as though it were a living thing that might feel our affection and return it.

Remembering how happy I had been to spend that day with Rosalie, a surge of sorrow rose within me.

"What's wrong?" Will asked again, guiding me to sit beside him on the sofa. "Tell me. Did Amir say why he came back?"

"He wants Horseshoe Cliff. And he wants to make Bear suffer." I didn't voice the other reason that Amir had returned. "You know how awful Bear was to us when we were kids, and he always treated Amir worse than he treated me. In a way, even once Amir left, the torturing didn't stop for him. He's been haunted by what Bear subjected him to, the physical and mental abuse. I think he'd like to ruin Bear's life."

Will put his arm around my shoulders. "Oh, Merrow."

"I don't blame him. Most of me believes that Bear deserves whatever is coming to him."

"Most of you?"

I swallowed. "Amir said that my brother is drunk all the time. It's even worse than it was when we were kids. And he's ruined what was left of our home, the garden, and the orchard."

I knew from Will's expression that he was wondering what was left to be ruined—in his eyes, the property was already a wreck the one time he'd seen it nine years earlier. My pride stung. But Will was unfailingly polite; he didn't say what he was thinking if there was a chance it would be hurtful. I supposed that, in a way, he had taught me to do the same.

"Amir loves Horseshoe Cliff. When he came to live with us, he immediately felt a connection to the land. He's like my father in that way."

"And you, too," Will said. "I know how special it was for you."

I did not dare look him in the eye for fear that he would see what I was thinking: that he could never really understand what Horseshoe Cliff meant to me. "Amir says he won Bear's portion of the land in a poker game. Bear signed a contract."

Will's eyes widened. "Poker? Was Bear drunk?"

"Amir says Bear doesn't even care that he lost the land. He says there are witnesses, and that Bear isn't fighting it." I twisted my fingers together in my lap. "The Bear I know would have fought anyone about anything. Especially Amir." I sighed. "And now Amir wants to kick Bear off the land he's lived on his whole life. But the thing is, I still own one-third of Horseshoe Cliff."

The side of Will's jaw twitched. "So Amir's plan is that the two of you own the land together."

"I could let Bear stay. If I decided that's what I wanted to do."

"And have you decided?"

I shook my head. "I can't honestly believe I'm considering helping him. He's a monster."

Will's expression, shifting throughout our conversation, settled now into one of sympathy. "But you're wondering if maybe he *was* a monster, and now he's just a drunk getting swindled out of his home."

"I don't know! I don't know. I think I have to go up there. I need to see him for myself." I looked down at the ugly rug below our feet. "Amir is driving up in the morning. I'd be back tomorrow night."

A pause swelled in the air. After a moment, Will kissed my shoulder. "Do you want me to go with you? I don't like the thought of you getting in the middle of something between those two."

I almost laughed. I had been in the middle of something between Bear and Amir since the moment Amir stepped out of my father's truck with his mother's big blue coat. Bear had always been set on punishing Amir for making me happy, and on hurting me by torturing Amir. Amir and I were two parts of a braid, and Bear had always been the third.

"I'll be fine." I leaned into Will. He readjusted himself, settling into the sofa as though for a nap, and I stretched out beside him. I felt his chest rise and fall. Even after our late night of drinking and dancing, I was too agitated to rest. My skin felt so warm that I wondered if I was getting sick. After a moment, I stood. Will's eyes flicked open.

"I'm going for a swim," I whispered.

His eyes shut again. I thought he'd fallen asleep, but as I left the den, I heard him murmur for me to be careful.

I was still wet from my swim and had my towel draped around my shoulders, the cool sand below me, when I picked up my phone. I had three missed calls from Emma. Instead of returning her calls, I called Ronnie. My thoughts had raced in circles, a dog chasing its tail, the entire time I'd been in the water. Ronnie had met Amir briefly at the party the night before, and I had seen in the way her gaze moved from him to me that she was curious about our relationship. She knew a little of my childhood, but I had never spoken of Amir—she knew only that I had grown up on a farm and that my parents had died when I was young.

"It's him, isn't it?" she asked rather breathlessly as she answered the phone. "Back in college, I was always so sure you were pining for some mysterious guy from your past . . . and then when I met Will I thought, *This is the guy!* But Will isn't the guy, is he?"

"No."

"It's Amir!"

"Ronnie—"

"What happened between the two of you? Why didn't it work out?"

The cold water had invigorated me. I thought I could feel my blood pumping more strongly through my veins. "It's complicated. I believed for a long time that he did something . . . something truly terrible . . . and then he disappeared. He's been gone nine years. I found out this morning that I was wrong. He didn't do it. And he disappeared because he thought I was leaving him, which I never would have done . . ." I trailed off. "I haven't been home in all that time. But there's something going on with my brother, so we're going to drive up there tomorrow."

"You and Amir? Just the two of you?"

"Yes."

I could practically hear Ronnie's sharp mind ticking away like a timer winnowing down on a set moment. I supposed this was why I had called her.

"And Will isn't bothered by this?" she asked. "You going away with the guy who it turns out didn't do the awful thing? Who didn't actually mean to break your heart? Who was looking at you last night like the Prince of Troy catching his first glimpse of Helen?"

"Will offered to come with me."

"But he didn't insist? When the Prince of Troy took Helen, her husband launched a thousand ships and started a war."

"Ronnie, no one is *taking* me—"

"I know, I know. But don't you think it's strange that Will doesn't seem to think it's possible to lose you? That he didn't even notice how *you* were looking at Amir?"

My face grew warm as we both fell silent.

After a moment, Ronnie said, "Oh, Merrow. What are you going to do?"

A hand on my shoulder made me jump. When I looked up, I saw Emma. She wore large sunglasses and a wan smile. *Can we talk?* she mouthed.

"Emma's here," I told Ronnie, promising that I would call her again soon.

Emma sank down to the sand beside me. "I've been calling you! Will said I'd find you here. I've been so embarrassed all day." She touched her fingers to her forehead and moaned. "I drank too much last night. Did I make a fool of myself? Did you see Amir this morning? What did he say? I hope he doesn't think too poorly of me! Does he?"

I felt a rush of sympathy for Emma, who had always been more interested in her studies than in boys, and who had now, by all appearances, fallen in love with Amir overnight. "Of course not. You were fine. It was a party. Everyone had too much to drink."

She cocked her head. "Amir *did* say something, didn't he?" Her cheeks grew pink. "It's okay. You don't have to tell me what he said."

"Really," I said softly. "He didn't say anything about you." I realized I had not thought of Emma even once while I had sat with Amir on the beach that morning. Any twinges of jealousy had fled my mind the moment I'd looked at him and felt how he looked at me. Now, I wished only to put my friend out of her misery as gently as possible.

"Oh." She took off her sunglasses and fiddled with them for

a moment before putting them back on. "Was he always so handsome? I really only met him that one time we stayed in Osha, didn't I? I don't remember him looking like *that*." Her face twisted. I could not tell if she was embarrassed or distraught. She attempted to laugh. "I'm sorry. Is that gross for you to think about? I wouldn't like to think about my brother as hot, either. He's just Will."

"Amir isn't my brother."

There was a pause.

"What do you call him?"

"He's—" I realized with a start that I had been about to snap: *He's mine.* "We grew up together."

Emma stopped smiling. "Are you . . . upset with me, Merrow? Did I do something wrong?"

"No." I tried to smooth the edges from my voice and could not. "I'm sorry. It was a late night."

"Oh." She pushed the sand around with her feet. "Sometimes I wonder if you still think of me as just a little girl."

I could not tell her that Amir and I would always belong more to each other than to anyone else. That I loved Will, but we were not welded together in the way that Amir and I were. That the thought of Amir being with another woman, even someone whom I liked as much as I liked Emma, was unbearable.

"I'm sorry," I said again. The cool feeling of the sea on my skin had dissipated. A queer sensation had overtaken me since Amir had returned. It was as though my blood were moving faster, its rush an insistent thrum in my ears. I stood and held out my hand to help Emma to her feet. "I'm sorry."

CHAPTER TWENTY

I did not sleep well that night. I awoke in the middle of the night with Bear's voice in my ear and my fingers balled into tight, sweat-filled fists. After that, sleep eluded me.

I was anxious, too, to see my home. In my memory, Horseshoe Cliff glowed as though in amber, a place of powerful and ethereal beauty. The ocean there was larger and more soulful, its crash more in rhythm with my own heart, than any other ocean. But now that I had seen the beauty that could be found in so many other parts of the world, and now that I had my own house by the sea in San Francisco, would Horseshoe Cliff still offer the same enchantment? I was not entirely sure I was ready to find out.

In the morning, Amir picked me up in a truck that was the same color as the stones we used to stack on the beach. The city looked different from its cab. The buildings seemed thin and huddled, the people small. Amir turned out to be a confident driver, but he took his time. There was something gallant in the way he halted for dawdling pedestrians who approached the curb, making eye contact and nodding politely to the elderly and to the young mothers with toddlers in tow.

I looked at his profile, the cut of his cheekbone, the beautiful shape of his dark-lashed eyes. Nine years had changed him, but in his eyes I would always find the boy he had been. It was a relief just to be near him again, like a wrong had at last been righted.

"You have a new admirer," I told him. "Emma."

Amir steered the truck onto the Golden Gate Bridge. I sensed the water far below us, churning where bay met sea. He glanced at me with a sidelong smile. "Are you jealous?"

"No. She's nineteen."

"That's practically ancient compared to how old you were when you met Will."

"Will and I didn't start dating for years after we met."

Amir raised an eyebrow but did not shift his gaze from the road ahead. "She's not my type," he said after a moment.

I could not help smiling at this. "No? She's beautiful."

"I'm sure a lot of people think that. But the woman I'm meant to be with has a different sort of beauty. She's not like anyone else."

I could not pull my eyes from his face. The corner of his mouth settled into a small smile as he continued. "The woman I'm meant to be with is a strong swimmer, and she can ride a horse without reins. She's moved by how the needs of children are as simple as they are profound. She's happiest by the sea. She loves, and knows how to tell, a good story. Oh," he said, his eyes flicking over my face for too short a spell of time, "and she has a sixth sense for unlocked windows."

I swallowed. "That's very specific. She might be hard to find."

"Finding her," Amir said, "has never been the problem."

I studied him. "You know, in these years that we've been apart, there have been moments when I've felt like someone was watching me."

"Your mother? You used to sense her watching you when you were on the beach."

"It wasn't you? You haven't followed me?"

He shook his head. "Do you think I could have seen you and not said anything? It took everything in my power to keep my distance from you. I thought it was what you wanted. When I heard you tell Rei that you were leaving, it didn't sound like you planned to look back."

"Then why seek me out now?"

"Your engagement. There was something about it in a magazine."

I was confused for a moment before remembering that a local magazine had published a piece about Rosalie's philanthropic work, and she'd insisted that I be included in the family photograph that ran with the profile. I was listed as Merrow Shawe, fiancée of William Langford.

I looked through the window. Suburban neighborhoods gave way to cow pastures and rolling hills.

"I *was* always good at finding an open window, wasn't I?"

Amir's smile lit his entire face in the way the light from the rising sun used to burst through the cracks of the shed. "You needed to see how other people lived. You needed to know."

It had been Amir who had led me into that first house, knowing how it would distract me from the grief I experienced when Pal died, the rage I felt for my brother, the swirl of darkness that had risen within me.

"I don't think I understood just how little we had until I walked around those homes," I said.

Amir's smile faded. "I don't think I ever understood how *much* I had until I saw how mesmerized you were by those houses. I realized then what the stakes were, and what exactly I had to lose. Breaking into those houses never felt harmless to me. Even before we wound up at the Langfords', I sensed where things were headed."

His words worried me. "I hope you don't think I'm marrying Will just because he's rich."

Amir shrugged. "He makes you feel safe. You lived your entire childhood not knowing what the next minute would hold, and with him you can see your whole future. Who could blame you for wanting that? He's giving you everything you think you want."

"Will is smart and curious and kind, Amir. He's a good person."

His jaw hardened as he stared at the road ahead of us. After some time had passed, he said, in a voice more gentle than I expected, "Will *is* a good person. His entire family has looked after you—I see that now. But you can be grateful to the Langfords without owing them the rest of your life."

I did not respond. Was it so wrong to love someone because they made you feel safe? Because you were grateful for how they changed your life? And if it wasn't love that I felt for Will, what was it? I remembered my panic when I'd awakened in Venice to find him gone. I remembered watching Will with his sister and mother in that house in Osha, the glow that seemed to surround them and how I wished that it would surround me, too. I remembered the first dress that Rosalie had given me, the delight I had felt when she'd said I could keep it. It had swirled around my knees and my heart had swelled in response. I kept that dress wrapped in tissue, and when I looked at it from time to time what struck me was how simple it was, and how I loved it, and how much I hoped it would never be taken from me.

AT FIRST GLANCE, it appeared little had changed in Osha. The co-op still had a box out front labeled FREE, but when I looked closer, I realized it was no longer a cardboard box but a sturdy-looking wooden crate. I felt a jolt of pleasure at the sight of Little Earth Schoolhouse, which had been a respite for me for too few years. It had the same pretty slanted roof and porch, the same tidy yard, but a new sign now with crisp blue lettering and an illustration of Earth in place of the *o* in *house*. I thought of the journal that Teacher Julie had handed me, my first, telling me that I was "nearly bursting" with stories.

As we neared Horseshoe Cliff, I felt myself leaning forward in my seat. Amir swung the truck off the road, and right there in the middle of the dirt driveway, Bear's truck—my father's truck, now stained with rust and pocked by broken headlights—glowered at us like an old blind watchdog. In a weedy plot of dirt just off the driveway hunkered a camper not much bigger than a one-horse trailer. I held my breath, waiting to see the door of the camper thrown open to reveal the looming silhouette of my brother. Behind the grimy window, the curtains did not move.

"Keep going," I whispered.

Amir looked at me. "He can't hurt us." He put his hand on mine.

I laced my fingers through his and drew in a long breath. "Keep going," I said again.

The truck dipped off the driveway into the scrub grasses as he maneuvered it around Bear's truck. Immediately, the cottage came into view.

On the night I'd run away, the cottage had appeared to teeter on the edge of the world. Now, it looked sunken, less in danger of falling into the sea than of melting into the earth. Half of the porch had crumbled, leaving a dark pile of rotten wood that had not been cleared. Parts of the roof had crumbled, too, and what remained was covered in moss. Even in decrepitude, that cottage clung as stubbornly to the earth as the earth clung to the cottage. The sight made my heart clench.

I had never forgotten that when I was a child lying in my bed at night, the wilderness had seemed to creep closer in the darkness and howl against my windowpane. Nor had I forgotten that in the morning I would stand at that same window and look out at the land that had filled me with terror the night before, and my heart would swell with love for it.

Amir stopped the truck in front of the cottage. In the distance, the gray satin blanket of ocean rippled. I stepped outside. The air smelled of the sea and of the land, exactly as it always had. The breeze against my cheek felt like a kiss; I was overwhelmed with the sense that my father and my mother were beside me. I looked up, searching for a red bird, but saw only the white blue of the vast coastal sky. The constant murmur of the ocean offered an inhale and an exhale.

"I know," Amir said, coming around the truck to join me. He wrapped me in a hug.

I laughed, wiping away the tears that pricked my eyes. "I haven't cried in years but suddenly it's all I do."

Amir looked down at me but did not wipe the tears from my cheeks. "Bear hated when you cried, so you stopped."

Should I have been ashamed to feel as relieved as I felt to be in Amir's arms, to feel both at peace and deliriously adrift, to feel my heart beating toward his? Maybe, but I was suddenly, overwhelmingly, sick of shame. Amir knew me, and I knew him. We had been connected from the moment we had first held hands in the darkness of my bedroom on the night he arrived at Horseshoe Cliff, when he'd seemed equally dampened by grief and brightened by hope.

He put his hand under my chin, cupping it, and the touch of his fingers sent a charge down my spine. I moved toward him. My eyes, locked on his, began to close.

In my pocket, my phone vibrated. I didn't look at it, but the thought that it might have been Will calling made my eyes flick open.

"Let's walk." I stepped out of Amir's arms and set off toward the ocean.

The garden had become a weedy tangle, too overgrown to see if the raised boxes that my father had built were still underneath. When we approached the shed, I was surprised to see that it had withstood the years of neglect better than the cottage and garden. The door creaked loudly when I opened it. The walls were bare, my father's tools gone. A chunk of the ceiling in one corner had fallen, letting in a bright stream of dust-flecked light.

It was so small.

I stepped across the dirt floor, remembering how Amir and I had huddled together with Pal for warmth.

Amir looked around. When he spoke, his voice was laced with quiet anger. "I'll never understand how he could have forced a kid to sleep out here."

"We were always happier than he was. He couldn't stand it."

We left the shed and closed the door behind us. Where the chicken coop had once stood, there was a bare patch of earth. Amir said that Bear must have sold the coop, and I felt a stab of regret that another piece of my father was lost to us forever. The horse pasture fence and lean-to were still there, at least. On the side of the lean-to, my mother's peace sign was so faint that at first I thought I imagined it. The ring of paint was warm below my palm. *Someday someone is going to paint the peace sign that does the trick,* my mother had said. *And who is to say that person won't be me?*

I remembered my father bringing me to the lean-to on my fifth birthday, the delight of finding Pal there, waiting for me. When I took a deep breath, I could have sworn I smelled the dusty warmth of Old Mister and Guthrie.

"We should get horses again," said Amir. I looked at him in surprise. I didn't answer, but the sun caught my eye, and when it did I saw two horses in that pasture. I saw children, too, though they were not Amir and I. They were Marty and Keira and Assim and all the children from Learning Together. How they would love to spend a day at Horseshoe Cliff, exploring, losing themselves in the thrill of adventure that the wild expanse offered.

I opened my eyes and jogged a few steps to keep up with Amir. The air grew blustery, the sound of the waves crashing against the shore more distinct.

"Oh!" I said, stopping. Where land had once been, it was no longer. The shape of the cliff had changed; the smooth horseshoe curve was now a jagged V with sudden ledges that made the cliff seem even more precarious than it had been during our childhood. I remembered running along that cliff, shouting into the wind, laughing whenever Rei told me it was dangerous to play so close to the edge.

"There must have been a storm." Amir peered over the new line of the cliff, unafraid. The strip of sand below was wider than it had been in some places and narrower in others. The waves hurled themselves at the beach. Amir looked sadly back in the direction of the cottage. I knew, without him saying it, that he was wondering how long it would be until all of Horseshoe Cliff was gone.

"Do you remember," I asked, "why Rei thought this property was named Horseshoe Cliff? 'It's the *inside* of a horseshoe that is lucky, not the horseshoe itself,' she'd say. The horseshoe just holds the luck. If you hang a horseshoe upside down, the good stuff spills out like wine from an overturned cup. She thought that whoever named Horseshoe Cliff had believed that it was the *ocean* that was lucky, not the land. It was the ocean that would outlast everything else.

"'This is why the ocean brings us peace,' Rei said. When we are by the sea, we are in the presence of something eternal. There is strange comfort in feeling small beside the vast ocean. 'In the face of Forever,' Rei said, 'we become more grateful for the vital heartbeat of Now.'"

The light turned Amir's brown eyes a dark shade of honey. To look at him was to feel his love for me, and—always, always—my love for him.

"The one thing I don't agree with," I said, "is the idea that Horseshoe Cliff is unlucky. My father never believed that, and neither do I. Even when I was away, I felt the pull of this land, and of you. I have always felt you with me, Amir, even when you're not."

There was so much more I wanted to say, but Amir's gaze flicked away from mine. His face tightened. Across the bluff, staggering toward us, half broken by the wind, was an old man.

"Who is that?" I asked.

Amir reached for my hand, lacing his fingers through mine. "Bear."

My stomach lurched. The wind made my ears ache. I took a step back, and Amir's grip tightened around mine.

"Careful," he said. I had not realized just how close I'd come to the rim of the cliff.

My old impulse to run from Bear was as strong as it had ever been, and it took all of my willpower to remain still as he approached. When he drew closer, I saw that the halting stride I'd mistaken for the gait of an older man was in actuality the stumbling pace of someone who'd had too much to drink. Bear's flannel shirt hung off his wasted frame. Where was the massive bulk of a man who used to cast such a large shadow? I could not believe how thin he had become, how deeply time was etched upon his forehead. His changed appearance did little to ease my nerves; the Bear I knew would always find a way to seize my joy.

I steeled myself, but when my brother finally arrived at the cliff's edge, I was shocked to see that his eyes held not knives but tears. With his hollowed cheeks and surprisingly dark beard, he looked so much like my father that I felt shaken. I could not believe he was thirty-five, only a little older than Will.

"What are you doing here?" he said to me. He had slurred for nearly as long as I could remember, but now he spoke as though he had sand in his mouth. It was difficult to understand him.

"We're here because this place is ours," said Amir, stepping between us.

Bear glowered. I could see that my brother's hatred for Amir was still there, even if his tears dampened its intensity. He waved his hand in the air as though Amir's words were a spiderweb that was easily broken.

"I mean *here*. Right here!" He looked at me and blinked, forcing more tears to roll down his cheeks. He seemed confused. "What are *you* doing *here*? Don't stand so close to the edge! How many times do I have to tell you?"

Amir and I exchanged a baffled look. Bear had never once, that I could remember, told me not to do something for fear of my safety. We watched as he began to sway from foot to foot.

"You should know it's too dangerous. You should know!" He muttered something I could not make out. His lips were wet with tears.

In my entire life, I had never seen Bear cry. The sight ripped something open inside of me.

"Because of Mom?" I asked. He didn't seem to hear me. The wind was relentless; far below, the crashing waves echoed against the cliffs. I didn't want to raise my voice, but I did. "Because this is where Mom fell?"

"Mom?" Bear seemed startled. He raked his hands through the mess of his hair and stared at the edge of the cliff and then raised his watery red eyes to meet mine. "She cried all the time. All the time. She didn't used to, not before you were born." He looked down again, moving his feet as though the earth were hot below them. "She was happy. I remember her happy. After you were born, she didn't get out of bed. She held you and she cried all the time. When I hugged her, she would cry. When Dad talked to her, she cried. Her face was different. She had been beautiful. So beautiful." His voice choked. He looked at me and his face drained of color. I had the sense that he believed, for a moment, that I was our mother. Then he shook his head forcefully, swiping at his tears. His swaying grew more agitated. He began to walk, pacing right to the edge of the cliff he'd warned me away from.

"She went gray after you were born. Her skin, her face, her eyes. All gray." Below Bear's feet, rocks skittered out and over the cliff's edge. My hand shot out and managed to grab his wrist. He shook himself loose of me with more strength than I would have thought he could muster, but he stepped away from the edge of the cliff. His eyes filled with tears faster than he could wipe them. I had never felt as scared of the cliff's edge as I did in that moment, watching Bear stumble near it.

Amir and I exchanged a glance. It was being reminded of my mother's tears that had made Bear hate mine so much, I understood now. My birth must have triggered something within her, releasing a dark fog of depression. I wondered why my father—or Rei—had never told me this piece of the story. Perhaps they thought that for a motherless child the story of her mother's death was simply sad enough on its own, without the details filled in.

"Why don't we walk back toward the house?" I asked.

Bear blinked at me. "She told me you were going for a walk that day."

I shook my head. "No. I was a baby. I couldn't walk yet."

"You and Mom," Bear said. "Mom and you. She hadn't taken a walk in weeks. Dad was in the orchard. She said she was going to take you for a walk, but I . . ." He trailed off.

"What?" I asked.

He narrowed his eyes and I saw a hint of the old daggers in there, dull below his tears. "I didn't like it. Something about the way she said it."

"You thought she was going to hurt herself."

Bear's tears came faster. "And you. She was taking you."

Amir reached for my hand. If Bear noticed, he didn't say anything.

"What happened?" I asked.

"I told her not to go. But she left anyway. She walked out onto the back porch and down the stairs and she was crying and then you were crying. I said, 'Mama, let me hold Merrow,' and she did because I was good at getting you to stop crying. I always made you laugh."

I stared at him. I had no memory of Bear ever making me laugh. I had only the memories of his hatred for me. But I had no memory of Bear as a ten-year-old boy. I could not picture myself in his arms. I could not imagine his face smiling into mine. I could not imagine him loving me. The person he was describing was not the Bear that I knew.

"She handed you to me. She said she would be back soon. I looked down at you and tried to get you to laugh, but that day you just kept crying and crying. When I looked up, she was far away, walking toward the cliff, and then she was gone."

"Oh, Bear. You saw her fall?"

"She didn't fall. She just kept walking until there was no-where left to walk."

I had never really considered exactly what our mother's death had done to my brother. I had not had time to know her, but Bear had had ten years with her. My father had told me that my mother was magnetic, that once you met her you could not imagine life without her, that her smile warmed its lucky re-cipient from hair to heel. Bear had known our mother, really known her, and he had watched her walk away. He had known, somewhere deep inside himself, where she was going, and he had saved me. But he had not been able to save her. He'd lived with that guilt his whole life. As long as I'd known him, he had never been anything but unhappy. He had never had a single friend. He had no one, and I had my love for the sea and the earth and my animals. And I had Amir.

If one of the kids at Learning Together had told me this story, I would have had all the sympathy in the world for what he had been through. I would have forgiven him for any crime.

"Thank you," I told Bear. "Thank you for saving your baby sister. You were a good brother."

He sucked in a big breath that seemed to rattle his entire body. And then he stumbled closer to the edge of the cliff. He steadied himself and moved away from the edge, eyeing me.

"I don't want you to worry about where you're going to live," I said. "You can have my third of Horseshoe Cliff. This land is yours every bit as much as it is mine and Amir's."

Bear released a laugh that dissolved into a hacking cough

that sounded unnervingly like my father's. "You think I want this piece of shit land? I don't! Never have. This land never brought our family anything but trouble. Good riddance!" He threw his hands toward the sky and when he did his leg slid out from under him, pushing into a piece of earth that was suddenly not there. A strangled cry hung in the sky—it might have belonged to any of us—and then Bear was gone.

I sprang to the edge of the cliff. Amir yelled my name. There was Bear: his hands clutching the side of the cliff, his feet scrambling for a hold. I dropped to my stomach and wrapped my hands around his forearms. "I have you," I said, though my heart thundered in my ears. My brother's eyes were round with fear. Earth crumbled out from under him and tumbled down forty feet to the beach below. Amir was beside me then, reaching his long, strong arms toward Bear. At the sight of him, Bear's face twisted, curdling like wasted milk.

"Let me go," he said in a low growl. "Don't touch me."

Amir immediately released him. Bear shuddered a few inches down the side of the cliff, his arms sliding through my hands. I grabbed his wrists. A line of red bloomed on his chin where his face scraped the cliff.

I yelled for Amir to help, but Amir did not move. "Look at me," I begged him.

Amir's face churned with a terrible mix of anger and pain and love. I did not want to ask him to save his abuser, but I had no choice. Bear slipped another inch in my hands. I gasped as I slid forward with him, dragging my toes against the ground behind me. My nails sunk into Bear's skin. His head sagged down onto his chest, and I worried he was on the verge of pass-ing out.

"Don't do it for him," I said to Amir. "Do it for me. Please."

The anger on Amir's face was replaced, almost immediately, with resolve. He reached down again and grabbed Bear's fore-arms.

"No," Bear groaned, rearing his head. "Let me go. Let me go!" He began to struggle against Amir's grip, but I knew that Amir would not let him go now. Together, we yanked Bear up and over the edge of the cliff even with him thrashing and cursing us. We fell into a pile together, breathing heavily. Bear rolled away, muttering a stream of hateful curses. He managed to stand. Streaks of blood webbed his chin and arms. He stared out at the sea, his chest rising and falling violently. My heart pounded. He could jump off the edge of the cliff whenever he chose.

"Bear—"

He looked down at me as though he did not recognize me, but his eyes were the same green-brown color as mine, as our mother's. "Leave me alone," he said. He turned away from us, and from the sea, and began a meandering path back toward the road.

Amir put his arm around my shoulders. I leaned against him.

"Your poor mother," he said.

"I don't remember any of that. I was just a baby, but still . . . I wish I could remember the last time she held me." In the distance, a gull floated on the water, bobbing up and down as the sea moved below him, carrying him steadily away from the spot where he'd landed. "She must have been in so much pain. I'm sure she walked off in search of peace. I can't imagine being Bear . . . seeing that . . ."

"It's hard to imagine that he was once a little boy."

"If he hadn't stepped in, my mother might have brought me over that cliff with her." I looked at Amir. It was impossible to think that I might have lost the chance to meet him. My mother had given me life, but my brother had insisted that I keep it.

"So all this time I have owed Bear everything," Amir said. With his eyes on mine, a molten sort of warmth spread through me. I knew what he was thinking because I was thinking it, too. We had always been like this—our thoughts were not identical, but they were symbiotic, each one of us drawing inspiration, joy, and hope from the other. My passion felt deeper when I was with him, my appreciation for and connection to the natural world more profound.

"All these years," I murmured wonderingly, "I really thought you were watching me. I could feel you there."

Amir's hands moved to the sides of my face. "You felt me near you because I never left you, Merrow," he said. "I was always with you, just as you were with me."

My eyes filled with tears. I knew that I could not marry Will. I loved Amir. I had always loved Amir. Sitting beside him on that cliff, with the sea tumbling below us and the wind in my hair, my entire being felt alive with my love for him. I did not want to go another day without knowing where he was, without feeling the heat of his skin against mine.

Amir moved to kiss me, and though my body wanted desperately to meet him in that kiss, I managed to shake my head. "I have to tell Will," I said. "He deserves it . . . and we do, too. I was always made to feel so ashamed of how I felt about you when we were younger, and I don't want shame to ever come near my feelings for you again. I want to be with you, wholly, without anything hanging over us."

I knew that Will would be hurt whether or not I kissed Amir. I had betrayed him already in far more meaningful ways. But it would be hard enough to face Will without the memory of Amir's kiss playing in my mind.

"I hate the thought of waiting another second," Amir said. "But I will. I'll wait as long as you need me to wait."

CHAPTER TWENTY-ONE

It was nearly midnight by the time we returned to the city. Amir and I sat for a few minutes in the cab of his truck.

"You'll call me tomorrow?" he asked.

"Yes." I leaned over to kiss his cheek, and when I did, he wrapped his arm around my waist and held me there with my cheek against his. It felt so right to be in his arms that it was nearly impossible to pull away. "I have to talk to Will," I said softly.

Amir nodded, but I could see that he was unhappy. I ran my finger over his cheek and he gave me a sad smile.

When I stepped inside, the house was so still and quiet that I wondered if Will was even there. I walked up the stairs and opened our bedroom door. The room was awash with moonlight. Will was in bed. The covers rose and fell with his silent breaths. I whispered his name, but he did not stir.

In the bathroom, I washed my face and changed into my pajamas. I lay down beside Will on the bed, above the covers. I blinked up at the ceiling. I rolled onto my side and tried to sleep, but sleep would not come. I watched Will. My lovely Will, who was so generous with his love. My chest ached at the sight of him, vulnerable in sleep, the sweep of his blond hair against his forehead. I ran the events of the last few days over and over again in my mind. On another night, I might have pressed my head against Will's chest and let the beat of his heart, the steady catch and release of his breath, calm me. But I could not do that now. Eventually, I rose from the bed. I scribbled a note on a slip of paper and left it on my pillow.

I'm home, it said. *Can't sleep.*

Downstairs, I took a throw blanket from the den and walked out to the patio. The moon was so bright that the flagstones glowed beneath my bare feet. I curled onto a lounge chair and wrapped myself in the blanket. The sea was a vast mirror, the glinting shards of light an echo of the moon and stars. Far below the patio, the waves hit the shore with a gentle hush, and in the sound, I heard my mother murmur, *It's okay. It's okay. It's okay.* I had no memory of the sound of her voice, but I was sure it was her, that the ocean held her, was her, that I swam daily in her embrace, that she had never left me but had, in fact, been with me all along.

I AWOKE TO find Will looking down at me with an amused expression.

"There you are," he said. He sat at the end of the chair and pulled my feet onto his lap. The sky behind him was draped in pink gauze.

I straightened. "What time is it?"

"Almost seven. Were you out here all night? Weren't you cold?"

I shook my head. "The strangest thing happened." I told him how I had heard my mother's voice in the sound of the waves against the shore. I waited for him to make a joke about my mystical powers.

Instead, after a beat, he asked what my mother said to me.

"She said, 'It's okay.'"

"'It's okay,'" he echoed. "What do you think she meant?"

I swallowed. "I think she was trying to comfort me."

Will had been slowly rubbing my calves, but now he stopped. His hands became so still that I wondered if he was holding his breath. I wondered if he knew, if there was a part of him that had always known.

"Will."

"What happened up there?" he asked quickly. "Did you see Bear?"

I nodded. "He's not the same. I hardly recognized him. I told him he should stay at Horseshoe Cliff, that he could have my share of the land."

Relief washed over Will's face. He reached for my hand, and I felt the press of my engagement ring against my skin. "So Bear and Amir will own the land together."

I looked down at our entwined fingers. When I spoke, my voice was strained with emotion. "No. It will still belong to all three of us."

"I don't understand."

I forced myself to lift my chin and look at him. I saw a

flicker of understanding and hurt in Will's gaze before it hardened in anger.

"What happened up there, Merrow?" he asked again.

"I don't know how to explain it," I said. "Except to say that I . . . I realized that I need to be with Amir. Now that he's back—"

Will yanked his hand from mine. "You need to be with Amir? The person who disappeared when you needed him most?"

"He thought I was leaving him. He heard me—"

Will shook his head. "You know what, I don't care. I don't care about what happened between you and Amir when you were kids." His expression softened. "I love you, Merrow. I love our life together. Amir is your past, but I am your future. Don't you see that?"

"I thought I did. I was ready to live the rest of my life with you."

Will's shoulders sank. "Love isn't something that you turn on and off like a light switch."

"You're right," I said quietly. There was so much that I could not bear to say to Will because I could not stand the thought of hurting him any more than I already was. I could answer his question and tell him that what had changed was only that Amir had returned, and all the years that we'd spent apart had simply fallen away. That the overwhelming love I'd felt for Amir when I was a girl I still felt now as a woman, and more so. That my life and Amir's life were bound together—by fate, by nature, by sorrow and cruelty and comfort and joy and profound understanding.

Would explaining the depth of my love for Amir have helped

Will to process why I was leaving? Perhaps. But I did not want to risk bringing him more pain. I did not want to reveal to Will that my feelings for him were a tidy pasture, green and lovely, but that my love for Amir was a vast, unruly landscape with a wild sea and windswept land from which, against all odds, beauty and sustenance grew. It was a love that I would be pulled toward my entire life, a love that I felt in the very core of my being. Our love felt transcendent; it was a protection from sadness, a gift of being wholly seen, wholly known. My life was this love, and this love, my life.

"Nothing has changed," I said, my eyes filling with tears, "but somehow everything has changed. I know I owe you so much better of an explanation than that. I'm truly sorry."

He stared at me. After a beat, he stood. "I can't believe you're doing this, Merrow. There is so much love here. I can feel it. Can't you?"

I stood, too. My body ached, from the long car rides back and forth to Horseshoe Cliff, from the exertion of pulling Bear from the cliff's edge, from the fitful hours of sleep on the lounge chair, from the agony of hurting someone for whom I cared so deeply.

"Yes," I said. "I can feel it."

Will's face twisted. "I gave you your house by the sea. I gave you space to write. I wanted you to have a beautiful life, free of all the awful things that happened to you during your childhood. I wanted to take care of you and make sure you never felt pain again. You're choosing the hardest path when the one I've offered you is so easy. I gave you everything, and it's not enough, is it?"

Years earlier, Rosalie had told me that sometimes you had to leave your home, and everything you loved, to discover who you really were. Over the years I had been away from Horseshoe Cliff, I had become an adult. There were things that I'd wanted as a child that I no longer wanted. I had traveled to many places and my love for Horseshoe Cliff had only deepened. As a child, my feelings for my home had confused me, but I was no longer confused. I knew who I was. I knew what I wanted.

"No," I said quietly. "I'm sorry."

He walked away from me and stood at the edge of the patio, his arms crossed over his chest. I wanted to walk to him, to comfort him, but I knew that I shouldn't. "We never belonged to each other the way I thought we did." He spoke without turning toward me. "I don't think you ever loved me the way I loved you."

His words made me feel limp with sorrow. "That's not true," I said, but the truth was he might have been right. The entire time that I had loved Will, I had also loved Amir. I had been wrong to promise to love Will forever.

"It *is* true." When he turned to me, his face was hard.

"Oh, Will. I am so sorry. I hate hurting you." I took a step toward him, but he stepped back.

"You should go. I'd like you to leave now."

I swallowed, nodding. I wished that I could hug him, and say a real goodbye, but it was clear that he could not stand to look at me, and for this I could not blame him. I walked to the patio door. When my hand touched the handle, I turned. He stood at the edge of the patio with his back to me. The rising sun made his blond hair appear full of light.

"Goodbye, Will," I said.

His gaze was set on the horizon. He didn't move. "Goodbye," he said.

It was still early in the morning when I left our house. *Will's* house. I walked through the city, squinting against the sun. Twenty blocks. Forty blocks. An hour later I realized that I had walked straight to the Langfords' house. Rosalie was an early riser, and I knew she would be awake.

When I rang the bell, Rosalie's dog, Midas, barked furiously. The sound carried me back in time to Osha, the shock of Tiger's teeth sinking into my flesh. This new dog, Midas, knew me as a member of the family. He stopped barking and happily trotted toward me the moment Rosalie opened the door.

"Merrow! What on earth . . ." Rosalie peered into my face. "Come in, sweetheart. Come in."

I shook my head. I could not let her comfort me, not after breaking her son's heart. "I'm so sorry," I said, wiping away the fresh tears that had sprung to my eyes the moment she'd said my name. "You have always been so kind to me. I don't know what I would have done without you."

Rosalie waved away the thought. "What's all this? Why don't you come inside and sit down? You're upset."

"I can't. I really can't. I just needed to see you, and to tell you that knowing you has meant so much to me. Your belief in me, the way you told me your story and you listened to mine . . . it changed my life. I've learned so much from you, Rosalie. I hope I can do the same for other children in need."

Rosalie smiled. "But you already are. You're making a difference in the lives of so many children at Learning Together."

I swallowed. "I don't think I'll be working there any longer."

"Really? Why not?"

I took a breath. Rosalie and Wayne had left our party before Amir had arrived. I asked her if she remembered him.

She blinked. "Amir." She said his name slowly. "The boy who was rich of heart. Of course I remember him."

"He's here. He's come back."

The skin around Rosalie's lips seemed to tighten. "And what does that have to do with anything?"

"I . . . I love him, Rosalie," I said helplessly.

She sucked in her breath.

"I needed to tell you myself. I needed to tell you how sorry I am for the pain I'm causing your family. I want to thank you for everything you have done for me. I'm afraid that you will never know how much you mean to me. I'm afraid that you will only remember me as the girl who betrayed you. And I am so sorry for that."

Rosalie stood very still. I had the sense that she was torn between slamming the door in my face and embracing me. I was relieved when she crossed her arms over her chest. She sighed deeply. It was not a hug, but it was not a closed door, either.

"I don't know what to say. I'd like to talk to my son."

I nodded. Rosalie put her hand on the door as though to close it, but then stopped. She drummed her fingers on the door, her brow furrowed with thought. I waited.

"There was a time," she said at last, "when I advised you to leave the past behind. I fear now that I pushed you into a relationship with Will—"

"No, no. I *loved* Will, though I know he'll never believe it now."

"But if I hadn't encouraged you, you might have waited for Amir."

"Rosalie, I loved Will," I said again. "You have no blame in this."

"Hmm. Maybe." She straightened taller. "I need to call Will."

I nodded. As I turned away, I felt her hand on my shoulder.

"You know, Merrow," she said, "somehow, at some point, it's going to be okay."

They were simple words, but they were the same ones I'd heard my mother say the night before. They made me think of the push and pull of the surf against the sand.

"Thank you," I told her, and then we said goodbye.

CHAPTER TWENTY-TWO

That evening, the first thing I noticed when Amir and I turned onto Horseshoe Cliff's driveway was that Bear's truck and trailer were gone. Amir slowed to a stop. We stared at the patch of dirt where my brother had recently lived.

"Where do you think he went?" I asked.

Amir shook his head. "I don't know."

"He doesn't have any money."

"He does, actually. I wrote a check for his share of our inheritance from Rei before we left yesterday. I put it under his door."

I stared at him. "Oh, Amir."

He looked away. I knew how hard it must have been for him to do something kind for Bear. I put my hand on his, tucking away my worry for Bear for the moment. I could not deny the relief I felt that my brother was not nearby. Even though I had a sense now why he had become the person he had become, and even though I'd forgiven him for much of his cruelty, I knew that neither Amir nor I would ever feel at ease with him nearby. He had caused us too much pain.

We drove toward the ruined cottage. It was just the two of us for miles in any direction, surrounded by land and sea. When I stepped out of the truck, I felt the possibility of the earth below my feet, just as my father had said he'd felt all those years ago.

I looked over at Amir and grinned. The glow of the sunset was luminous on his skin. I held his hand, and we began to walk toward the cliffs.

The sun hovered at the horizon, moments from dipping into the sea. Up and down the coast, the cliffs were bathed in a glaze of honeyed light, glistening and majestic. I was sure that Horseshoe Cliff had never looked as beautiful as it did then. Standing there with Amir's hand in mine, on the edge of our new life together, I felt the shame that I'd felt for so long about my feelings for him finally crumble. We had met each other when we were eight years old; we had grown up together; we had fallen in love.

Amir turned to me, his gaze flooded with desire. When I kissed him, my mind emptied of everything but the urgent press of my lips to his at last, the taste of his mouth, the electricity of his hands moving through my hair and then down to the small of my back, pulling me ever closer to him. Eventually, I led him by the hand along the path that cut down to the beach. Rocks scuttled out from under our feet. On the sand, his kisses moved from my ear to my neck to my collarbone. The pleasure of feeling his skin below my hands traveled through me like a pulse of light. I reached below his shirt and lifted it off him, and then mine was off, too, and we were pressed against the shield of that golden cliff, lost entirely in each other, our sounds buoyed for a moment on the air above us before tumbling out to join the sounds of the sea.

AFTERWARD, WE DRESSED slowly, reluctantly, our hands continually seeking out the touch of the other. We leaned against the cliff, Amir's arms around me. I kissed his neck, inhaling his scent. Our attraction for each other was so strong that it felt like an animal pacing the beach, slinking breathlessly between us.

When I opened my eyes, I saw the cave. Amir followed my gaze.

"Do you think they're still there?" he asked.

After we stopped sleeping in the shed, we'd moved the red birds that Amir had carved and I had painted to a high ledge deep within the cave where we knew Bear would not find them. The shape of the cliff had changed since then, and with it the cave: the mouth was smaller now, more a whistle than a wail.

The birds were still in the cave, or they weren't. It did not matter. They were everywhere.

"Yes," I said. "They're here."

It was then that we began to talk about our future.

Amir thought that we should use Rei's money to build a new house for ourselves on Horseshoe Cliff, along with a bunkhouse so that we could establish a teaching farm.

I thought that in the summer we could run a camp for kids who were involved in programs like Learning Together, kids without a place to spend their days when school let out.

"It would mean so much to those kids to have room to run and explore," I said. "And to dig in the dirt and learn to work together to grow things. To learn that some plants that look fragile actually aren't at all; they can grow with little water, in places no one would believe that they could."

"Think of the stories you'll tell them," Amir said, his arm still around me.

"And the ones they'll tell the kids back home." The stories would be, as they had always been, like stones that, warmed by one hand, are passed on to warm another.

Nine years had passed since Amir and I had last been on that beach together. In some ways it felt like a much longer span of time than that, and in other ways it felt like we had never left. The tide was pulling away from us, revealing a larger swath of beach and rocks covered in seaweed, as if reminding us how much more there was to discover, and how much we had to share. I rested my head against Amir's shoulder and thought of children running on that sand, children who would sink their small heels into the vast land, making their joyful mark in the precious moments before the sea returned.

ACKNOWLEDGMENTS

First and foremost, an enormous and everlasting thank-you to my readers.

Countless hardworking people have helped this tale become a book. Thank you to my stellar agent and friend, Elisabeth Weed, dispenser of rock-solid advice, as well as to Hallie Schaeffer and everyone at the Book Group. Thank you to my editor, Emily Krump, for her insight, encouragement, and kindness. For being such hardworking and creative champions of the written word, I'm grateful to so many at William Morrow, including Liate Stehlik, Jen Hart, Julia Elliott, Bianca Flores, Amelia Wood, Rachel Meyers, Elsie Lyons, Diahann Sturge, and Amy Vreeland.

I am forever grateful to my loving parents, Carol Mager and James Donohue. For their support and affection, thank you also to Jackie Mager, Barbara and Charles Preuss, Brianna Andersen and Jay Donohue, Maritere and Charles Preuss, Jennifer and Tom Hudner, and the entire Donohue, Mager, and

Preuss gang. A special note of love for my delightful nieces and nephew: Lily, TJ, Hailey, Clara, and Reese.

Thank you to my brilliant, book-loving friends Emily Elder, Issabella Shields Grantham, Jeanette Perez, Alex Wang, and Liza Zassenhaus for reading this novel at various stages and providing invaluable feedback, sugarcoated with friendship and delivered with cocktails.

Thank you also to my dear friend and soul sister Mary-Ellis Arnold for being an encouraging early reader as well as a subject-matter expert. Despite her attempt to set me straight, there are likely some poultry-related inaccuracies in this work.

An immeasurable thank-you to Emily Brontë for writing the extraordinarily strange and wonderful *Wuthering Heights*. Stories have shaped my life, and Brontë's novel has left a particular and indelible mark. *You, Me, and the Sea*—and, really, all my work—is in her debt.

Finally, my eternal love and gratitude to Phil, Finley, Avey, Hayden, and our dogs, Cole and Wally. You are my home and my heart.

P.S.

Insights,
Interviews
& More . . .

*

Meet Meg Donohue

Sarah Deragon

MEG DONOHUE is the *USA Today* bestselling author of *Every Wild Heart, Dog Crazy, All the Summer Girls,* and *How to Eat a Cupcake.* Born and raised in Philadelphia, she now lives in San Francisco with her husband, three daughters, and two dogs. ᥫ

Wuthering Heights: The Novel That Haunts Me

"Whatever our souls are made of, his and mine are the same. . . ."
> —Emily Brontë, *Wuthering Heights*

Cathy: a headstrong, brave, complicated heroine. Heathcliff: a passionate, brooding hero . . . or is he an antihero? From my first reading of *Wuthering Heights* over twenty years ago, I have been fascinated by Emily Brontë's infamous pair. The intensity of their relationship—and the dramatic setting that Brontë so evocatively depicts— cast an indelible mark on my memory. As Heathcliff found himself haunted by Cathy, I have found myself, and my own stories, haunted by Brontë's novel.

I was mentally creating *Wuthering Heights* fan fiction long before I knew the genre existed. There is a particular plot point in *Wuthering Heights* that has always charged my imagination, spurring it to invent different paths for the characters than those carved by Brontë. When Heathcliff returns from a mysterious disappearance, Cathy is forced to choose between him and Edgar, the man she has recently ▶

married. Before Cathy can resolve this dilemma—spoiler alert!—she dies. The second half of Brontë's novel recounts the ways that the children of these central characters become intertwined . . . and, well, reader, forgive me, but I have always found it difficult to care much about the offspring of Cathy, Heathcliff, and Edgar. I love the heightened drama of *Wuthering Heights*, its eccentricity and unconventionality . . . but on this one point (the love triangle), my mind yearns to imagine alternative futures for the characters.

What if Cathy had not fallen ill after Heathcliff's return? I ask myself. If Cathy had lived, she would have been forced to choose between Edgar, the man who gave her the life she thought she always wanted, and Heathcliff, the great love from her childhood.

As a writer, you can wonder about these sorts of things for only so long before they become fodder for your next novel. And so—at the risk of provoking Brontë to howl from her grave—while writing *You, Me, and the Sea,* I set out to answer the question that has rattled around my mind for over twenty years: What if Cathy had lived?

I recast Cathy as Merrow, Heathcliff as Amir, and Edgar as Will. While

Wuthering Heights is told largely from the perspective of a servant named Nelly, I wanted to explore Merrow's point of view and decided her voice should carry the story.

My novels always have a strong sense of place. I'm sure I owe this tendency, in part, to my love of Brontë, who uses setting to reflect the inner lives of her characters and heighten her narrative's drama. Instead of the mist-shrouded moors of England, I set *You, Me, and the Sea* on the coast of Northern California, which, in addition to being a wonderfully romantic setting for a novel, happens to be where I live. While writing, I began to think of the sea and the land as two parts of an eternal pair, constantly shifting, changing the shape of each other and their embrace over centuries—an apt metaphor for a story about love.

The more I wrote, the more I allowed myself the freedom to play loosely with the plot of *Wuthering Heights,* turning it into something new. While I hope readers familiar with the classic will enjoy spotting the threads of connection to that novel, there are places where I've made definite departures. I place my characters in (mostly) present day, at a point in history that affords Merrow opportunities a girl in the late 1700s ▶

Wuthering Heights: **The Novel That Haunts Me** (continued)

would not have had. I cannot resist a bit of mystery, so I wove fresh intrigue into Merrow's story. And since I am both a romantic and an optimist, I could not help but sprinkle a fair amount of hope, and even magic, onto these pages.

I'm happy to report that writing this novel has not stopped me from feeling haunted by *Wuthering Heights*. It's a novel I will always return to, finding new insight with each reading, and I'm sure it will continue to inspire me, popping up here and there in my future writing. After all, as Merrow's father says in *You, Me, and the Sea*, "The past never leaves us. It only changes shape." ◠

Questions for Discussion

These questions reveal plot points and are best read upon completion of the novel.

1. The central characters in *You, Me, and the Sea* have strong connections to the sea. For some, the sea brings a sense of peace; for others, heartache. How would you describe Merrow's relationship with the sea? How would you describe her father's? Her mother's? Bear's? Amir's?

2. Consider this quote: "My father used to tell me that each touch from the sea, even one as soft as an exhaled breath, forever changed not only the land, but the shape of the sea itself. *True love's embrace,* my father called it. *Ever-changing. Eternal.*" In what ways do the relationships in the novel mirror the relationship of the sea and the land? In what ways does falling in love change the lives of these characters? In what ways does the love between these characters change over time, and in what ways is it eternal?

3. As a teenager, Merrow is made to feel ashamed of her feelings for Amir, though she is not related to him by blood. How would you describe their connection? ▶

4. Stories are an important part of this novel. Through folklore, Merrow's father came to believe in the healing power of the sea. What is the significance of stories to Merrow? How does her love for stories relate to her desire to work with children?

5. While Merrow has a connection to the sea, Amir has a connection to the land. Consider this quote: "Dad told us how our trees—trees that drank the coastal fog—grew deep roots in order to find moisture where they could, seeking out hidden reserves far below the dry surface soil. *Adversity makes them stronger,* my father said. *Heartier.*" In what ways does this passage shed light on Amir's connection to Horseshoe Cliff?

6. In one of the final scenes, Merrow learns important information about her brother, Bear. How does this knowledge change her feelings for her brother and her understanding of the past? In what ways, if any, did this revelation change how you felt about Bear and his actions throughout the novel?

7. For those who have read *Wuthering Heights*, what are some of the similarities that you notice between Emily Brontë's novel and *You, Me, and the Sea*? What are some of the differences?

8. Will's family helps Merrow leave a dangerous situation. What are some of the other aspects of Will and Merrow's relationship that make it strong? What do they see in each other?

9. In what ways does the setting of *You, Me, and the Sea* reflect the inner lives of the characters and heighten the narrative's drama?

10. Do you like where—and with whom—the characters found themselves at the end of the novel? Do you think Merrow made the right decision? If you were to rewrite this novel's ending, what would you change? ◠

More Books by Meg Donohue

EVERY WILD HEART

Passionate and funny, radio personality Gail Gideon is a true original. Nine years ago when Gail's husband announced that he wanted a divorce, her ensuing on-air rant propelled her local radio show into the national spotlight. Now, *The Gail Gideon Show* is beloved by millions of single women who tune in for her advice on the power of self-reinvention. But fame comes at a price, and escalating threats from a troubled fan make Gail worry for the safety of her daughter, Nic.

Fourteen-year-old Nic has always felt that she pales in comparison to her vibrant, outgoing mother. Plagued by a fear of social situations, she is most comfortable at the stable where she spends her afternoons. But when a riding accident lands Nic in the hospital, she awakens from her coma changed. Suddenly, she has no fear at all, and her disconcerting behavior lands her in one risky situation after another. And no one, least of all her mother, can guess what she will do next.

"*Every Wild Heart* should be on every reader's list of new books to savor. It's a heartfelt, funny, poignant, and suspenseful story of a good woman trying her best, making mistakes, picking up the pieces, and moving on—a celebration of what it means to be a working mother."
—Susan Wiggs, #1 *New York Times* bestselling author of *Family Tree* ▶

More Books by Meg Donohue (*continued*)

DOG CRAZY

As a pet bereavement counselor, Maggie Brennan uses a combination of empathy, insight, and humor to help patients cope with the anguish of losing their beloved four-legged friends. Though she has a gift for guiding others through difficult situations, Maggie has major troubles of her own that threaten the success of her counseling practice and her volunteer work with a dog rescue organization.

Everything changes when a distraught woman shows up at Maggie's office and claims that her dog has been stolen. Searching the streets of San Francisco for the missing pooch, Maggie finds herself entangled in a mystery that forces her to finally face her biggest fear—and to open her heart to new love.

"Even if my daughter hadn't recently rescued a dog, our first, I would have fallen in love with Meg Donohue's *Dog Crazy*. On these pages you will find love, healing, forgiveness, and pure unbridled joy of the human and canine kind."

—Adriana Trigiani, *New York Times* bestselling author of *The Shoemaker's Wife*

In Philadelphia, good girl Kate is dumped by her fiancé the day she learns she is pregnant with his child. In New York City, beautiful stay-at-home mom Vanessa finds herself obsessively searching the internet for news of an old flame. And in San Francisco, Dani, the wild child and aspiring writer who can't seem to put down a book—or a cocktail—long enough to open her laptop, has just been fired . . . again.

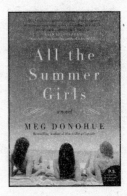

In an effort to regroup, Kate, Vanessa, and Dani retreat to the New Jersey beach town where they once spent their summers. Emboldened by the seductive cadences of the shore, the women begin to realize just how much their lives, and friendships, have been shaped by the choices they made one fateful night on the beach eight years earlier—and the secrets that only now threaten to surface.

"Beach Book Extraordinaire! Donohue's three protagonists are irresistibly sympathetic as they try to unbury their true selves from the ruinous secrets of their shared past."
—Elin Hilderbrand, *New York Times* bestselling author of *Beautiful Day* and *The Matchmaker* ▶

13

More Books by Meg Donohue (*continued*)

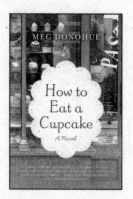

HOW TO EAT A CUPCAKE

Free-spirited Annie Quintana and sophisticated Julia St. Clair come from two different worlds. Yet, as the daughter of the St. Clairs' housekeeper, Annie grew up in Julia's San Francisco mansion and they forged a bond that only two little girls oblivious to class differences could—until a life-altering betrayal destroyed their friendship.

A decade later, Annie bakes to fill the void left in her heart by her mother's death, and a painful secret jeopardizes Julia's engagement to the man she loves. A chance reunion prompts the unlikely duo to open a cupcakery, but when a mysterious saboteur opens old wounds, they must finally face the truth about their past or risk losing everything.

"Beautifully written and quietly wise, *How to Eat a Cupcake* is an achingly honest portrayal of the many layers of friendship—a story so vividly told, you can (almost) taste the buttercream."

—Sarah Jio, *New York Times* bestselling author of *The Violets of March* and *Blackberry Winter* ❧